RIGHT TO
KILL

RIGHT TO
KILL

A **NATHAN MCBRIDE** NOVEL

ANDREW
PETERSON

THOMAS & MERCER

Text copyright © 2016 by Andrew Peterson
All rights reserved.

Published by Thomas & Mercer, Seattle

www.apub.com

Amazon, the Amazon logo, and Thomas & Mercer are trademarks of Amazon.com, Inc., or its affiliates.

ISBN-13: 1503940373
ISBN-10: 9781503940376

Cover design by Stewart A. Williams

Printed in the United States of America

First edition

To the memory of Special Warfare Operator 1st Class Charles Keating IV—KIA in Iraq on May 2, 2016. I didn't know Charles Keating IV, but I am forever in this Navy SEAL's debt.

CHAPTER 1

Linda Genneken threw off the fog of sleep as fast as her arms threw off the covers.

Earthquake?

No. Something worse.

Only one thing triggered the bed's alarm feature: her custom-built security system. By design, it worked silently and in isolation. She'd long ago decided to deal with intruders herself and leave the police out of the equation. Besides, response time to her house would be ten minutes at best, probably more like twenty, especially at the brink of midnight on New Year's Eve.

Assuming this wasn't a false alarm, the odds of this being a random break-in to steal cash or jewelry in this La Jolla neighborhood? A hundred thousand to one.

She sensed her husband stir and pressed a button on the remote, killing the bed's vibration. Left with the stillness of the room, she heard only the light patter of rain against the skylights.

"Linda, what's going on?"

"Get up and stay low."

"Wait. What—"

"Prowlers."

"Prowlers? You mean—"

"Yes."

He didn't move.

She put command in her voice. "Damn it, Glen, *now*."

"What about our dogs?"

Their dogs . . . ? First things first, but he was right: she shouldn't leave them running loose. She whispered their names, herded them into the closet, and closed the door. Her two German shepherd rescues were visually intimidating, but that was all. They had no tactical or combat training. Although she'd do her best to protect them, she wouldn't risk her life, or Glen's, in the process.

"We can't leave them—"

"Stay close and don't make any noise. I need absolute silence."

She grabbed her Beretta M9 from the nightstand drawer, thumbed off its safety, and verified the suppressor was tight. After powering its laser, she gave it a quick test to be sure it worked.

It did.

She also took her night-vision scope. The M9's tritium sights glowed brightly, but she wanted a bigger advantage. Used in tandem with the NV, her laser-sighted Beretta became a more effective weapon. A pressure switch on the grip activated the laser; otherwise it stayed dark.

Dressed only in her underwear, she had no place to put the extra magazines, so she took a few seconds to throw on a pair of cargo shorts and a T-shirt. Having extra ammo might be the difference between living or not.

***

Nathan McBride's cell didn't ring with its normal tone. The distinct sound meant only one thing—an activated alarm. He unlocked it, looked at the screen, and knew he needed to respond.

Right now.

He scrambled up from the floor, where he'd been curled up with his two giant schnauzers, and started a mental countdown. Fully alert, Grant and Sherman trailed him into the closet.

His security company had installed state-of-the-art systems for many of his Marine Corps and CIA colleagues, and when their alarms triggered, notifications appeared on his computer and mobile devices.

This alert originated from Linda Genneken's home.

An image of her compact form flashed through his mind. Five feet tall. Athletic. Long brown hair. Hazel-green eyes. Confident. Capable. Although Nathan was younger and towered over her by a good seventeen inches, pound for pound, LG was one of the toughest human beings on the planet. In her mid-fifties, she could go hand to hand against 99.99 percent of the earth's population and win the fights, but given the opportunity, she preferred shooting her combatants.

Truth be told, so did Nathan.

Before being promoted to chief of Latin American operations, she'd successfully completed every type of field mission known to the Agency. She possessed survival training in all environments, held black belts in multiple fighting arts, and could fire everything from a pellet gun to a TOW anti-tank missile.

Three . . . two . . . one . . . *right on time.*

He answered Harv's call. "I see it."

The voice on the other end held its usual calm baritone. "Is there any chance of convincing you to wait for me?"

"None."

"Yeah, I kinda figured."

Harv was his closest friend. Friendship to Nathan meant giving your life for the other; nothing else defined it. Harv had been the spotter in their two-man sniper team in the Marines and then his teammate in the CIA. Now, many years post-service, Harv and he owned a highly successful private security company. The bond they shared went beyond friendship, beyond family. At times, Nathan swore they shared a single consciousness. Although his connection to Genneken wasn't as strong, it didn't matter.

Nathan switched to speaker, set his phone down, and hustled into black 5.11 Tactical clothes. "She's one of us. I need to get over there."

"You're seeing what I'm seeing, right? All her thermal imagers picked up heat signatures within two minutes of each other. If only one of them had been triggered . . ."

"It could be a stray animal. All of them means trouble."

"Right, so if the TIs are picking up warm bodies, why aren't the motion detectors and IR beams going off?"

"Good question. We'd better wear vests."

"Cops?" Harv asked.

"She wouldn't want them; they'd only get in her way. And ours."

"I really think you should wait for me."

"A lot can happen in twenty minutes. Send her a text. I'm heading out the door in the next thirty seconds. ETA five minutes."

"Been slumming it in La Jolla with the mutts?"

"I got a little bored in Clairemont." Nathan owned two homes. His Clairemont residence was tiny compared to his La Jolla digs, but the smaller house somehow fit him better. He spent most of his time there.

"You? Bored?"

"You know what I mean."

"Yeah, I do. My text might distract her."

"Send it anyway, I'm sure she's silenced her phone. Look for my car. I'll park near the hairpin on El Camino Del Teatro and approach her place from the canyon."

"That could be the bad guys' route in and out."

"I'm counting on it."

That would be the end of it. Harv wouldn't say anything to undermine his resolve or confidence. They didn't operate that way.

Wearing an armored vest, he bounded down the stairs with his emergency bag in hand. "See you in twenty. And Harv?"

"Yeah?"

"Tell LG not to shoot me."

Harv didn't say anything.

"One more thing."

"What's that?"

"Happy New Year."

***

Linda set her pistol and NV down on the bed, unlocked her phone, and put it in vibration mode. A tap of the flashing security app showed a site map of her property. She squinted at the blinking red lights, each representing the location of a triggered thermal imager.

She knew it wasn't normal, but in situations like this, she didn't feel fear, only resolve. The adrenaline rush reminded her how much she missed being a covert-ops officer. She'd never shared that sentiment with her husband because, quite frankly, Glen would never understand it. It didn't matter. As cold as it sounded, his understanding wasn't required. The simple fact was, once activated, she became an efficient killer. She didn't question it, debate it, or regret it.

Whoever these intruders were, they had the house surrounded. She tapped a menu button and the screen changed to the motion-detector map. Oddly, it showed no activity. Neither did the infrared beam screen. Could her system be malfunctioning? It seemed unlikely.

Using the night-vision scope, she took a quick look through the blinds but saw no movement in the rear yard. She tapped her phone again, calling up a grid-like mosaic of live thermal-image feeds.

There.

She tapped the west-facing feed and enlarged the image.

Like a grim reaper, a glowing hooded figure stood in her yard, facing the house.

She felt her skin tighten. Creepy didn't begin to describe how the intruder looked.

Cursing her carelessness, she lowered into a crouch and hoped her lit face hadn't been seen. If any of them had NV . . .

She took another look at her phone. The man outside still hadn't moved.

What the hell's he doing?

Three more feeds showed the same thing—stationary figures, standing in her yard like statues. Wearing knee-length rain ponchos, they appeared as bright objects compared to the ambient background temperature. The thermal imager overlooking the pool area showed two more. She scrolled through all the other feeds and saw three additional threats.

Were they waiting for a command to rush forward in a simultaneous attack? No, that didn't make sense. Some of them were already inside the grid of IR beams and all were inside the range of the motion detectors.

How could they have gotten that far without—

Then she knew.

She switched back to the first TI feed, enlarged the image to maximum, and focused on the man's boots. The guy's position had changed slightly. He stood about a foot closer to the house.

This is big trouble.

With their heels pressed together, the intruders were shuffling forward at ultraslow speed to avoid triggering the motion detectors. An extremely disciplined task. To the untrained eye, they wouldn't appear to be moving at all. She knew a time lapse would look oddly beautiful—stationary figures gliding along the ground as if hovering.

Whoever these guys were, they obviously weren't aware her security system employed TIs. Clearly, they knew about the other security measures; that's why the prowler on the west side of the house had dropped to the ground. He was in the process of crawling underneath the beam, which meant they had night-vision equipment. A third-generation or newer NV scope could see an IR beam.

Based on their progress, they'd reach her walls within five minutes.

Her phone vibrated. Once. A text or email alert, not a call. Thinking it was an automated alert from her system, she ignored it.

Linda eased toward the bedroom door, gun up, and listened. She didn't think any of them were inside the house yet. Her dogs would've heard or smelled them, and they couldn't penetrate her last line of security without setting off additional alarms. So far, only the exterior TIs had picked up activity.

She felt her phone vibrate again and decided to take a look. The message was from Harvey Fontana, a name she hadn't thought about in years. His security company had installed her system and rigged the custom vibration feature. She squinted at the screen, remembering her system linked to McBride's and Fontana's phones.

```
echo five eta in five - don't shoot him
```

She squinted at the screen. Echo Five had been McBride's CIA moniker when they'd worked in Central and South America. Fontana was Echo Four, and she'd been Echo One.

"Who is it?" Glen asked.

Now she had to worry about shooting a friendly. At least McBride's size would make him easy to ID. Not too many men stood six foot five, 240 pounds. Her size was quite the opposite—another saving grace: McBride would never mistake her for one of the intruders, especially dressed as she was.

She pressed the microphone icon and didn't bother including the punctuation. "Eight or more intruders I'm going silent." She hit Send.

"Who is that? Who are you texting?"

"Glen, be quiet."

She regretted her tone but couldn't afford the added distraction. At least she knew a friendly was on the way—an extremely capable friendly. McBride was many things, but sloppy and careless weren't two of them. He'd be fully aware of her concerns. She didn't fear death, but she *did* fear the manner of her death, and dying can be an agonizing business—every operations officer's worst nightmare, especially a female's.

At least McBride's security system did its job. If she lived through this, she'd buy him a lifetime's worth of Nordstrom gift cards. The man needed some serious wardrobe coaching.

She reached back, gave Glen's arm a squeeze, and wished there was something she could say to ease his nerves. If the intent of the intruders was to kill or capture her, they wouldn't leave a witness behind.

If she died, Glen died.

And likely, badly.

For both their sakes, she needed to find a good defensive position before the intruders breached her walls.

***

Nathan pushed the limits of control on the way to LG's, but he had to be extra careful because of the wet roadways. The increased speed and heightened sense of peril made the experience tolerable. He hated driving, even when the streets were deserted. His distaste of driving was so severe that he didn't even drive the golf cart when he and Harv hit the links. He liked flying, though. Was it self-indulgent to own a helicopter? Of course, but screw it, he'd earned it. His Bell 407 was an awesome ship, and the pleasure he derived from flying far outweighed the expense. It was, after all, his sole indulgence in life.

Nathan answered Harv's call as he accelerated to seventy miles an hour down Nautilus. "I'm fifteen minutes out. You?"

"Two minutes," Nathan said.

"I had to plug her address into the nav. I haven't been there in years."

"Did she get back to you?"

"She said she's facing at least eight intruders and going silent. You'll need to be extra careful, or you'll find yourself on the business end of her Beretta."

"The thought had crossed my mind. She's always liked that M9."

"And she's a crack shot with it, better than me."

"No one's better than you."

"I found where you're going to park. Let's hope she hangs in there until you arrive. She'll be glad to see you."

"Hardly. She never liked me."

"I happen to know for a fact that isn't true. It wasn't true then and it isn't true now."

"Then why the cold shoulder?"

"What? You mean not everyone warms to your fuzzy personality?"

"It's more than that. She was . . . I don't know . . . indifferent."

"She wasn't indifferent. She was disengaged. You of all people should understand that."

"So we're the same, LG and me?"

Harv didn't say anything, which was an answer.

"It's a wonder she ever spoke to me."

"Come on, Nate, that's not fair. Most of our missions weren't fought on battlefields. How many times did we make a single kill, then bug out?"

"A bunch." Nathan knew the exact number. It was hard to forget. "And . . ."

"I know, I know. We've had this discussion many times. Someone had to do it, I get that, but it doesn't make it any easier to live with."

"LG did the same stuff we did. Worse. She was also a trained inter-rogator. Did it ever occur to you that she probably thought *you* never liked *her*?"

"I liked her. I would've given my life for her."

"You nearly did."

"Maybe it's a chemistry thing, but a man can tell when a woman doesn't like him."

"I still say you're imagining things."

"Do you remember when I first met Holly?"

"Is there a tattoo in the NBA?"

"Okay, dumb question. Even though we got off to a rough start, I just knew she liked me." He braked hard for the turn onto Muirlands.

"She's attracted to tall, introverted men with long, deep scars on their faces. I mean, what woman isn't?"

Nathan smiled, glad Harv couldn't see it. "I'll be careful."

"No unnecessary risks, Nate. I like my world with you in it."

He wanted to say, *Define unnecessary*, but didn't. "Come in dark and text me right after you park. Better yet, use your radio. I'll be wired for auto-transmit. We'll use channel seventeen and speak Russian. The intruders might have a scanner."

"Good thought. LG never did any ops over there, so it's unlikely they speak Russian."

"I'm almost at the hairpin. See you in a few minutes." Nathan ended the call, remembering how he'd felt being around Genneken.

Quicksand.

Her intense gaze, combined with that arctic demeanor, made her impossible to read. There'd been times when he couldn't tell if she'd been pissed off or happy. Who knew? Maybe she'd been both.

Harv was right. He and Linda were the same. Different genders but identical at the core. Despite LG's icy persona, he meant what he'd said. He'd give his life for her and knew she'd do the same for him. The bond they'd formed in Venezuela hadn't been watered down over the years. She might not like him, but loyalty outweighed personal differences. Whether she wanted it or not, LG was getting his help tonight.

Like Harv said, the trick would be avoiding the wrong end of her M9.

***

"We're going downstairs," Linda whispered. "Keep your hand on my back."

"I know what to do."

"Absolute silence unless I say otherwise. When I tell you something, tap me twice to confirm you heard."

She felt two pokes on her back. If this wasn't such a serious situation, she might've laughed. For once in his life, her husband was in complete marital-listening mode.

Until McBride arrived, her only hope of making it through this involved dealing with the intruders decisively, with deadly force. If one lived, she'd interrogate him, but she planned to kill, not capture. Physically and mentally, she possessed everything needed to defend herself.

She hoped Glen wouldn't become a problem, but if he did, she'd have to knock him unconscious. As much as she hated the thought, she couldn't allow him to slow her down. The classified information in her head could cost lives and topple governments. Being captured wasn't an option, even at the expense of her husband.

So Glen's an expense? Like paying a bill?

It felt like a slap to the face, but she never twisted the truth to fit her needs. She'd do everything possible to save his life, but she'd sworn an oath long before Glen entered her life. Besides, he knew the score. He'd married her knowing what she'd done for a living, knowing this could happen someday.

Well, someday had arrived.

Except for the hum of the refrigerator, the house remained quiet. She doubted anyone had seen her during the brief interval her face had been illuminated by her phone. They'd never make themselves such easy targets, especially if they believed they'd been spotted.

They've got balls; she conceded that much.

So who were they and why now? She'd been retired for more than seven years. If people connected to her past wanted her dead, why the delay? Linda had enemies all over Latin America, but none of them should've been able to find her.

Shaped like a cross, her house featured a central stairwell that served all three levels. Currently, she was just outside the master bedroom on the second level. Even though every second-floor room had a door accessing the linear veranda encircling the house, it wouldn't do much good if the intruders decided to torch the place. She and Glen could use the veranda to escape the house fire, but that would expose them to sniper fire.

Linda inhaled through her nose but didn't smell anything. Professionals knew better than to smoke before an op or use strong deodorant or cologne. These guys would be totally odorless and silent. Had the thermal imagers not picked them up, they would've been invisible too.

In a stealthy handgun duel, getting eyes on the enemy first usually meant living or not. She'd managed that much, but the worst was yet to come. If she and her husband didn't survive, she hoped the intruders would spare her dogs. An image from the movie *John Wick* invaded her mind and she forced it aside.

Halfway down the stairs, the silence ended.

The crash of breaking glass came from every direction at once, even behind her in the bedroom. Something thumped along the hardwood floor.

Shit! No time to warn Glen.

She crouched, closed her eyes, and buried her face in the fold of her arm.

CHAPTER 2

Nathan climbed out, used his night-vision scope to scan Linda's house, and saw no sign of movement. Along with a dozen other estate homes, Linda's place sat atop the south ridgeline of a small canyon. He estimated her house was about five hundred feet distant and fifty to sixty feet higher in elevation.

Her backyard and pool area were equally quiet, as were the houses adjacent to hers. A twenty-foot vertical cliff fortified her home from the canyon. Like the access between decks of a Navy ship, near-vertical stairs ran down the sandstone cliff; he knew he'd have to ascend them cautiously. Harv was right: that could be the intruders' route in and out of her property. Working quickly, he checked the wiring of his radio, inserted the earpiece, and turned the volume to a medium setting. He tested it with a few clicks and then increased it slightly.

He glanced at his watch. More than six minutes had passed since LG's alarm system had alerted his phone.

He wasn't worried about anyone driving past this location. This was a sparsely populated area of Mount Soledad, dominated by huge homes spaced well apart from one another. Most were screened from the street by mature landscaping and security walls. A few windows glowed with the bluish light of televisions, but otherwise this neighborhood remained comatose.

He froze when he thought he heard glass breaking.

And it came from the direction of Linda's house.

What he saw next looked like something from a horror movie.

As if controlled by demonic forces, all her windows ignited in stroboscopic flashes.

Half a second later, the muffled thumps reached his position.

Nathan sprang into high gear.

He quickly transferred some additional items to his belly pack and took a series of deep breaths. After locking the car, he placed the keys on top of the front left tire.

This wasn't a long-gun mission. He didn't have his Remington 700. Tonight's action would be up close and personal—the way he preferred it.

Hoping he wasn't too late, he entered the canyon.

Hang tough, LG. I'm on my way.

***

A concussive shock wave hammered all of Linda's senses, especially her hearing.

The M84's detonation felt like a blow to her kidneys.

Glen bent and cursed, having taken the worst of the nonlethal blast.

She gave silent thanks that it hadn't been a frag or incendiary, then reconsidered her gratitude. They wanted her alive. Not a pleasant thought.

"Get in the linen closet."

"I can't see!" he whispered loudly.

"Feel along the wall."

"Shit, Linda!"

"Do it, or we're both dead."

She'd thought about arming him with a handgun, but he possessed zero combat training. Far better to keep him concealed and quiet.

Looking like a blind person in an unfamiliar house, Glen felt his way up the stairs and disappeared around the corner.

The dogs were going berserk.

If she turned them loose, they'd provide a tactical advantage by distracting the intruders, but it also meant sacrificing their lives. The deciding factor was time. She couldn't afford the eight seconds required to hustle to the closet and back.

A blaring siren began shrieking. Shit, she'd forgotten to disable it. The breached-door or -window alarm worked separately from the perimeter alarm that had triggered the bed's vibration. She found the right screen on her phone and entered the code.

The howling ended as quickly as it started.

Fortunately, it hadn't been active long enough to alert McBride's answering service or the San Diego Police Department. It would be chalked up to a mishap.

To avoid being trapped in no-man's-land, she descended the stairs, being careful to keep the silver beads at the ends of her braids from ticking. She stopped short of the landing in the kitchen, brought her NV scope up to her eye, but didn't activate the pistol's laser yet.

Peering around the corner, she saw the east-facing French door was shattered, its tempered glass scattered across the floor.

Movement caught her attention and she aimed in that direction. Weaving through the living room furniture, a single gunman advanced directly toward her. She saw the distinct outline of night-vision goggles and something far more chilling.

Confirming what she suspected, he held a TASER, not a handgun.

In addition to the TASER, a suppressed MP5 hung across the gunman's chest, probably set to its three-round-burst mode.

She lined up on his form, saw body armor, then adjusted her aim to the man's face. He hadn't spotted her yet.

Linda activated her laser.

In the green image of her NV, a bright star blossomed on the man's nose.

She squeezed the trigger in a controlled pull.

Her weapon bucked and the expended casing clinked off the wall.

The man didn't move.

Had she missed? No way. She'd drilled him for sure.

Then the gunman shuddered as though a chill raked his body. He tried to stay on his feet but collapsed to the floor.

One man down, fifteen rounds left. She always kept a bullet in the chamber, giving her an extra shot.

Contrary to how Hollywood portrays it, her suppressed pistol wasn't silent, even with subsonic ammunition. The report sounded like two Bibles being slapped together. To a combat vet, it was an unmistakable sound.

She pivoted to the opposite side of the stairwell and scanned the library.

There!

Another gunman lurked in one of the bookshelf alcoves.

And, like his fallen comrade, he hadn't seen her.

He definitely knew someone had fired a round, but he didn't know where it had come from. The man was looking for movement, hoping to locate the source of the shot.

Linda intended to give him movement, in the form of 124 grains of 9mm copper and lead traveling at three football fields per second.

She bench-rested her M9 against the wall, painted the laser just below his NV goggles, and pulled the trigger.

The gunman's head jerked and his arms went stiff.

The man fell sideways and began a death spasm, something she'd seen more times than she cared to admit.

Me or them, she reminded herself.

Two down, fourteen rounds left.

Time to relocate.

She entered the kitchen and sandwiched herself between two bar stools that served the island. The French door from the kitchen into the backyard was also shattered, but she didn't see an intruder.

Then she heard the crunch of glass.

Someone was already in the kitchen.

Directly opposite her position, a gunman had to be crouched on the far side of the island. He must've ducked for cover when the shooting started.

Linda had a huge advantage by knowing the contents of the island; if she fired through the cabinet at a precise height and location, her bullet would penetrate the panels and exit the other side. With a little luck, the bullet would have enough energy left to do some damage.

Worth the risk.

Eighteen inches below the granite countertop's height, she aimed the pistol for a level shot. At the same instant she pulled the trigger, she lowered her face to avoid taking any splinters to her eyes.

The wood veneer ruptured and she felt something smack the top of her head.

She heard a grunt of pain and seized the moment to circle the island.

A single gunman lay on his side, clutching a wounded shoulder. He reached for the TASER, but she stomped his forearm.

With his bloody hand, he tried to unsling his MP5.

Yeah, right. She finished him with a single round through the back of his neck, just below his helmet.

Three men down, twelve shots left in her pistol.

She held her position and listened for several seconds but heard only the muffled tirade of the dogs. At least if they were barking, they were still alive. For now, Glen was safe in the closet, but that could change.

She reached up to her head, where a piece of the cabinet had grazed her scalp, and felt blood, but it wasn't too bad. If it began dripping into her eyes, she'd have to deal with it. Staying low, she grabbed the dish towel hanging on the trash compactor's handle and stuffed it into her waistband.

Hearing nothing, she took a few seconds to evaluate her dead opponent.

Black face paint hid his facial features, but she got the distinct impression he was Hispanic. A closer look revealed a collar mike and earpiece, a digital-camo uniform, and all the trimmings of a Special Forces soldier. Had she been targeted by her own government? No way. And his camo didn't look like a US Army or Marine Corps digital pattern. Besides, if CIA Director Cantrell wanted her to come in, all she had to do was ask.

Not knowing whether the gunman's helmet employed a micro camera, she stayed out of its sight line, reached down, and turned the gunman's head to the side, facing away from her. She set her NV scope down and quickly searched the man. He carried no wallet, had no rank insignia, or any other discernible characteristic that allowed her to identify his country of origin. No surprises there.

The dogs erupted again.

Directly above her position, their muffled barking reached a new fury.

One or more gunmen were in the master bedroom.

Would they kill her dogs? She hoped not. Putting herself in their mind-set, she ran some scenarios through her head. To shoot the dogs, they'd have to open the door a crack or blindly fire into the closet, but they wouldn't risk that if they wanted a live prisoner to interrogate.

Cracking the door to shoot the dogs held risk. They could be facing the muzzle of a gun. It was more likely they'd leave someone to monitor the closet while the others continued sweeping the house.

Returning her attention to the dead man in front of her, she unclipped his radio with the intent of taking it, but realized it would give her location away without the corresponding earpiece. From the look of things, the wire was routed under his vest. Professionals always secured the wire by tying it to a piece of clothing—like a belt or buttonhole—to prevent the wire from being yanked due to a snag. A tug confirmed her suspicion: the wire wouldn't pull free. Besides, they'd likely be in compromised-radio mode and either go silent or communicate in code.

Her best course of action was to remain mobile, keep picking them off one by one, and hold out until McBride arrived. With a little luck, all her old colleague would find was a mop-up job.

An idea formed.

She turned the radio's volume down to its bare minimum and began a series of intermittent clicks, mixed with the deepest mumbling sound she could make. Whoever was hearing the broken traffic might think the transmitting radio was malfunctioning.

She heard it then, a short code phrase. *"Cambie al bravo del plan."* She spoke fluent Spanish: *Switch to plan bravo.*

Linda pulled the radio's earpiece wire from its jack, cranked the volume to maximum, and set it inside the kitchen sink, where it couldn't be seen. Next, she eased around the island to a location where she could see the dining room, part of the living room, and the stairs' landing.

If these gunmen were part of—

Heavy clunking sounds interrupted the silence.

Someone bounded down the stairs in a big hurry.

Could that be Glen? No way, he'd never be that reckless. Or stupid.

She'd have to hold fire until she was certain. If they'd taken him hostage and were using him as a human shield, she'd do her best to avoid shooting him, but bullets were going to fly. Hindsight was always 20/20, and she now wished she'd kept Glen with her.

Whoever descended the stairs stopped at the same place she'd used to nail the first two gunmen. Keeping her laser dark, she lined up at the corner and waited.

Gradually, a pair of night-vision goggles crept into view as the wearer peered around the corner.

A sudden transmission from the radio in the sink startled the arriving gunman. He swept his TASER toward the sound.

Linda lined up on the intruder's nose, and fired her fifth round.

The gunman's head snapped back from the kinetic energy.

A pop echoed through the house as the gunman squeezed the TASER's trigger. The tiny prongs cracked the glass window behind her.

His brain scrambled, the man fell forward to his knees, then plopped sideways. Four men down, eleven rounds left in her M9.

Not enough.

She ejected the magazine, pocketed it, and inserted a full one in its place. Because the chamber already held a round, she didn't need to cycle the slide.

Time to relocate again.

She studied her immediate area with the NV scope and detected no movement. Part of her hoped the others would flee, but the dominant part of her wanted to exterminate them. All she had to do was picture herself bound and naked while they took turns. No, these intruders deserved to die. And she wouldn't stop there: she'd hunt down whoever ordered this assault and kill them as well.

She eased across the front of the oven and took up a new position at the corner of the island. To her left, the dining room table and chairs offered some cover.

The radio came to life again.

"Todas unidades, informen!"

All units, report. Linda was sorely tempted to grab the radio and tell the ringleader what she thought of his mother, his sisters, and his lack of physical manhood. But caution won the moment.

Five voices copied the transmission; meaning she still faced at least six intruders. The ringleader would likely be driving the getaway vehicle—a commander who didn't want his hands dirty. It didn't matter. He'd soon be joining his friends in the underworld.

Decision time.

Wait for the remaining gunmen to come to her, or go on the offensive and take the fight to the enemy? Both held risks, but she decided to fight a defensive battle. Thankfully, they hadn't torched or teargassed the house to force her out. She hoped she hadn't just jinxed herself thinking about it.

The dining room chairs had fairly solid backs. If she stretched her body across the far row of them, she'd be far less visible but also less mobile. She decided to risk it because she didn't think the intruders would be expecting anyone to hide like that.

Staying low, she moved across the dining room to the far side of the table. The chairs felt cold against her skin and caused a shiver, but she got herself into a horizontal position across the top of them easily enough.

Now it became a waiting game.

Like a spider anticipating prey, she merged with the furniture and remained focused on the stairwell's landing.

Nothing happened.

Patience, she told herself.

Her wait wasn't long. Something thumped down the stairs.

And it wasn't footsteps.

CHAPTER 3

Her ears . . . she couldn't cover them in time.

She lowered her head and closed her eyes.

One-one-thousand . . .

Two-one-thousand . . .

The device detonated.

A blinding red glare penetrated her eyelids.

Unprotected, her hearing took the full force of the explosion and she nearly cried out. The banger did its job flawlessly, making all of her senses scream in protest. She felt, more than heard, two gunmen thump down the stairs.

This was it.

Survival or extinction.

As before, the footsteps stopped short of the landing.

She aimed her Beretta at the corner where the gunmen would appear.

A pair of NVGs slowly eased out from the corner.

It took all the self-control she possessed to resist squeezing the trigger.

If she shot the first gunman before getting eyes on the second, her job grew in difficulty by a factor of ten.

The goggles looked down at the dead man, came back up, then slipped behind the stairwell's corner.

Patience. He'll be back. Wait him out . . .

Her eyes felt dry and raw. She blinked a few times.

Lying here immobile, she felt terribly vulnerable. Now wasn't the time to second-guess herself. She'd chosen this spot and she'd make it work.

Any second now.

As if on cue, the goggles reappeared, followed by the gunman's body.

He slinked around the corner and took a knee, crouched at a forty-five-degree angle to her position. A second gunman came into view, looked in her direction, and froze.

Time seemed to stretch as the second gunman swept his TASER back and forth through the dust and smoke, the green line of its laser plainly visible in her NV scope.

Linda projected herself into her opponents' perspective again. They obviously knew their prey was down here somewhere. The dead man at their feet was all the proof they needed. They had to be nervous, knowing a bullet could come from any direction at any second. They also had to be considering abandoning the fight. Four of their teammates had gone silent, presumably dead, and they didn't want to be the next casualties.

The second gunman stayed put and pivoted toward the living room. Without standing, the first gunman lined up in the opposite direction, covering his friend's back.

Then they both froze and their lasers went dark.

Was she blown? Had they seen her?

She held her breath and squinted in concentration. The angle she had on the second gunman wasn't ideal but better than nothing.

Should she wait or shoot?

The pressure to nail the first guy felt agonizing.

Risking everything, she decided to delay a few more seconds.

And was glad she did.

The second man eased to the left of his comrade, giving her perfect lines of sight on both of them.

She'd never get a better chance.

She began a gradual increase of pressure on the Beretta's trigger, giving it about half what it needed. Part of her felt pity for them, but she reminded herself of what could happen.

Tied and bound while they took turns.

That's not happening. Not tonight. Not ever.

She increased to three-quarters pressure and squinted in concentration.

Now.

She activated the laser, painted the second gunman's cheek, and executed a controlled tug of the trigger.

Her pistol bucked.

The bullet flew true.

It slammed home, jolting the guy's head sideways. The blood spatter on the wall confirmed the kill.

The lead gunman reacted quickly. Caught in the open, he used his collapsing comrade as a shield and brought his TASER up.

With no clear shot to his head, Linda fired twice at the man's thigh and scored two hits. The guy grunted in pain but kept bringing his TASER up.

Have it your way. She fired twice more, aiming slightly lower.

Following a string of Spanish obscenities, the gunman dropped the TASER, shoved his human shield aside, and pulled a semi-auto pistol from a hip holster.

Before he could line up on her, she drilled him in the face.

Cartilage, bone, and brains were no match for high-speed, copper-jacketed slugs moving at nine hundred feet per second. Another spray pattern decorated her wall. She'd put a nice picture frame around it, then sign and date it.

Instinctively, she kept a tactical tally. Eleven total shots fired. Ten rounds left in her weapon. And six stiffs. Not a bad evening's work so far.

Time to reposition.

Moving slowly, she eased off the dining room chairs and crouched, facing the living room.

The radio on the counter came to life at the same time the glass window behind her shattered inward.

Shit. SHIT!

Before she could turn to face the threat, she heard the pop of a TASER and knew what would follow.

The tiny prongs stabbed her flesh just below the nape of her neck.

Oh, crap. That's a bad location.

Fifty thousand volts coursed through her like hundreds of wasp stings.

The result was hideous.

Her body went stiff as every muscle contracted. She'd only been zapped once during her training, but it had seemed far less painful then. All her voluntary functions—such as remaining on her feet—instantly short-circuited.

She wanted to curse the triggerman but all that came out was a teeth-clenched yelp. Like a poisoned insect, she curled into the fetal position, willing the agony to stop.

It didn't.

He'd given her a full dose: five seconds' worth.

Somewhere in the red haze of consciousness, she fought to keep some sense of awareness. If she could keep them from pouncing on her, she might have a fighting chance.

She'd thrown off most of the electrical disruption to her brain, but her large muscle groups wouldn't respond. She could form a fist, but her arm wouldn't obey. She could wiggle her foot, but her leg wouldn't move.

How could she have been so careless and not cleared her six? A costly mistake that would cost Glen his life. With her out of the fight, they'd search the house and find him. An overwhelming feeling of rage surfaced, but she forced it aside. Now wasn't the time for a meltdown.

All she needed was a little more time to recover.

It didn't happen.

A gunman charged into the dining room from the direction of the library.

He put a knee on her back and leaned in close. She felt his hot breath on her neck as he said, "The boss is going to have a good time with you, Little Peach, and I'll be joining the fun. We all will."

Little Peach? Only one person in the world had ever called her that. She felt her skin tighten. *Oh, dear God, not him.* Had she been able, she would've pointed her weapon at her own temple and pulled the trigger.

Instead, she tried to whip her head and smash the man's nose, but her body didn't answer the call.

He yanked her hands behind her back and used disposable handcuffs to bind her wrists. The buzz of the cuffs locking overshadowed the barking from upstairs. At least the dogs were still alive.

Taking his time, her captor ran his hands across her breasts and made an *Mmmm* sound.

She hated the thought of this greasy maggot having his way.

If only she'd let her dogs out. They might've given her the precious seconds she'd needed.

Her arms working now, she tested the plastic bindings. No good. They wouldn't budge.

"Save your strength," he said. "You're gonna need it."

"If you walk away right now," she shot back, "I'll spare one of your balls."

The gunman laughed. "How generous of you."

His hands continued down her stomach and stopped at her groin.

She played possum until the last second, then tried to knee him in the face. She made contact but struck only a glancing blow.

He backhanded her across the face.

Without good motor function yet, she did the only thing she could think of.

She spat a bloody wad.

The man stood, backed up a step, and wiped his eyes. A look of pure malevolence took his expression, evident even through the black face paint.

He reared back and kicked her torso—hard enough to rupture organs.

The result was blinding. Nauseating and sharp.

He performed a ballet-like pirouette and offered a prolonged yell of "Goooaaaal."

What an asshole.

She supposed she should be grateful he hadn't kicked her in the mouth. No doubt, they'd work on her face later.

It came on suddenly. There was no stopping it. The contents of her stomach spewed.

"Disgusting," her attacker said. He walked to the sink, filled a glass of water, and dowsed her face. "Better?"

"You're really tough against a helpless woman."

"That comes later. Right now, my colleagues are going to find your husband and peel his skin off in front of you."

"He's not here."

He smiled with an expression of *nice try*.

Part of her hoped the guy had perforated her intestines or stomach with that kick. With a little luck, she'd be septic within twelve hours and dead a day later. But thirty-six hours could be an eternity. Somehow, someway, she'd find the strength to endure whatever they had in store for her. She'd never been tested like McBride, and she wondered how she'd hold up.

McBride.

He was still coming. All she had to do was buy some time. But the only way to do that was through pain. She had nothing else left to barter with. The question was, how?

Think, Genneken, think. What did most Latino men treasure? Their macho self-image. And she knew how to tear that down to size.

"Tell me something," she said in Spanish. "Was your mother drunk?"

"What?"

"You know, the pig in the pink dress. How old were you the first time? Was she passed out or did your brothers have to hold her down?"

"You've got quite a mouth. You'll be taught how to use it later."

"I'll bet you couldn't get it up, even with all your sisters working as fluffers."

He just stared, then said, "Keep it up and I'll sew your lips shut with a fishhook and sixty-pound line."

"I've got something to tell you, but you might have a hard time accepting it."

He stared for a few seconds, then spoke into his collar mike, updating his comrades.

"Maybe I shouldn't tell you, you'd just kick me again. Cowards like you get off hurting women. It's a shame, though. It's really something your boss would want to know."

"Tell me," he said. "What would my boss want to know?"

She smiled. "The best part of you ran down the crack of your sister's ass and left a wet spot on the dirt floor."

She watched the man's expression change from amused to angry. She unclenched her teeth just in time. He kicked her in the thigh hard enough to create a bone-deep bruise. The impact spun her head into the island, face first. Her vision grayed as her nose took the force. Blood began flowing, its distinctive taste far from new.

He leaned in close again. "You'll be begging for death, but you won't get your wish. My boss is going to keep you alive for a long, long time." He reached into his backpack, produced a nasty-looking syringe, removed the cap, and plunged it into a vial. "Here's some Special K to keep you manageable, but don't worry: I'll make sure you're fully awake when the fun starts."

Ketamine.

Not giving him an easy target for the needle, she began struggling against her cuffs.

She never saw it coming, but the blow to the side of her head crippled her mind.

The sound of duct tape being pulled from a roll brought her back. Struggling to stay coherent, she felt pressure on her ankles, but she couldn't focus.

A bee sting nailed her in the back of her thigh.

He's injecting me.

The next thing she sensed was another intruder racing down the stairs.

Great, she thought, *just I what need: another dickhead joining the party.*

Would they rape her right now, or wait until later?

She hardened her resolve, telling herself she wouldn't give them the satisfaction of seeing her sob and beg for mercy. Wishful thinking. Every human had a breaking point and a good interrogator always found it. It was only a matter of time. She'd been through interrogation-resistance training, but that was a joke compared to what was coming.

Then she heard a man yell, a guttural roar of anger.

Glen?

They'd found him.

She began an all-out struggle to free her feet, thrashing around like a gaffed fish.

Glen yelled again, louder.

She looked up and saw an impossible sight.

Glen wasn't being dragged down the stairs; he charged down them.

Her assailant tossed the syringe aside and tried to pull his MP5.

Too late.

Glen body slammed him to the floor. Her husband wasn't a large man, by any means, but he'd been a championship wrestler in college.

"Run, Glen, get out!"

The gunman's face ended up near her bound feet and she kicked out with all the force she had.

And missed.

Her attacker smashed his elbow into the side of Glen's head, but her husband didn't let go. In admiration, she watched Glen sink his teeth into the outside of the guy's shoulder and shake his head like a dog trying to tear a chunk free.

The gunman growled as the two of them became an entangled blur of flailing arms and legs. Linda used the opportunity to curl her legs tight to her chest. She needed to loop her bound wrists over her feet so her hands would be free in front of her body.

Her bruised thigh erupted with fresh agony, and her stomach followed suit.

She blew out all the air from her lungs to make more room and kept forcing her feet toward her body. She clenched her teeth as the dual throbbing reached a crescendo.

Needing more than courage to get this done, she allowed anger to flood her thoughts, embracing it for what it was.

For the first time in her life, Linda Genneken experienced absolute rage. Like a cattle brand, the emotion scorched her soul.

She pulled her legs in harder, screaming like a warrior.

Just . . . one . . . more . . . inch . . .

Success!

Her hands were now in front of her. She twisted to her knees, grabbed a steak knife from the countertop, and quickly sliced the tape binding her ankles.

There was no way she could break or sever the plastic handcuffs without a tool, but she'd practiced hand-to-hand combat with bound wrists many times.

She heard it, then: the unmistakable claps of a suppressed handgun.

Three quick shots, as fast as a trigger can be pulled.

Something sprayed her face.

In the bluish light from the microwave's clock, she couldn't see much detail, but she knew the spray had to be blood. And if Glen was on top . . .

Oh, please, no.

Her fear became reality when a black stain rapidly expanded around torn holes in the fabric of Glen's T-shirt.

The bullets must've punched through Glen's chest and exited out his back. Despite the mortal wounds, Glen tried to keep his forearm around the gunman's neck, but his strength seemed to be gone. Her husband did his best to stay on top but quickly lost the battle.

The gunman pistol-whipped him on the side of the head. Glen's mouth formed an *O* shape, but no sound emerged.

As cold as the thought was, she hoped one of the slugs had pierced his heart. If so, he'd be losing consciousness within the next fifteen seconds. At least his death would be quick, and he wouldn't have to watch her being tortured.

That's a nice, cheery thought, Genneken.

Stop, she told herself. She was far from beaten. She wouldn't allow her husband's sacrifice to be in vain. Glen had bought her the precious seconds she needed with his life and she intended to cash them in.

The gunman aimed his pistol at her.

She rolled toward the oven.

This could be it.

The bullet missed, puncturing the refrigerator.

Her attacker adjusted his aim for another shot.

Hating herself for doing it, she kicked Glen's body. Her husband grunted in pain, but she got the effect she wanted. Like a billiard shot, the energy of her kick transferred through Glen into the gunman, jarring his aim. Again, the bullet missed; glass from the oven's door rained onto her head. She closed her eyes and shook her hair, dislodging the biggest pieces.

The gunman cursed and shoved Glen aside. When he tried to line up on her again, Glen somehow found the strength to grab at the man's forearm.

She gained her feet before her attacker could fire a third shot and felt a piece of glass puncture the sole of her foot. Ignoring the stinging pain, she kicked her attacker in the face.

The man's head slammed into the cabinet.

She followed up by stomping on his gun arm and felt the ulna and radius bones snap. The pistol skittered away on the floor, and she saw it was her own weapon.

Seeing the man's exposed groin, she delivered a solid kick.

The air rushed from his lungs like a punctured beach ball.

She bent over and whispered, "Welcome to *my* world. You should've taken my offer." She reared back and kicked him in the groin again, this time hard enough to rupture his nuts.

This wasn't over. The gunman who'd nailed her with the TASER must still be outside. Why hadn't he attacked? Maybe McBride was already here.

Wishful thinking, LG. You need to pretend McBride's not coming and fight your way out of this.

She took a few seconds to listen for sound. All she heard was Glen's raspy breathing, growing more strained and weak with each passing second. He'd be gone inside a minute.

The only other sound in the house was the muffled baying of her dogs.

Her husband's voice startled her.

"Linda, I'm sorry . . ."

"Breathe, Glen, just keep breathing."

"Our dogs . . . Get them out . . ." He coughed up blood.

He's dying and he's worried about our dogs?

"Love you . . ."

"I'm calling an ambulance." It was a white lie she could live with. Calling 911 wouldn't save him.

How could this be happening? A few minutes ago, she'd been asleep in her bed. Now, Glen bled out on the kitchen floor. She'd doled out her share of death, but she'd never been on the wrong side of it so personally. It felt so brutal and unfair, Glen being murdered for something connected to her past.

Another wave of anger swelled, but she couldn't grasp the feeling with much force. She ought to be able to tap its red energy and use it to harden her resolve, but it slipped away.

The Ketamine.

Stay focused, Genneken.

What were her options? More gunmen remained. At least two more. She thought it unlikely any of her neighbors had heard the flash bangs, given the rainy weather, the distance between the houses, and the fact that the detonations occurred inside. And even if they had, the sounds could easily be dismissed as kids playing with fireworks. Smart idea, her attackers choosing New Year's Eve for their assault.

She found another set of disposable handcuffs in her attacker's backpack and secured the guy's hands behind his back. She then took a dish towel and gagged him, tying it tightly around the back of his head.

To her horror, a wave of warmth grabbed her.

No. Not yet . . .

CHAPTER 4

Nathan felt it, the butterflies of mortal combat. This wasn't a video game where you morphed back to life. This was the real deal.

Real bullets.

Real death.

Understanding the danger allowed adrenaline to do its vital work, preparing him for battle.

He wished he could advance through the canyon more quickly, but he had to keep clearing his surrounding area. If the enemy got eyes on him first, the result wouldn't be good. Even if his vest stopped a bullet, he'd be in a bad way.

At the base of the vertical bluff below her backyard, he took a few seconds to listen and swore he heard the faint pop of suppressed handgun fire.

He moved west along the cliff over to the stairs. A small locked gate guarded the landing, but he easily hopped it.

Nathan kept his Sig Sauer nine millimeter in his hand and tested a step. The wood didn't creak and he began his ascent.

Near the top, he slowed and peered over. Detecting no one, he hurried up the last seven treads and ran over to a line of oleander bushes along the fence, screening Linda's pool from prying eyes. Beyond the fence, groups of patio furniture sat on the concrete deck. He used the NV to scan the house and saw a shattered French door. Other than that, things looked undamaged. He caught the faint odor of burned power, probably left over from the stun grenades. He reached into his waist pack for his thermal imager, but didn't find it. Crap. In his haste to get up here, after seeing Linda's windows ignite, he'd forgotten to grab it.

Way to go, McBride.

Without warning, the entire ground floor of Linda's house flashed at the same instant he heard the thump. At least if the intruders were still deploying bangers, it meant they hadn't killed or captured her yet.

Nathan estimated her house stood a good fifty yards away from his current position. He considered making an all-out sprint, but without knowing how many gunmen he faced or their locations, it could be the last thing he ever did.

He paralleled the oleander bushes, working his way toward the western boundary of the property, where an eight-foot stucco wall separated her place from the neighbor's. Planted along the wall, a row of citrus trees offered him a good way to advance toward the house with some cover.

He looked at the shattered French door and froze when he heard a suppressed pistol shot from somewhere inside. His night vision picked up more flashes from suppressed shots, followed by several more. In Spanish, a man yelled a crude string of words about LG's mother. Nathan didn't hear a sixth shot over the hollering, but his NV registered the flash. The foul language ended.

Linda was likely alive and, from the sound of things, engaged in a handgun battle.

The next thing he heard was glass breaking and a different kind of sound. He couldn't be sure, but it sounded like a TASER. A distinctive pop-like sound, quite different from a suppressed handgun. If the intruders were using nonlethal grenades, it made sense they'd also be using nonlethal handguns, with the intent to take her prisoner.

Thirty feet ahead, the pool fence changed direction and ran north toward the house. Fortunately, the oleander bushes followed the fence. If anyone were inside the pool area, the bushes gave Nathan good concealment.

He'd been about to dash over to the line of citrus trees when he sensed immediate danger. Call it intuition, or ESP, or just dumb luck, but something made him look to his left.

Good thing he did.

On the expanse of grass, Nathan saw the faint outline of a man running toward the shattered French door. Nathan knew the gunman had spotted him because the guy stopped and didn't fire. The man needed a few seconds to determine whether Nathan was a friendly.

A costly delay.

In the NV image, Nathan saw the gunman's laser come to life and sweep across the grass directly toward him.

Nathan dived to a prone position, ignored the punch to his stomach from the waist pack, and brought his Sig to bear.

Nathan fired first.

And missed.

Damn it! He should've made that shot.

Although his bullet flew off-target, it caused the gunman to flinch, which bought him half a second for a follow-up shot.

His opponent shuddered as the bullet punched his body armor.

Not wanting to risk missing a headshot at this distance, Nathan drilled him again. And again. Subsonic rounds didn't pack the energy of their supersonic counterparts, but they still hurt like hell. The gunman dropped to the grass to stop the assault on his rib cage.

Nathan didn't oblige him.

He bench-rested his pistol and fired three more rounds as fast as he could accurately pull the trigger. One of them found the gunman's neck.

His cervical column severed, the gunman stopped moving. Taking no chances, Nathan aimed just under the guy's NVGs and fired his eighth bullet. The gunman's head jerked from the impact.

Not knowing if anyone had lined up on his muzzle flashes, he rolled left. Fortunately, no return fire came his way. He sprinted across the open expanse of lawn toward the first citrus tree along LG's western property line.

After reloading his Sig, he heard it: a female scream of pure rage.

***

Linda felt the sensation arrive in the form of a gentle surge, like the end of a foamy wave soaking into the sand. She knew the next one would be bigger and longer. An intramuscular injection took five to ten minutes, maybe less, depending on the dose. There was nothing she could do. Medical chemistry couldn't be defeated through willpower alone.

She had a date with oblivion.

Making matters worse, Glen's labored breathing stopped.

Doing CPR on him might extend his life by a few minutes, but she couldn't do that and fight the intruders at the same time. And what was the point? CPR would only delay the inevitable. Glen wasn't coming back.

She wiped a tear and focused on her threat vectors: the dining room, the kitchen door, and the stairwell's landing. She believed at least two more gunmen still stalked her property. Or was it three? How many had she killed?

Another feeling of warmth engulfed her.

Linda looked at the microwave's clock: 12:07 a.m. Within five minutes, she'd be semiconscious and quite helpless. With a little luck, her white knight would arrive by then. She hoped he'd find more than bloody smears on the floor.

Her assailant moaned and tried to get to his knees. Keeping her head up, she approached the kitchen counter where a wooden block of Cutco knives sat next to the toaster. She grabbed the block and shook the knives onto the floor. Shit, the clanging sounds were too damned loud. Screw it. Like swinging an axe to split firewood, she drove the block of oak onto the bound gunman's jaw and felt bone crack. The man went slack.

Who's begging for death now, asshole?

She turned from the guy and grabbed the biggest serrated knife.

What she needed to do wouldn't be easy or quick. Working against the clock, she held the knife between her feet with its sharp edge pointing upward. Annoyingly, the knife kept slipping because of the blood from her punctured foot. She used the dish towel she'd stuffed in her waistband to wrap the knife's handle, which seemed to do the trick. Leaning forward, she began moving the plasticuffs back and forth along the blade, sawing through the plastic. If she used too much downward pressure, she ran the risk of the blade slipping sideways—into one of her wrists. Not a bad way to go, given the alternative.

She made progress, but disposable cuffs weren't like common zip ties. They were thick and tough.

What was that salty taste in her mouth?

She tried to think.

It had something to do with her thigh . . . Her thigh? That didn't make sense. Then she remembered being kicked, spinning toward the island. Her nose had smashed into the cabinet.

It happened without warning.

A massive swell of light-headedness took her to a place she didn't want to go, but it felt oddly compelling to drift with it. *Oh, man, that feels good.* Something else . . . All of her pain had vanished. She closed her eyes but snapped them back open. Behind the descending curtain of fog, she knew the Special K had wormed its way into her brain, slowly peeling away her will to resist.

The knife slipped from between her feet and she stared at its strange form.

What's that knife for?

She reached for it, but both hands moved forward at the same time.

Weird . . . Why did both hands move?

Her wrists.

They were bound by disposable handcuffs.

She'd been using the knife to cut through them.

Casting caution aside, she re-braced the knife between her feet and forcefully sawed back and forth. In a last-ditch effort, she gritted her teeth and pressed harder. The plastic gave and her hands smacked the floor. She reached up, found the tiny wires connected to the back of her neck, and yanked the prongs free.

She slumped against the cabinets, exhausted.

The pool of blood under Glen's body looked too small. Why did that matter?

Think, Linda!

His heart. It wasn't pumping with much force. If he had any hope of living, the puddle ought to be bigger.

Wait, his heart wasn't pumping at all.

He'd been shot.

When her eyes started to roll back, she whipped her head from side to side, trying to clear her mind.

It only made things worse.

The kitchen's cabinets looked out of kilter. She straightened her head and cabinets leveled out.

This really sucks.

Any second now, another gunman was going to appear and take her prisoner. Would he laugh at her? Kick her around first?

Her Beretta seemed so far away. She reached out, but her hand fell to her lap. *What's that charred odor?* It smelled like burned wiring and sulfur. Was the house on fire? No, not fire . . . stun grenades.

Were those fireworks outside?

One of her neighbors must be popping off firecrackers or bottle rockets.

Idiots, she thought. *Don't they know about the wildfire danger? Oh, wait, it's raining. Brilliant thought, Linda . . .*

More pops.

From outside.

If she could hear the neighbor's fireworks, then maybe they'd heard the bangers and called the police.

Sadness washed through her.

This was so unfair to Glen. He hadn't been a bad man. They'd had some really bad arguments, but she'd try not to remember him that way.

Keeping her eyes open became its own battle as she felt her world begin to compress. She hoped Glen's death wouldn't be in vain.

I'll see you again . . . but not tonight.

She needed to remember something, something important.

Someone was coming.

Someone really big.

***

A few pops from nearby fireworks broke the silence.

With his night-vision scope still deployed, Nathan sprinted across the open lawn and stopped at the broken French door.

If he didn't warn LG he was coming in, he might get shot. But warning LG meant complicating her situation. She'd have to worry about shooting a friendly and might hesitate at the moment of truth. She knew he was coming; she just didn't know when. Weighing the consequences both ways, he made the decision.

Staying to the side of the door, he yelled, "LG! Friendly coming in!"

He waited for a barrage of small-arms fire, but nothing happened. Maybe they'd already taken her and bugged out. It hadn't been more than a minute since he heard the suppressed pistol shots. Only one way to find out.

He peered around the edge and scanned the interior. This part of LG's house was a library. He remembered it from when he and Harv had installed her security system. Floor-to-ceiling bookshelves lined the walls, augmented by three-sided alcoves.

He saw the upper half of a downed man. The rest of the body lay inside one of the book alcoves. He adjusted the focus and saw the same digital camo, armored vest, and backpack that the gunman he'd killed at the pool wore. A small puddle of blood encircled the man's head. At least LG had gotten one of them. He moved deeper into the library and ducked behind the pool table.

The acidic odor of burned powder hung in the air. Somewhere from deep inside the house, a dog barked. Check that, several dogs. It wasn't vicious sounding, more like frustrated.

So far, LG hadn't responded. He'd announced his entrance and he wouldn't do it again. If LG were still alive, she might be engaged and responding to his call would reveal her location.

He'd hold position for a few more seconds before advancing. He summoned a mental image of Linda's house. He hadn't been here in years, but her house was one of the first to employ their MSS, multi-sensor system, linked to mobile devices. It still baffled Nathan why the motion sensors hadn't been triggered. Maybe LG had turned the system off once the thermals picked up the threats.

Working his way deeper inside, he stopped at a short hallway that led to the kitchen and dining room.

Ahead, three bodies lay at the landing of a stairwell and he couldn't help but notice her marksmanship. The spray patterns on the walls were a reminder of how deadly LG was.

And still is, it seemed.

He needed to make a second announcement and had an idea. It was worth a try. He offered a warbling whistle, like a whip-poor-will.

The response came in a loud, slurred whisper. "McBride . . . is that you?"

"Yes."

"In the kitchen."

Her tone sounded oddly relaxed. He peered around the corner, saw the island but no sign of LG. She had to be on the opposite side.

Keeping his head up, he circled the island and found another dead gunman in front of the sink. Two more men lay next to Linda, one of them looking exactly like the guy near the sink, but this one was still breathing. The other man, not breathing, had to be her husband. His bloodstained T-shirt told Nathan why.

Slumped against the island, Linda rested her head against a cabinet door. Her face and white Sea World T-shirt were smeared with blood. She'd changed her appearance from what he remembered. Her dark hair, weaved in cornrows and hanging braids, accented her facial features perfectly. The ends of her braids were secured by metal beads the size of small marbles. Severed plasticuffs encircled her wrists. He hated the visual of this woman being slowly tortured to death.

From what Nathan could gather, she'd gone hand to hand, and the gunman at her feet clearly lost the bout; his mouth still oozed blood.

"Is the house clear?" he whispered.

"Probably not." She sounded drugged.

"Can you walk?"

She shook her head and motioned at the syringe next to her. "Special K."

Nathan squinted at the term. The street name for Ketamine.

"How long ago?"

"Dunno . . . What took you so long?"

"I stopped for coffee."

She nodded at the unconscious gunman. "Finish him."

"Linda, he's out of the fight."

"Going to rape me . . . they all were. He . . . murdered Glen."

Nathan stared, his mind working. Clearly, this man had committed murder and planned to sexually torture Linda. He didn't know what was going on, or why these men had attacked her, but murder was a capital offense and this guy had a date with a needle.

Gut check time.

Who was Nathan McBride? Judge, jury, and executioner? Or a Marine with ethics and a code of honor. Yes, he'd executed men in the past; but was it justified now?

She pointed to her pistol. "Use mine."

He didn't like the idea of killing a helpless man, but Linda wouldn't lie about Glen's murder or that this man intended to rape her. His trust was absolute. If Linda wanted him dead, that was good enough.

He picked up her pistol and tried to flip his mental switch, but it wouldn't budge.

Damn it, Linda. Why'd you ask me to do this?

Decision made, he clenched his teeth, activated the laser, and pulled the trigger for LG.

Not ideal, but he'd be able to sleep tonight.

Because Harv wouldn't arrive for at least another five to eight minutes, he needed to get Linda out of here and find a defensible position.

"My dogs . . . they okay?"

"I heard them barking. Where are they?"

"Closet."

"In your bedroom?"

She nodded. "Collars . . . leashes . . . in the drawer there." She tried to point, but her arm didn't make it up.

"I'll come back for them later."

"Promise?"

"I promise."

"They'll like your dogs."

"No doubt."

He stashed her pistol in his waist pack and scooped her off the floor.

"Hey, big boy," she mumbled. "Watch those hands."

CHAPTER 5

Nathan almost laughed at LG's comment. Still feisty, even after the Special K cocktail. Glen must've had his hands full. They had to be opposites or they would've killed each other. He shook his head: being married to LG would be like having a pet cobra.

At the broken glass door of the library, Nathan paused to clear his immediate threat zones.

No movement.

A glance toward the pool area confirmed the man he'd dropped hadn't moved. No surprises there. With Linda's limp form slung over his shoulder, he hustled across the lawn, the beads of her braids ticking as he ran. He reached the citrus trees and laid her down on the wet grass. Despite the weather, it wasn't overly cold. She'd be okay until Harv arrived.

"How many did you take down in the house?"

She offered a dreamy smile. "Fifty."

"You've been a busy . . . woman." He almost said girl, not woman. She'd made it clear on more than one occasion she didn't like being called a girl.

"You're a good man, McBride."

He grunted to acknowledge her, considering what to do next.

"I won't remember this . . ."

"Don't talk, okay?"

He considered holing up in the small pool house. It was such an obvious place to hide, he figured any remaining intruders wouldn't look there. He nixed that thought, preferring multiple options for relocating if needed.

If the police were on the way, he didn't hear any sirens. He held perfectly still for a good sixty seconds, listening and watching. Except for some sporadic fireworks, the neighborhood remained quiet.

"McBride?"

"Yeah, I'm here."

"I'm really glad it's you." Her voice had a dreamy, sensual tone.

"Why's that?"

"I'm going to be unconscious soon . . . and you were always such a gentleman . . . I shouldn't have given you a bad time . . . about opening doors for me . . . or getting my chair."

Her brain hadn't registered his request for no talking. "You can blame my mother."

She tried to poke his chest playfully. "Well, she raised you right."

"Stay quiet, okay? I need to text Director Cantrell."

"You can do that?"

He crouched low, shielded the glow from his phone, and dictated a text. The phone translated it perfectly and he didn't bother to fix the capital C.

```
echo five is sierra Charlie, make contact
ASAP!
```

He pressed Send and knew it would get her immediate attention. Sierra charlie represented the letters SC: code for *situation critical*. The last time he'd seen this, he'd been on the receiving end.

"McBride?"

He scanned the area with his NV again. All quiet. "Yeah?"

"Do you like me?"

"Of course I like you." Knowing her filters were down, he steered the conversation in a more germane direction. "I'm really sorry about your husband. Don't talk, okay? I'm going to clear the area. I'll be right back."

"Please. Don't go." She tried to grab his arm. "Stay."

"Sure, Linda, no problem."

"I'm feeling kinda good now. Are we . . . going to your house?"

He put a finger to her lips and issued a soft *shhh* sound.

His phone vibrated with a text from Cantrell.

one minute okay?

Sure, no problem, Rebecca. I'll just hang out right here guarding our former Latin American station chief from a small army of contract killers. Actually, that wasn't fair. He couldn't expect Cantrell to drop everything, debts or no debts. Besides, the IOUs went in both directions. She'd pulled some major strings over the years, keeping Harv and him out of trouble. *Trouble?* More like jail.

He texted back an okay.

He didn't know how many other retired operations officers were in Rebecca's speed-dial list, didn't really care. His access had been purchased with unspeakable pain and anguish. Besides, he never abused the privilege. Rebecca knew if he ever initiated contact like this, it meant a life-and-death situation.

And the reverse was true. If Rebecca ever needed them, Harv and he would drop everything and respond. No questions asked. And no money would exchange hands. She'd once told him, "You're never retired," and she'd meant it.

Even though Rebecca sat in the director's chair, she'd never lost touch with her roots as an operations officer, something he appreciated. Her rise through the CIA's ranks had been nothing short of phenomenal—a result of hard work and dedication, not of calling in political favors and brown-nosing. She sat in the director's chair because she'd earned it. Figuratively speaking, her fingernails had been—and still were—dirty.

He looked down at LG. *She's really quite striking.* He liked the Caribbean look, a lot, actually. He'd never seen the softer side of her. Even drunk, LG maintained a bulletproof veneer. In all the years he'd worked with her, she'd never let anyone in. He recalled being shocked at her wedding announcement. LG getting married? In what world?

His phone vibrated. Cantrell. He glanced at his watch: 12:10 a.m.

"I'm still sierra charlie," he said, keeping his voice low.

"Can you talk?"

"Yes, but I don't know for how long." He didn't need to say his end of the line wasn't secure.

"Give me your situation."

"I'm at Echo One's house. She's been assaulted by a squad of Special Forces types, at least ten in strength. Nationality unknown, but I heard Spanish. They're wearing unfamiliar digital camo and black face paint. They're also well armed and armored."

LG started to say something, but he gently covered her mouth. She didn't resist.

"Echo One's condition?"

"Alive but losing consciousness. They injected her with Ketamine before I arrived. How long will she be out of it?"

Cantrell paused. "Depending on the dose, around half an hour. She should be fully recovered in two hours, give or take. Does she have any injuries needing emergency care?"

"Not that I can see. Her nose looks broken and she might have some cracked ribs, but other than that, she seems okay. It's clear she went hand to hand at the end. Her husband's dead; it looks like he was involved in the scrum. It's clear they wanted her alive; the intruders brought TASERs. She'd already dropped half a dozen or more, and I got another one, but there could be holdouts lurking. Probably are. Echo Four's ETA is a few minutes. One more thing: There's an unconscious man in her kitchen."

"How unconscious?"

"I don't know. It looked like Echo One clocked him pretty hard. I didn't see evidence of any serious wounds. She wanted a more . . . permanent outcome for him. I didn't do it."

Cantrell didn't respond right away. "Smart move."

He knew what she was thinking; they now had a prisoner to interrogate, though neither of them would say it on an open cell line.

Her voice held resolve. "We need that man positively secured."

"I'd like to wait until Echo Four arrives to do that."

"*Now,* Echo Five."

Nathan took a deep breath. Cantrell was ordering him to reenter LG's house and make certain the guy couldn't escape. Not a thrilling assignment. He had an idea that held less risk. It also minimized his time inside the house. "You've got my exact locale?"

"Hang on a sec . . . You're on the west side of her property in a row of small trees. Concur?"

Nathan smiled. Digital technology never ceased to amaze him. She'd zeroed in on his cell phone. "Yeah, that's me. They're orange trees. I'll leave our guest secured under the skirt of the tree I'm next to. You're seeing that, right?"

"Yes."

"I'll tie him to the trunk and make sure he can't make any noise. Good enough?"

"That will work. You said they stuck Echo One with Ketamine?"

He knew what Cantrell wanted him to do. "The syringe is on the kitchen floor. I'll grab it and look for the vial. Is there any other activity in the area?"

"No. All quiet. They used flash bangs and timed their attack at midnight. Neighbors probably wrote off the sound as fireworks. Can you find out if SDPD's been dispatched?"

"Yes. I need to get some assets in motion. Stay on the line and hold your current position. It might be a minute or two."

"No problem." His phone went completely silent. What did he expect? Elevator music? He thought back to his initial missed shot and vowed to brush up on his combat shooting. There'd been a time when he wouldn't have missed. No need to tell Harv about it.

He was relieved Cantrell hadn't asked him to document the scene. That would've meant wiping off the intruders' face paint, taking photos, and texting them to her for the CIA's facial-recognition program. He'd also have to shoot tattoos, scars, or anything else that might ID them, including pictures of their uniforms and boots—cleat patterns and all. He knew the drill; he'd performed it many times.

LG's eyes opened. "Nathan, was that Cantrell?"

So it's Nathan now? "Yeah, Linda."

"How's she doing?"

"She's doing great."

"About Caracas . . . I never thanked you . . . You got shot."

"No need to thank me, it just kinda happened." That wasn't exactly true, but he didn't want to relive the memory right now.

Clinging to consciousness, she smiled again and touched a scar on his face. "I'm sorry about . . . Montez. What he did to you."

"It wasn't your fault, Linda. It happened, it's over."

"I never told you . . . how I felt about it."

Her hand dropped into his lap, and he moved it aside. It wasn't intentional; her brain was shutting down. Nathan knew her plight well—the twilight of pending unconsciousness. He was no stranger to surgery. Most people didn't mind the anesthetic buzz. Not him. It brought back wretched memories. Montez had given him all kinds of drugs. Heroine. LSD. Crack. Quaaludes. And yes, Special K. You name it, he'd gotten it. There'd been times when he didn't know what was real . . . even the torture. The grisly proof came later. Maybe Hell wasn't a physical place. Maybe it was an ethereal morass of twisted reality designed to tear a human mind to shreds. If so, Nathan was glad he'd never found out. He didn't blame LG for being captured in Nicaragua, never had. Yes, she'd been in command of the Echo missions, but unforeseen things happened. Not every contingency could be predicted.

He wanted to reconnoiter the area, but that meant leaving LG alone, something he wouldn't do until he went back inside for the unconscious intruder. More gunmen could be converging to this location.

He tested LG with a nudge and got no response. Gone. After circling to the opposite side of the tree, he took a knee in a defensive position from which he could see LG and the expanse of lawn extending to the house. If anyone approached from that direction, he'd see them. What he wouldn't give for a thermal imager right now.

That's two slip-ups tonight. He'd forgotten his TI and missed a shot.

There was no denying it: Being a CIA operations officer wasn't the same as riding a bike. True, you never forgot the basic skills, but others needed constant practice—like situational awareness. Fortunately, that particular skill wasn't rusty or he wouldn't have noticed movement to his right.

Advancing cautiously, another gunman wearing NVGs eased along the wall of Linda's home.

Good thing the guy didn't have a thermal imager, because he and LG would've been bright objects—impossible to miss.

An insecure shiver tightened his skin. Cantrell's call was still active! If she came back on . . .

Although his phone was set to vibrate and minimum brightness, a good pair of NVGs would still detect its glow, even through the fabric of his waist pack. The best mitigation he had was flipping it over, so the screen faced inward. Turning it off would take too much time.

Strike three. He was now at risk from his damned cell phone.

What's next?

He forced the thought aside and studied his new opponent. The gunman's movements were measured and sharp. Whoever these guys were, they weren't rank amateurs. Dressed and armed exactly like his fallen comrades, this guy was definitely one of the intruders.

Clearly, this gunman planned to enter LG's house; he was headed toward the library's door.

He estimated the distance at slightly more than thirty yards. Not ideal for night pistol work, but well within his effective range.

In ten more steps, the gunman would be at the door. Since Nathan still needed to reenter LG's house to secure the prisoner, he couldn't allow this man to go inside.

He made the decision. This was an enemy combatant who wasn't unconscious on the floor. If he didn't take this guy out right now, he'd regret it later. He had to think about LG's safety. And Harv's. Not to mention his own.

Using two hands to keep the branch from shuddering, he carefully picked an orange and hurled it behind the gunman.

It skipped off the grass and smacked the house.

The gunman spun and froze.

Perfect.

He used the tritium sights on his Sig to line up on the man's torso but held off activating the laser. He didn't want to paint his target until the last possible second. Lighting the guy up too soon would give his position away, especially to an opponent with NVGs. The gunman's ultrasensitive device would see his Sig's laser beam suspended in the light rain, providing a precise vector to his position. Once Nathan activated the laser, he'd have less than two seconds to send a bullet.

He steadied his elbow on a knee and pressed the laser's button.

In the image of his night-vision scope, a bright green dot formed on the man's chest.

Rather than react instantly by dropping to the ground or ducking for cover, the gunman looked down at himself.

Bad move.

Nathan adjusted his aim above the man's body armor and stopped at the gunman's neck to avoid hitting the NVGs or helmet.

By the time his opponent realized what was happening, it was too late.

Nathan squeezed the trigger.

The image brightened for an instant. Even suppressed, the Sig's discharge lit the area like a camera flash.

He reacquired the target, but a second bullet wasn't needed. The man was down, unmoving. Thankfully, Cantrell hadn't come back on his cell.

The instinct to relocate tugged at him, but he fought it off. He needed to stay close to LG. Given this was still an active site, carrying or dragging her to a new location wasn't a viable option.

He was about to check on her when his radio earpiece came to life with Harv's voice.

In perfect Russian, Harv said, *"I'm twenty seconds from the hairpin."*

Nathan responded in kind. "How fast did you come down the Five?"

"One-forty. I pissed off quite a few drivers."

He knew his friend would speed, but 140 miles per hour? "Keep going and park a few houses short of Linda's driveway to the east. We've still got an active site. I'm on the west side of her property, where I just dropped an intruder. Linda's been drugged, but she's okay. Her husband's KIA. There's a north–south row of citrus trees along the west wall. We're behind the second one on the north end. I'm staying put. Come in from the east and use your TI. These guys are hard to see with NV."

"Then we're already in a shoot-to-kill situation?"

"Yes. I'm on hold with our friend on the Potomac so I may have to cut this short. Proceed slowly. I'm secure for now. Check in as you progress through Linda's yard. I doubt they have a perimeter sniper or I'd be dead. Our bad guys look like SOFs. They're wearing digital camo with backpacks, waist packs, face paint, the works. They're also using NVGs, but I don't think they've got thermals."

"How are they armed?"

"Suppressed MP5s, probably set to three-round bursts."

"Copy. I'll check in once I'm approaching LG's property on foot. If there are any dogs around, they'll blow my stealth."

"I think we're in spoiled-dog territory. I doubt any of them sleep outside, especially in the rain."

"Yours sure don't."

"Point taken. Nobody barked at me as I came up the canyon. I think you'll be okay."

"On the satellite photos, I saw a security wall along the front of her property. I'll have to find a good place to scale it."

Nathan didn't like that idea. He'd rather have Harv climb over the wall where he could watch his friend's back. "Harv, I'm changing the plan. Leave your headlights on and cruise past her place. Park two hundred yards west of her driveway and hop the wall at the southwest corner."

"No problem. I just reached the hairpin."

"I've got you. I can see your bleed headlight in the treetops."

"Is LG with you?"

"Affirm. Did you hear any sirens?" Nathan knew Harv would've rolled his windows down once he got within half a mile.

"Not yet."

"I've got RC checking with local police to see if a unit's been dispatched. With a little luck, none are coming."

"She'll want her own people to secure Echo One's house."

"No doubt, but we aren't hanging around until they arrive. We're bugging out. Our friend is back on the line, gotta go."

He put the phone to his ear.

"Was that Russian?" Cantrell asked. "What's going on?"

"Just me talking to Echo Four. We're using our radios."

"SDPD hasn't been dispatched. I've got a team on the way and I don't want you there when they arrive."

"I was hoping you'd say that."

"Count on twenty-five minutes. Take Echo One with you. Can you transport her?"

"Yes."

"Is she unconscious?"

"Yes. With your team coming, I assume you don't need us to photograph the intruders?"

"My team will handle that. In twenty-three minutes, I want you to clear her property and observe from safe distance. As soon as you see two vehicles enter her driveway, take off and don't look back. Echo One's in your care until we sort out the security breach."

"I hear you. No one should've been able to get her home address, especially foreign nationals."

"I seriously doubt Echo One accidentally leaked it. From this point on, the only people who will know her whereabouts are you, Echo Four, and me. Meanwhile, I've dispatched a specialist to handle the intruder. Maybe we'll get somewhere with him."

Nathan knew what she meant. "That won't break my heart. Do you know what this is about?"

"Not over the phone. Remember when I said you're never retired?"

Nathan didn't need to say anything.

"You and Echo Four are vested in this," Rebecca said. "Secure our guest and call me after my team arrives."

"I promised Echo One I'd look after her dogs until she's back on her feet."

"Low priority."

"I gave her my word."

Cantrell didn't respond and Nathan didn't interrupt the silence.

"Where are they?" she asked at last.

"Upstairs, in the bedroom closet."

"Let my team handle them."

"Echo One said their collars and leashes are in a kitchen drawer."

"I'll pass it on. One of my officers will pack up the dogs and meet you later for the exchange."

His phone went dark.

I should be careful what I wish for. I told Harv I was bored.

CHAPTER 6

Two minutes later, Nathan's earpiece came to life with Harv's voice, still in Russian. *"I'm parked. I'll be at the corner of her property in under a minute."*

"Copy that. I'm looking at the spot where you'll hop the wall."

Linda's eyes were closed and she took long, slow breaths. If not totally unconscious, she was in a twilight state.

Again, he wondered why she'd been targeted, and why now? Rebecca said she had an idea about what was going on and Nathan intended to find out. Someone had gone to a great deal of trouble attempting to get their hands on her.

"Okay, I'm at the corner of the wall."

"Stand by, Harv. I'm going to relocate to the closest citrus tree. Ten seconds. I'll be able to see the entire front and side yards from there."

"There's no activity out here."

Nathan clicked his radio and hustled south along the row of trees. Detecting no one, he radioed the all clear to Harv.

His friend appeared at the top of the wall and, without hesitating, dropped to the grass. *He hasn't lost much.* Scaling a solid eight-foot wall took strength and skill and Harv made it look easy.

Nathan stepped into Harv's line of sight. "You got me?"

"You're hard to miss."

"Do a thermal scan from there. You'll see two casualties."

"I've got them. I'm not detecting anyone else."

"Then come join the party."

Without NV, Nathan wouldn't have seen Harv. His friend's black 5.11 clothing and gear mirrored his own, making him all but invisible to the naked eye. Harv also wore a night-vision visor, but his friend's scope was flipped up.

They both crouched at the base of the tree. "If there are more intruders in here, they've gone to ground," Nathan said.

"Where's LG?"

"Sixth tree."

"Let's play it safe and leapfrog. I'll go first."

"Sounds good."

Using a technique they'd mastered on countless ops, they advanced to LG's position. So far, so good: no one had shot at them.

Harv pivoted his NV scope down to his eye, powered on the device, and adjusted the focus. "Looks like she went a few rounds."

"It was up close and personal at the end. Her husband took a few in the chest."

"That's a bad deal. You know LG . . . she's gonna want some payback."

He nodded and updated Harv on what he'd seen, including his conversation with Cantrell. "I need to go back in there and haul that unconscious guy out."

"That's a terrible idea for a lot of reasons," Harv said.

"We're a little short on options."

ANDREW PETERSON

"If I position myself next to the door, I'll be able to cover LG's position from there and make sure no one follows you in."

"You'll be exposed. There's no cover."

"I'll be okay," Harv said. "Get going, I'll be right behind you."

With Harv watching his back, the sprint across the open expanse of lawn didn't feel nearly as perilous. Even the distance seemed shorter. He took a knee next to the library door and said, "Sit tight for a sec and give me ten seconds of radio silence." He heard Harv's acknowledgment click.

Everything looked the same, but the house was totally silent. Linda's dogs no longer barked. That could be good or bad.

He keyed his mike and told Harv to advance.

"Change in plan," Nathan whispered when Harv arrived. "I don't like how quiet it is in there. We'll leapfrog our entry. I'll stop at the far side of the pool table, you continue straight into the kitchen. You'll see an island. Our bad guy's on the far side, in front of the oven. Grab his backpack. We're gonna need it. You ready?"

"And if I say no?" Harv asked.

"We're going anyway."

"I knew you'd say that. What about LG?"

"We'll be in and out in under a minute. She'll be okay."

As it turned out, it only took forty-five seconds.

With Harv covering, Nathan retrieved the unconscious gunman and hauled him in a firefighter's carry out to LG's position at the citrus tree. Harv arrived a few seconds later.

Nathan turned his NV to maximum gain and rifled through the gunman's pack. Sure enough, he found a vial labeled in Spanish: *Ketamina* 1000mg/10 ml *Solución Inyectable*. He rifled through the backpack for a syringe but didn't find one.

"Harv, did you grab the syringe from the floor?"

"No, you didn't ask me to."

"We need it. I'm going back."

58

"Stay with Linda, I'll go." His friend grinned. "I'm faster than you."

"Like hell you are. Your legs are shorter. So's everything else."

"It's not the size, it's the motion."

"Just get going, jarhead."

"Aye aye, sir."

He had to admit, Harv could haul ass. Of course, not wanting to get shot was a strong motivator.

Alone with Linda and the intruder, he again thought about what this dirtbag would've done to her. Maybe he should've killed him. Then again, enduring Cantrell's interrogator would be punishment enough.

He suddenly realized he had no idea how much Ketamine to use. He was a pretty good judge of weight and figured this guy weighed about 175 pounds. If he injected too much, it might kill him.

"Harv, I need to call Cantrell for the right dosage."

"Hang on. I'm on my way out. I read an article about Special K's recreational use in China not too long ago."

Harv arrived thirty seconds later, handed him the syringe, and conducted another thermal scan.

"Do you know the dose?"

"The article said one hundred milligrams."

"We need to be certain." Nathan adjusted the focus of his NV scope. "That number doesn't do us much good. This syringe is measured in milliliters, not milligrams. We need to know the conversion. Maintain our perimeter. I'm calling Cantrell."

"I'm on the other line," Cantrell said. "What's going on?"

"We need a dose in milliliters for the Ketamine in a big hurry. Our guest weighs about 175 pounds."

"Hold the line. I'll be right back."

The call went silent again.

"I'm on hold."

"We can't carry LG down the driveway. We'd be in plain sight. What about the canyon?"

He shook his head. "The stairs going down the bluff are too steep and narrow. We'll just have to manhandle her over the wall. The trees along the street will give us some cover. It's a good thing she's unconscious."

"For us or her?"

"We're getting her over that wall without worrying about where we touch her."

"If you say so . . ."

Waiting for Cantrell, Nathan supposed he could call Dr. Reavie. The doctor's wife, Jane, worked as the nurse-anesthetist in their plastic-surgery practice. Strike that. What was he thinking? He couldn't call Doug in the middle of the night and ask about a Ketamine dose. Doug would want an explanation; anything less would put his friend on the wrong side of the ethical equation. Besides, Cantrell wouldn't sanction Doug's involvement or knowledge in what could be a major CIA security breach.

She came back on the line. "What's the label say? It comes in different strengths."

He read it to her.

"Okay, use two point six milliliters. Inject him in the thigh slowly, over ten seconds or so."

"Will do," Nathan said.

"Call me when you've cleared the area."

Nathan filled the syringe to the specified amount, stuck it into the man's thigh, and slowly pressed the plunger. Next, he dragged the man under the citrus tree, used his knife to cut the cuffs LG had used, and secured his wrists behind the trunk with another set of disposable cuffs he'd found in the man's backpack.

"All right," Nathan said. "Let's move out." LG made no sound as he scooped her off the wet lawn. *Good thing,* he thought. Fractured or bruised ribs tended to be extremely painful. "I'll carry her over to the corner where you hopped the wall."

"I'm right behind you."

Thirty yards of open lawn lay between them and the wall, but there was no avoiding it.

With LG slung around his neck like the Wounded Warriors logo, he took off in a dead run. Unfortunately, it took both hands to safely carry her. He hadn't used this technique when he'd carried her out of the house because he'd needed a free gun hand. If bullets flew his way, he'd be relying on Harv to lay down suppression fire. Before he reached the base of the wall, Harv said, *"I'm on the move. Right behind you, covering your left."*

Nathan stopped at the wall and kept LG slung around his neck.

Harv joined him a few seconds later. "You know, we might just make it outta here without getting shot."

"Yeah, that's the general idea."

Harv did a quick sweep with the TI. "We're good."

"You go first and straddle the top. I'll lift her up by her armpits. Once you've got her arms, I'll switch to her legs."

Nathan laid LG down, grabbed her under her armpits, and power lifted her like a father hoisting a toddler over his head. Her head lolled forward and hit the wall, but it wasn't a hard blow. Harv reached down and grabbed her arms just above her elbows. When Harv pulled, LG's T-shirt lifted over her head.

Nathan didn't divert his eyes in time, but given the circumstances, he felt certain she wouldn't care. Once Harv had her stabilized, he scaled the wall and straddled it, facing Harv. He grabbed her thighs and balanced her weight on the top of the wall.

"You got her?"

Harv said he did.

Nathan dropped into the front yard and Harv lowered her into his grasp. It was ten times easier getting her down.

"I'll cover our six again," Harv said.

With one hundred and ten pounds draped around his neck, it would be a long, two-hundred-yard run to Harv's car. He took careful strides to avoid falling as he hustled along the trees lining the street.

He thought about what she'd gone through. Would she blame herself for Glen's death? What would her mental state be when she regained awareness? From what he'd observed in the house, she'd done incredibly well, considering the odds she'd faced. At least their security system did its job. She'd been given enough advance warning to—

Just short of Harv's sedan, he heard the sudden roar of an engine.

CHAPTER 7

From the direction of Linda's house, some kind of compact sedan raced straight toward him and its headlights were dark. Making matters worse, a gunman hung out the passenger window, his weapon plainly visible. There was no way he'd have time to set Linda down, pull his Sig, and line up on the threat.

He didn't have to.

Harv appeared out of nowhere as the compact closed to thirty yards.

Nathan watched in admiration as his friend took a Weaver stance in the middle of the street and popped off three quick shots. The compact's windshield took a tight group of impacts at the exact height of the driver's head.

Great shooting, Harv.

As if mechanically wounded, the vehicle sped past Harv's position, veered to the left, hopped the curb on the opposite side of the street, and spun 360 degrees. Still moving at a good clip, it sheared a mailbox and plowed into an imperial palm. The compact went from thirty miles an hour to zero in less than a second. The loud crunch of deforming metal and shattering plastic reverberated off every house in the area.

"So much for getting out of here quietly," he said.

"Yep, we're blown for sure. I'm in the open, I need to find cover."

"I'll take LG the rest of the way. Stay on the compact."

"I'm on it."

At Harv's Mercedes, Nathan laid LG on the grass next to the curb and pulled his Sig.

The passenger door of the compact flew open and a gunman—dressed exactly like his comrades—crawled out. Nathan knew the air bag detonation had hammered him. The guy rolled onto his side and cursed. He then unslung his compact machine gun, scurried around the vehicle, and hid behind its collapsed hood.

Nathan didn't have a shot without risking a stray into the house beyond. Because the driver's door of the compact faced away from Harv's position, Nathan wasn't certain his friend had seen the gunman crawl out.

To protect Harv, he yelled in Spanish, "Hey, numb nuts, over here!"

That drew the gunman's attention, just as he'd planned. *Better me than Harv,* Nathan thought. His friend had a family to think about.

His earpiece came to life with *"Damn it, Nate. What the hell are you—"*

The gunman's suppressed weapon spat javelins of light.

Maybe this wasn't such a good idea.

Nathan lay flat between LG and the shooter. If any bullets found their way through Harv's hundred-thousand-dollar Mercedes, he hoped they'd find him, not Linda. He covered his head with his arms. Although his ballistic vest protected his torso, everything else remained exposed.

The gunman's aim wasn't perfect but good enough.

Several three-round bursts slammed into Harv's car. The thumps happened so quickly, they sounded like single impacts. Two more volleys pounded the Mercedes. *Harv's gonna be pissed.* Some of the bullets went high, shattering the rear passenger windows. Tempered glass showered them. For now, all Nathan could do was protect LG until the barrage ended.

"I'm pinned and your car's taking a beating." He heard two suppressed reports from Harv's Sig. The neighborhood fell silent for a few seconds.

Then the sound of the bursts changed as the gunman returned fire at Harv.

Time to enter the fight.

Nathan peered through the broken windows and saw Harv charging the compact, shooting as he ran. Nathan's night vision registered each of Harv's discharges, making his friend's handgun look like some kind of high-tech EMP weapon. The gunman kept shooting, forcing Harv to dodge right into the cover of some eucalyptus trees.

Nathan said, "Giving you cover fire."

"I could use it!"

Staying low, Nathan moved to his right, bench-rested his Sig on the hood, and activated the laser. He painted the near side of the wrecked compact and fired three times into the door panel. Intentionally skipping them off the street, he sent several bullets underneath the chassis. He felt confident his subsonic ball ammo wouldn't have much energy left to penetrate the walls of the house beyond. Confident, but not positive. He had no choice. Harv needed help. Nathan's goal was to kill the gunman, but he'd settle for making the guy duck for cover and stop shooting.

It didn't work.

Nathan reloaded his Sig and began a continuous barrage, firing a bullet every second. He adjusted his aim and put bullets through the vehicle's windows.

The gunman stopped firing.

Nathan keyed his mike. "Status?"

"I'm in the trees at your ten o'clock," Harv said. *"I'll be in position to take him out in five seconds. Give me more cover fire."*

Nathan clicked his radio and changed magazines again. Fresh holes appeared in the door panels and front fender as he walked his shots along the length of the compact. Contrary to the way Hollywood depicted things, cars didn't explode from small-arms fire.

Halfway through his salvo, the gunman bolted.

"He's on the move," Nathan said. "Running west, across my twelve o'clock. I don't have a clear shot without risking a stray into someone's living room."

"I'm on him."

"I'll parallel you on this side of the street." Although their exchange of gunfire wasn't loud, the car crash had been. Dogs continued barking and porch lights snapped on. It wouldn't be long before every cop within a ten-mile radius sped to this location. Even though this firefight was nearly two hundred yards west of Linda's house, it would complicate things for Rebecca's team. She'd wanted Harv and him to observe from a distance until her people arrived; well, that was off the table now.

Harv fired four quick shots.

The gunman tumbled.

"He's down," Harv said.

"I've got eyes on him. He's crawling toward a hedge. He's wearing body armor so assume he's still in the fight. I'll check the compact's driver."

"Copy."

Nathan backtracked along the same route he'd taken while carrying LG. When he crossed the street, he sensed the presence of prying eyes from every window. Behind him, he heard the gunman and Harv exchange more fire. Keeping his head down, he approached the steaming vehicle. A glance through the passenger window confirmed Harv's marksmanship was second to none. The gunman's destroyed face was slumped against the deflated air bag. No need to check for a pulse. Even if by some miracle this poor sap lived, he'd never eat with a knife and fork again.

Several more three-round bursts reverberated off the houses.

"I'm okay, he's firing blindly."

"Cover fire?"

"No need. I've got this. Get LG into the car. I'll be there in thirty seconds."

Just then, the owner of the house where Harv had the gunman pinned appeared at the front door with a pump shotgun. Nathan recognized its distinct shape.

The man leveled the gun at Harv, and Nathan had no way to know if he intended to pull the trigger, or just make a macho show of force.

Not chancing it, Nathan painted the wall above the homeowner's head and sent three bullets.

The surface exploded, showering the homeowner with pulverized chunks of stucco. The guy cursed and retreated back into his house.

Harv's handgun clapped twice more. *"Thanks for the help; the rabbit's toast."*

Nathan clicked his radio and hustled back to Harv's sedan. He picked up LG, but then saw all the broken glass on the rear seat. Figuring he had a few seconds before Harv arrived, he set her down and used a gloved hand to sweep the shards onto the carpet.

When Harv arrived, he said, "Oh, man, my car . . ."

"Yeah, it's a shame all right."

"How's LG?"

"Down for the count. I'm afraid we skinned her knee on the stucco getting her over the wall, but it's not too bad. It'll be the least of her worries."

"No doubt. She just lost her husband. Like you said, she's gonna want some payback."

"Wouldn't you?"

Harv started the car. "Absolutely."

"There's no telling how this is going to affect her."

"She's tough, but we'll see how she acts once she's awake."

"I need to send Cantrell a text about being ambushed out here. I've got a strong signal. Let's roll, but slowly." He dictated a brief summary, indicating that the area two hundred yards west of LG's house would become a major crime scene and that her team would need to use the canyon to get onto LG's property.

A few seconds later, he received a response.

```
clear the area ASAP and lose all weapons
associated with tonight's action.
```

He read Cantrell's text to Harv and sent an acknowledgment, but he had no intention of discarding perfectly good Sig Sauers. They had plenty of extra barrels and firing pins. Besides, he liked this particular weapon; it had a proven history with him.

Wind gushed through the shattered windows as Harv accelerated. Neither of them said anything for a few seconds. Nathan knew they were both thinking the same thing.

"So, are we all in?" Harv asked.

"Need I repeat your NBA line?"

"And if Cantrell's not aboard?"

"We do it without her."

"Nate, we need to think about this. It would be nice to know what we're diving into. Getting Cantrell's support may depend upon who's behind this attack, assuming she either knows or can find out."

Nathan knew Harv would agree to help LG, even without Cantrell's support. His friend was simply doing what he always did: being the voice of reason and calm. Nathan had already grabbed the proverbial pitchforks and lighted the torches, but he knew his temper was getting the best of him. There was no need to press the issue with Harv right now.

His friend continued. "Whoever's behind the assault on LG sent a small army. We did a dozen ops with LG. We might be in the crosshairs too."

"I've considered that. We made lots of enemies, but none of them should be able to find us, or her."

"Not without some inside help."

"We should get some of our security guards to watch our homes, just in case."

"I'm on it."

While Harv made the call, Nathan tried to recall the various ops they'd performed with, and for, LG. Although he remembered the general stuff, most of the specific details escaped him. It was scary how much memory got recycled with time. Nathan hadn't even turned fifty yet; that milestone was still years distant. Still, he'd test his strength and stamina against kids one-third his age and win 98 percent of the contests. If he needed to review the debriefing reports from LG's ops, the details would come back. He'd written the damned things—his least favorite part of the job.

"Let's divert down to the hairpin and get my car." He looked at LG. "How's she doing?"

"Fine."

"You okay?"

"Crap, Harv. I'm full of piss and vinegar right now. That assault team wanted her alive, and if they'd taken her alive . . ." He didn't finish his sentence. Didn't have to.

"Yeah, it's a bad visual all right. She's tough, but they'd eventually peel her, which means they'd have a link to us and everyone else she worked with."

"Which may have been their plan all along. LG might not be their endgame, it might be us—"

"And they went after her because they couldn't find us."

"All the more reason to end this threat before it goes any further. You're a family man, Harv."

"Need I remind you that you are too?"

"I'm not a parent. You and Candace have two sons in college."

"And you have a teenaged niece and half sister. Let's not forget your mother, and a father who nearly made a bid for the presidency."

"I know. I just meant I don't have a wife or kids."

"Lauren thinks of you as her adopted dad."

"I surrender. You win. I'm a bona fide family man."

"How did it feel saying that?"

"I'll live."

Harv dropped him at his car, and a few minutes later, they arrived at his La Jolla home's electric security gate. Stretching beyond the reach of Harv's headlights, his driveway snaked its way up to the residence. Harv radioed that their security guards would be arriving in twenty minutes. If anything happened before the extra manpower arrived, they'd deal with it.

He told Harv to sit tight until Angelica, his live-in housekeeper, could let his dogs out to patrol the property. In the event tonight's action wasn't limited to LG's house, his tactically trained giant schnauzers would detect anyone inside the fence line. *Better to be safe than sorry.* Of course, a sniper could be hidden anywhere beyond his property, but he gave that low odds. LG's intruders wanted her alive, after all.

Angelica's "all clear" call came two minutes later. He watched Harv press his forefinger to the security pad at the bottom of the drive. The capacitance scanner identified him and asked for a six-digit code. It took both the fingerprint and the numeric code to open the gate.

Near the top, his earpiece came to life. *"No matter how many times I come up here, I don't think I'll ever get used to how beautiful your place is."*

"If it's any consolation, Harv, I feel the same way."

"When are you going to sell it to me?"

"Never. You get it when I die."

Harv didn't respond.

"Don't even think it."

"Hey, I didn't say anything."

Harv's house in Rancho Santa Fe was equally striking and bigger. It just didn't have this view. Looking north from Mount Soledad, the La Jolla coastline looked spectacular, even through the light rain. In the distance, dominating the northwestern sky, the orange glow from the Los Angeles basin lay on the horizon.

Nathan's house was humbling and he never took it for granted. It looked like a combination of a World War II pillbox, blended with Frank Lloyd Wright's Fallingwater. Each section of the house was a pie-shaped piece that was literally carved into the hillside. Each cantilevered wedge created dark shade and shadow. Three chimneys, along with other vertical features, offered nice contrasts to the horizontal lines and curves. The uppermost wedges of the design were covered by earth. The native vegetation literally grew right to the edge of his roofline above the windows. He had to admit the place looked really cool, especially at night with its glowing windows. Several years ago, he'd even constructed a helipad. It wasn't big, but it allowed a six- to eight-seat Bell to land without obstruction.

The Civil War cannons flanking the front door sealed the deal. Nathan's fascination with that conflict had started in childhood. He found that particular conflict to be as intriguing as it had been barbaric. Wholesale slaughter didn't begin to describe the major battles of the War between the States. Every time he thought about his own physical trauma, it paled in comparison to what those soldiers went through.

Silently, two black giant schnauzers bounded out of the darkness and hustled over to Harv's sedan, their docked tails wagging. Because they knew Harv and the unique sound and smell of his Mercedes, he'd be able to get out. But anybody his dogs didn't recognize wouldn't be allowed to exit their vehicle. Although tactically trained, they were big sweethearts at their cores. To keep them sharp, he and Harv worked with them often.

Nathan climbed out. "Hey, who feeds you guys?"

They trotted over. He ran his hand over Sherman's back, told him he was a good boy, then did the same for Grant. His dogs were an integral part of his life and he couldn't imagine his world without them. They kept him grounded, reminded him of a simpler life, in which only basic needs had to be met. He'd once told Harv he could be just as happy living in a remote cabin with no electricity or plumbing. He had nothing against Kleenex, cell phones, and luxury cars, but he often longed for a simpler existence.

Angelica stood near the front door with a concerned expression. Nathan offered a smile and a wave. He and Harv had known her since their early Nicaraguan missions. Before his botched mission, he'd arranged—demanded really—that her US citizenship application be expedited. Her entire family had been slaughtered by Sandinista holdouts. On their fourth Echo mission, they found her wandering the jungle. Hungry and homeless, she'd been near death. They gave her food and water, tended to her feet, and secured her a seat on their helicopter flight out to the Navy frigate. Leaving Angelica behind would've been a death sentence.

In her mid-seventies, she displayed classic Central American genes. Barely five feet tall, she had kind brown eyes, matching skin, and shoulder-length, graying hair. Harv and he thought of her as their adopted mother. In many ways, he was closer to Angelica than his own mom. But that was purely a matter of how much time he spent with her.

With the command word *alert*, Nathan put his dogs back into tactical mode. They disappeared into the darkness beyond the porch light's reach. If they detected anyone, they'd pin them in place and begin ferociously barking. It took a different command to make them inflict damage.

Harv carried Linda through the front door as if she weighed next to nothing. His friend was deceptively strong. At six foot one, Harv was the tallest Latino he knew . . . granted, these days he didn't know all that many.

He confirmed Angelica had a pot of coffee brewing when he entered the house. She obviously suspected they were going to have a long night. *One of many in my life.* The pangs of fatigue had already set in. Sometime within the next twelve hours, he'd need serious shut-eye.

He followed Harv into the ground-floor study that connected to the library and opened the sofa bed. Linda showed no signs of awareness as Harv placed her on top of the blanket. *If only I could sleep so soundly.* He estimated she'd been out for ten minutes or so. If Cantrell's estimate was right, she ought to be showing signs of awareness within the next twenty minutes, and a full recovery in two hours or so.

He asked Angelica to clean up her face and use hydrogen peroxide on her skinned knee.

After Angelica left the study, Nathan said, "We need to call Cantrell and make arrangements to get Linda's dogs, but let's give her a little time. No doubt she's multitasking at the moment."

"Did LG say much before she lost consciousness?"

"Not really," he said. "She was in a twilight state when I found her. The drugs bypassed her filters. It was weird seeing the softer side of her." Nathan doubted she'd retain anything of their discussion just prior to her losing consciousness. He didn't know much about Ketamine, only that it had an amnesia effect.

"The softer side of her?" Harv asked.

"She was . . . unguarded. You know, nice to me. I've always suspected she had it in her, I'd just never seen it before."

"What did she say?"

Nathan's radar went up; he'd seen this before when he'd first started dating Holly. There was little Harv got away with.

"Come on, Harv, out with it."

"Remember when I said I knew for a fact she didn't hate you? After Nicaragua, she told me she didn't. The reason she acted so cold all the time is because she thought *you* hated *her*. Look, she was an interrogator, not like Montez, but she got kinda rough on occasion. Think about what we did to Ernie Bridgestone."

He did, all too vividly. It hadn't been something he'd enjoyed.

"Put yourself in her position. She knew what you went through. How do you think she felt every time you looked at her?"

"I was pretty messed up after Montez. It's hard to think about."

"She didn't know how to approach you."

"I was . . . unapproachable."

"Not to me. I didn't let you shut me out."

"You saved my life, Harv. If you hadn't stayed by my side, I would've killed myself."

They'd talked about this a lot over the years, so there was no need to dive into it again. His friend had spent countless hours at his hospital bed, talking him through the emotional turmoil. Nathan's case of PTSD had been as severe as it got.

At times, he felt like Harv was the only person in the world who truly understood him, knew the anger that constantly chewed on his soul. Nathan didn't live one day at a time; he lived one hour at a time. The long grooves marring his face were constant, visible reminders of his ordeal. Thankfully, the crisscrossing network of deep scars on his torso was hidden by clothes. Nathan never took his shirt off in public. Ever. People didn't intentionally stare; it just couldn't be helped. Children were the worst. Some pointed, others hid behind their parents.

A dark entity inside of him fought a near-constant battle to break free of its cage. He called it The Other, for lack of a better name, and it was made of pure rage. Nathan believed it to be a leftover survival mechanism—likely the only thing that had saved him during those endless days of Montez's torture. It no longer ruled him. In fact, he'd learned to tap its energy and use it for constructive purposes. But he had to be careful. As feral as this alternate personality was, it could also be intelligent and cunning. Thinking about what Linda would've gone through at the hands of her abductors, Nathan felt as though a tin cup were banging on the bars of The Other's cage.

Even now, he sensed its eyes snap open and stare straight ahead, unblinking.

No. Not without my permission.

He closed his eyes and took a deep breath.

Harv's voice startled him. "You okay?"

"Yeah, just cutting it off."

"How far did it get?"

"Eyes only, it didn't test the bars. How long was I zoned?"

Harv smiled. "Only a few seconds."

Just like that. No judgment. No calling him a freak. No condemnation. It was scary how well Harv understood him. Nathan couldn't begin to imagine the hole in his life should anything ever happen to his friend. "I owe you a lot."

"You're underestimating your own resolve. Look, I'm not trying to make you relive the past. Just know that Linda never hated you. She kept her distance to protect you."

"Protect me? From what?"

Harv didn't respond right away. "She was an interrogator, you were a victim. Let's just leave it at that."

"Okay, okay," Nathan said. "I get it. End of conversation. I won't bring it up again."

"I think that's best."

"So . . . she'll need a familiar face when she wakes up. In fifteen minutes, I'll take the first watch. She may not remember the fight in the kitchen. If she doesn't, I'll tell her about Glen."

"As I recall," Harv said, "he stayed in investment consulting after we rescued him. He must've been doing pretty well to own that house."

"No doubt."

"We need to call Cantrell. She hinted she knows what's going on."

"I'm curious too, but let's give her a few more minutes."

They fell into a comfortable silence for a good minute, as they often did. Neither of them filled the quiet with mindless small talk.

Angelica knocked softly and entered the study with a washcloth for LG's dried blood, a bottle of peroxide, and two giant schnauzers.

"Hey, you guys are supposed to be on patrol."

"I brought them in," Angelica said. "They're curious about your friend."

The dogs extended their noses over the top of the bed and scrutinized Linda's face.

"They don't get many visitors," Harv said.

"I need to take them out more often."

"I give them walks around the neighborhood," Angelica said.

"And I'm sure they appreciate it, but I need to take them to a dog park where they can run around and be dogs."

"They might thumb their noses at the riffraff," Harv said.

"Hey, a purebred will eat a dead gopher alongside the lowest of mongrels."

"You got that right. So will we, if we're hungry enough." His friend's expression changed. "Sorry."

"Forget it, Harv." Nathan walked toward the front door and looked back at the dogs. "Come, you guys, I need you outside a little longer." He made an arm gesture and the dogs bounded out in front of him.

Outside on his driveway, he tried not to think about his tormentor, but it happened anyway. Harv's comment triggered a dark memory. Montez had starved him to the brink of death. He'd been denied food and water for days at a time. Both were hideous, but his hunger hadn't been nearly as bad as the thirst. Being that parched became an enemy all its own. Montez liked to dine in front of him, but not just dine. The jerk had set up a mock five-star restaurant table, complete with nice flatware, wineglasses, cloth napkins, the works. He'd even procured a white tablecloth. Nathan remembered wondering where on earth Montez had gotten all that crap. It had been a cruel ploy, designed to destroy his will to resist. Even though he'd been hungry enough to eat the scraps like a dog, Nathan hadn't caved. Montez made a critical mistake during the interrogation: he'd made it personal, and nobody won a battle of willpower with Nathan McBride unless Nathan allowed it. His dad possessed the same stubborn attitude, the reason they butted heads so often.

To this day, Nathan never wasted food and it sickened him to see how callous Americans could be. Most meals at restaurants were big enough to share, but few did. He didn't condemn wasteful people; they were simply victims of the great disposable culture.

Change subjects, he told himself, but his thoughts had a mind of their own, returning to Rebecca Cantrell and the failed Nicaraguan mission that led to his capture. At the time, she hadn't been high in the CIA's brass, but she'd been involved with the planning of Operation Freedom's Echo from its inception to its demise. Once Nathan fell into Montez's hands, she'd immediately pulled the plug and recalled the other Echo teams. There'd been no choice.

Cantrell took the blame, but it hadn't been her fault. Had she tried to deflect responsibility, he wouldn't have the trust in her he now felt. He admired her willingness to say the buck stopped on her desk—a philosophy he also followed. When Nathan screwed up, he owned the mistake, apologized, and moved on. Simple as that. Narcissism wasn't in Nathan's personality and he hated narcissists with a passion. Harv's oldest brother was a textbook case and the arrogant idiot had alienated everyone in Harv's family.

He looked at the view of La Jolla and felt a pang of guilt about having such a beautiful place. He'd initially refused the CIA's generous offer of restitution, not wanting to gain financially from what he'd gone through. But Harv had stepped in with a different opinion. Not only did Harv insist Nathan take the money, he also got the CIA to triple the amount. Nathan said he'd agree on one condition: he and Harv had to split the money evenly. Harv had risked everything returning to the jungle to rescue him, and he'd told Harv he wouldn't accept any other terms. Harv agreed, investing 75 percent of their lump sum of three million dollars in Apple Inc. stock and the rest, as they say, is history.

Nathan returned to the study and found Harv sitting in a reading chair. "How's she doing?"

"Still down for the count. I really like her hair. It's a striking look, almost exotic."

"I wonder how long it takes to weave those cornrows."

"I'd have to guess hours."

Nathan's phone dinged with a text message. "Here we go," he said.

```
do you still have the encrypted phone?
```

He sent "yes."

```
turn it on. I have to reactivate it.
```

"She wants us to use the encrypted phone. Good thing she asked us to keep it."

"Yeah, good thing," Harv said slowly.

"Harv—"

His friend held up a hand. "Let's just say she knew we'd need it again."

Nathan sent:

```
2 minutes
```

"I'll be right back; it's in the basement." He kept a lot of survival gear down there, basically everything needed in the event of a complete civil breakdown. You never knew when you were going to need several thousand rounds of subsonic ammo, a thousand instant meals, or a secure cell phone to call the director of the CIA. For Nathan and Harv, the latter seemed to happen with alarming frequency—the price of being on Cantrell's speed-dial list.

He returned to the study and powered on the phone. He watched its screen go white, then work through a startup process. About forty-five seconds later, it was good to go.

"Maybe we'll get some answers," Nathan said.

"I'm not holding my breath."

"Still don't trust her?"

"Let's just say . . . no, I guess I don't. At least not completely."

Angelica made a final pass along LG's chin with a peroxide wipe, then excused herself from the room, closing the door as she left.

A few seconds later, Nathan's encrypted phone bleeped to life.

CHAPTER 8

Nathan knew Cantrell would get right to the point. She wasn't much for small talk. For one, she didn't have time for it, and two, it wasn't her style. He put the phone on speaker and said Harv was with him.

"What's Genneken's status?"

"She's still out of it."

"I trust you'll keep someone by her side at all times?"

"No problem, we're planning to."

"Is the gunman secure?"

"Yes, he's handcuffed to the trunk of the same orange tree where you saw my GPS coordinates. The cuffs are disposables."

"Good work. My team's ETA is ten minutes. In your best estimate, can they get in and out undetected?"

"Only from the canyon on the north side of her property. It's how I got in. All they'll need is night vision, it should be an easy entry."

"I'll let them know."

"I have a favor to ask," Nathan said.

"Name it."

"We've got several of our security guards on the way to our homes, but I'd like to supplement them with some FBI special agents."

"I'll need to clear this with Director Lansing first, but given the circumstances, it shouldn't be a problem."

"He's going to ask what it's all about."

"I'll deal with it. I'll see if I can get the same SAs as last time."

"Thank you. What about LG's dogs?" He knew his concern sounded trifling at a time like this, but he'd given Linda his word. Besides, he really liked dogs—more so than most people.

"You said they're in an upstairs closet, right?"

"That's what LG told me. Collars and leashes in a kitchen drawer. Can we make sure they aren't cooped up for more than three or four hours?"

"No problem. Harvey, you've been awfully quiet."

"I'm just thinking that whoever's behind this attack is going to know it didn't succeed, especially if no one from the assault team reports in."

"We'll search the intruders at Genneken's for cell phones and see if there's been any recent text or voice communications."

Nathan looked at Harv while he spoke. "We didn't think to check the men we killed on the street for phones. We should've. Sorry about that."

"Don't beat yourselves up. I didn't think of it either. I wanted you two out of there in a hurry. What's the situation inside Genneken's house?"

"It's a mess," Nathan said. "I saw six bodies and there're at least two more in the backyard. The French door to her kitchen is broken out. Probably some windows as well."

"Stay on the line, Nathan. I've got to take another call."

The call went silent.

"Sorry about your car, Harv. We'll park it in my garage until things calm down."

His friend gave him the keys.

"I'll be right back." He found Angelica in the kitchen, handed her the keys, and asked her to move it. Back in the study, he said, "That firefight on the street is going to be on every morning news channel. A gun battle in the middle of a La Jolla neighborhood on New Year's Eve will be the lead story. The news networks make their livings from this kinda stuff."

"No doubt," Harv said. "If those gunmen are foreign nationals, it's going to generate a Homeland Security investigation. All kinds of questions will be asked. Cantrell reports to the DNI and there's no way she'll withhold this. We might find ourselves out of the loop."

"LG's not gonna back down. They murdered her husband and—"

Cantrell came back on the line. "Sorry about that."

"No worries," Nathan said. "We were just talking about containment."

"Let me worry about that. Job one for you is to keep Genneken secure."

Nathan exchanged a glance with Harv. They were thinking the same thing. Now was not a good time to say LG will be looking for payback.

"I've got you at your home address in La Jolla. Stay there until you hear back from me."

"Before you go," said Nathan quickly, "when I asked earlier, it seemed you might know what this is about. This call's secure. Care to elaborate?"

"We've been getting reports of assassinations and kidnappings all over Central and South America over the last seven days. Until now, none of the bad guys have been killed or captured, so the police had little to go on. The victims cross all professions and economic groups. We think we've found a common element, but we're still analyzing the data. The methods of assassination also vary. Some are home invasions, some are bombings. There're also reports of arson and poisonings. Some people have just gone missing. It's clear whoever's behind the murders doesn't want a discernible pattern to be discovered."

"And you think tonight's action is somehow related to those other cases?" Harv asked.

"We're not 100 percent sure, but yes. We've been experimenting with a new computer algorithm that tracks this kind of thing. It's still in beta stage but we've had some success."

Nathan asked, "How does it work?"

"Needless to say, it's extremely complex. It analyzes tens of millions of pieces of information. It collects intel from our agents and sources and similar agencies worldwide, then looks for follow-up law-enforcement intel or criminal activity at those locations. Ranging from countries and cities, down to street-level addresses, it plots the last known locations of people we suspect, people we're watching, and people we know for certain are up to no good. Everything's displayed on a giant wall of monitors, like newsrooms have. I wish we could take credit for the concept, but it was developed by the Israelis and they've had very good results."

"Incredible," Harv said. "Does it predict locations of future criminal or terrorist attacks?"

"No, but it finds connections between people and events that would otherwise be invisible."

Harv said, "So the attack on LG connected her to some of these other incidents and addresses?"

"Correct."

"Then it should've connected us as well," Nathan said.

"It did. I just checked it."

"Then it's dynamic?" asked Harv. "Working in real time?"

"That's right. About a dozen new data points came up tonight and several dozen others have new connections. I'm not the best person to explain exactly how it works, but in a nutshell, it finds patterns in seemingly random events."

"I'd love to see your program in action," Harv said.

"The next time you guys are out this way, I'll arrange it."

"So where does this leave things?" Nathan asked. "I don't like the idea of an assault team coming after us."

"I think it's fair to say you guys just neutralized it," Cantrell said.

Nathan said, "LG gets the credit. She did most of the heavy lifting before we got there."

"Right. Now you guys hold tight and take care of her until you hear from me again. Stay alert, assume nothing, and be ready to move on a moment's notice. I need to contact DNI Benson and update him. If that was a foreign assault team at Genneken's house, it rises to his level of involvement. It will be his call."

Nathan looked at Harv as Cantrell voiced their earlier concern.

"His call about what? How to handle it?" Harv asked. "As in, with or without us?"

"It's entirely possible you guys may have to sit this one out. For the record, I'm not advocating that, but it's not my decision."

"We're in this now," Nathan said, "like your algorithm says. There's no reason to believe they won't make another attempt to capture Linda. And maybe Harv and me as well. LG told me the man she killed said they were going to take turns with her." Nathan hadn't wanted to mention that, but it seemed relevant now. Harv gave him an approving nod.

"I get that. All I'm saying is I have to be a team player. I can't—won't—do anything behind the DNI's back. I've got some pull with him and the two of you have a proven history with me and he knows who you are. You've both been to the Oval Office, where the only awards you received were handshakes. That carries weight with me, and the DNI. Lots, actually. I don't normally get involved at this level, but I make exceptions with you two."

"Thank you, Rebecca. We appreciate it."

"Under no circumstances is Genneken to go anywhere alone. What's her husband's name?"

"Glen."

"Tell Linda we'll take care of him, okay?"

"I will." Nathan admired how Cantrell had softened her tone. It showed class.

"We'll have both of your homes under constant surveillance within the next half hour or so. Harv, your sons are in college, right?"

"Yes."

"And I'm assuming you guys have state-of-the-art security systems?"

"Identical to LG's," said Harv. "For better or worse. I told Candace to be ready for a call. She can be out the door inside thirty seconds. Like Nathan, I have a pair of tactical dogs. Malinois."

"Belgian shepherds," said Cantrell. "Nice. Nathan, I want you to dictate a brief op report and text it to me. Include everything you remember Genneken saying, no matter how unimportant it seems. I realize she was drugged when you found her, but I want everything. Do that right away."

He exchanged another glance with Harv, and said, "Sure, no problem."

"We'll know more once we've interrogated the gunman from Genneken's house."

And just like that, the call went dark.

Cantrell rarely said goodbye. Nathan had asked her about it once; she'd said she was superstitious.

"Did that sound like what I think it sounded like?" Harv asked.

"Kinda. Cantrell has to look at the big picture. For the record, I think Genneken's clean."

"Me too." Harv motioned with his head. "I'll be outside keeping the mutts company until our personnel arrive."

He smiled. "Be sure you turn them off before bringing them back in. You know the command word."

"Indeed I do. I'd spell it, but I bet your dogs can read and write."

"Practically."

"I'll watch their backs."

"Thanks, Harv. We'll leave our radios on. I agree with Cantrell. I think we eliminated the threat, at least for now, but stay sharp anyway. Don't forget to call Candace and tell her you're okay."

"I will. When was the last time you talked with Holly?"

"I texted her yesterday, but we haven't spoken in several days."

"Everything okay?"

"As far as I know. She's just hopelessly buried. We've come to terms with the long-distance thing. She seems okay with it."

"Are you?"

"It's not like I have a choice."

"You dodged the question."

"Yeah, I guess I did . . ." At moments like these, he knew his friend wouldn't press. "Truthfully, I wish we could spend more time together. I need to get out there."

"Why don't you schedule it?"

"Let's get through the next forty-eight hours first."

Alone in the room with Linda, he studied her Slavic facial features. Her nose looked bad, but it wasn't deformed to one side or the other. She'd likely have two black eyes, though. For the first time he realized her resemblance to Holly was uncanny. They could easily have been distant relatives.

He felt a longing to call Holly. As the FBI's chief of staff, she worked inside the Hoover Building in DC. He owed Holly more than he'd ever be able to repay. She'd showed him he didn't have to be alone, that he could share his life with someone other than Harv and not be judged or condemned. They'd been an item ever since taking down the Bridgestone brothers. Back then, she'd been the special agent in charge of Sacramento's field office. During a drive into the Sierra Nevada, they'd both taken risks and opened their souls, neither being evasive nor judgmental. When she'd been critically wounded by a Semtex bomb that destroyed a huge section of her field office, he'd never felt that degree of heartache. Seeing her broken and burned body in the hospital bed had torn him open. He remembered thinking: *Is this what love feels like? If so, how do people survive it?* An hour at a time, he supposed.

Like tonight.

CHAPTER 9

The woman ran her fingers up her date's thigh but stopped short.

He tensed with anticipation. "Why'd you stop?"

"It's not midnight," she said.

What were the odds he'd meet a woman like this on New Year's Eve and end up in a hot tub with her? *Not that low,* he told himself. Wealthy men got all the beautiful women. It was the way the world worked. Funny thing was, he hadn't been looking for a date tonight. He'd gone to the country club for a few drinks, like he frequently did, and spotted this gorgeous brunette across the room. She'd offered a friendly smile and . . . here they were. He fancied himself an excellent lover. Admittedly, it wasn't all that difficult. Massage and kiss the right places and the cork pops free.

"Next year can't get here soon enough," he said.

"I'll make it worth the wait. It's only . . ." She glanced at her Rolex Ladies President. "Four more minutes."

"Nice watch."

"Thank you. It was a Christmas gift from my brother."

He raised a brow. "He must be doing pretty well."

"He died a few years ago."

"I'm sorry . . . I—"

She put a finger to his lips. "Shh. It's okay."

"It's just that you haven't told me anything about yourself."

"I'm a good listener."

He smiled. It seemed that was all he'd get. Besides, she seemed comfortable with small talk. If he pushed, it might spoil the mood. "I like your Spanish accent."

"Really? You aren't just saying that?"

"It's sexy."

She leaned over and gave his neck a long kiss. "You Americans . . ."

He moaned and tilted his head back.

"Is it true Americans shoot guns into the air on New Year's?"

"Not too many around here. This is Hollywood, not Jerkwater, Alabama."

"There's no such place," she said. "Is there?"

"It's just an expression for a rural area. I didn't mean to pick on Alabama. Every state has its rednecks."

"Rednecks?"

"Another expression."

"I've never shot a gun."

"Are you serious?"

She nodded. "Is it scary?"

"I suppose it could be if you don't know what you're doing. Guns are perfectly safe in the right hands. Believe it or not, driving is far more dangerous."

"Now you're teasing me."

"No, I'm completely serious."

"Will you take me shooting sometime?"

"Sure, it's easy. You'd like it."

"I'm not sure about that, but I'm willing to try."

"I've been out here on New Year's before. We'll hear a few guns go off."

Her expression changed to fear.

A quick recovery was needed. "It's more likely you'll win the lottery than have a bullet land on your head." He snuggled up to her. "Besides, you've got me protecting you."

She kissed him again and climbed out of the tub.

The view from water level was beyond exceptional.

"I need to use the little girls' room. I'll be right back."

"It's almost midnight . . ."

"Don't worry. I'll be back in time."

He watched her walk toward the pool house. Man, that's some motion. Halfway there, she turned back and blew a kiss. He felt himself stir.

Alone in the tub, he fantasized about the rest of the evening. Such pleasures were rare in life, regardless of wealth. He'd worked like a sled dog to get where he was. His independent oil company had just secured a five-year lease in Venezuela's Orinoco Belt. The price of crude would eventually climb out of the toilet. He wasn't worried. Raised in Texas, he'd been an oilman his entire life—third generation. Oil futures were just that. Besides, he had another business going on the side, an equally lucrative one.

This woman easily made him forget all that. She possessed charm equaling her beauty, a rare combination in any part of the world. She could've gone home with any man in the room, but she'd chosen him. Granted, most of the old farts at the country club were bald, wrinkled, and married but, given the opportunity, they'd slobber all over this woman. Sure, she could be on a fishing expedition . . . but so what? If she considered him a catch, who was he to argue?

He frowned at an odd sound.

Is that a swarm of bees? His whiskey-dulled mind wondered if bees flew at night and he was pretty sure they didn't.

Whatever it was, it grew louder.

A single object about the size of an umbrella materialized out of the blackness. It came to a hover thirty feet away. He sat up a little, his curiosity turning to anger at the intrusion. It was one of those eight-bladed drones. An omnicopter or some other dipshit name.

If this was a prank by one of his neighbors, it wasn't funny.

He climbed out of the tub.

The craft moved closer and he gave it the middle-finger salute.

The machine rocked back and forth like a waltzing dancer.

He heard it then, a different sound, also coming from the drone. A bizarre chuckling, like that of an old laughing bag toy from the seventies. It started as a low chitter and grew in volume until it overpowered the blades.

Yeah, right. Very funny, asshole.

The laughing stopped.

A voice from behind startled him.

"Happy New Year, my love."

He turned.

The woman he'd brought into his home stood ten feet away with a leveled shotgun, its menacing form tucked under her bikini-clad breast like a coddled newborn.

Gunshots began crackling from the surrounding neighborhoods.

"What are you—"

His mind registered the discharge, heard the boom, and told him his chest cavity had just been destroyed.

The impact thrust him back and he plunged into the water.

He tried to reason a way out of dying, but knew it was wishful thinking. *So this is it? This is how I die? Seriously?*

Strange how the mind worked at a time like this. The third-generation oil baron hoped the police would find his body before this damned hot tub turned him into stew.

***

Tomas Bustamonte pulled the tarp away from the drone. A beautifully engineered craft greeted him. Nothing but the best for the great Daniel Cornejo. Tomas had conducted dozens of missions, but this was definitely a first. He found it amusing that America's FAA was only now realizing the harm and damage that irresponsible drone operators can cause. New laws were in the works, but as with all government intervention, they would be too little, too late.

The good thing about drones? They ignored property lines. An inane thought, he knew. Drones didn't do anything without their operators.

After a quick preflight check to make sure all its components and parts were secure, he removed the drone from the back of the SUV and set it on the street. No one could see him; the neighborhood was quiet and dark.

He felt the stirring of excitement as he turned on the remote controller and flipped the drone's power switch. He settled into the passenger's seat and thumbed the altitude button. He was rewarded with a humming buzz as the device lifted off the ground. Its eight blades working in unison, it hovered in a stable position, awaiting orders.

His twin sister Ursula loved working with small engines, electrical motors, and servos. It had been a fairly complicated task, linking the night-vision scope into its camera system, but, as with all things, her perseverance had paid off. It was now a simple matter of transmitting the drone's video feed through his laptop, via a cell-phone hotspot to Cornejo.

He piloted the drone to an altitude of approximately one hundred feet and sent it in a southerly direction. Prior to the mission, he'd used the Google Earth program to memorize the terrain and houses between himself and the target. Familiar landscapes and landmarks scrolled across his laptop's screen. When the drone crossed Park Oak Drive, he began slowing its speed and dropping its altitude.

The terra-cotta roof of the target residence appeared and, a few seconds later, the backyard pool area materialized. He zoomed the camera and found his mark right where he should be.

Tomas used the hands-free feature of his phone to call Cornejo, who'd insisted on watching the action live. Tomas thought his boss's order a little eccentric, but it fit the arrogant man he'd known for years. There were, after all, personal vendettas to be settled. Not his concern. Tomas got paid the same, audience or not. Based on the money Cornejo threw at him, coming out of retirement hadn't been a difficult decision. Besides, he'd worked for worse people . . . actually, come to think of it, maybe not.

"Mr. Cornejo, are you receiving the feed?"

"Yes, thank you for going to all the trouble."

"Do I have a green light to proceed as planned?"

"Absolutely."

"Very well, sir. Stand by . . ."

"I like the night vision."

"Thank you. Ursula gets the credit. She's quite the technician."

"This is great. I think we'll do this again. It's exciting."

To each his own, Tomas thought. The drone operation made his job both easier and more difficult. Easier because he didn't have to scramble over any walls or bypass any security systems to get a camera on the action. Difficult because the drone had to be purchased, assembled, and all the electronics had to be configured and tested. Again, Ursula's job.

Tomas had to admit to enjoying this as well. He especially liked the irritated expression on the man's face. The evening's ambiance had been spoiled. Too bad for him. *Just wait, it gets worse.* Tomas clicked a button on his laptop, activating the laughing sound. He couldn't hear it, but it had worked perfectly on the test run.

Cornejo laughed. "This is priceless."

Actually, it was quite expensive. Chump change to Cornejo. The man made millions every day.

Ursula's date got out of the hot tub and flipped the bird at the machine. *If looks could kill.* Tomas wiggled the joystick, making the craft rock back and forth.

At that moment, Tomas heard fireworks crackle and pop. Bigger sounds too—some of them probably from guns.

His sister entered the camera's field of view.

The man turned.

The shotgun flashed. Tomas heard the report a full second later.

Arms flailing, the man fell into the hot tub. Water surged over the edges.

Ursula waved to the machine, then walked out of camera shot.

"You can expect a large bonus for a job well done, Tomas."

"Thank you, sir."

"It's a shame he received such a quick death."

"We were willing to do it the old-fashioned way."

"I appreciate that," Cornejo said, "but it's important to avoid patterns. I trust you'll safely dispose of the drone?"

"Of course."

"Your next assignment in New York City will be much more personal, the way you like it. Do you have any word from La Jolla?"

"Not yet. I'm expecting a call any minute."

"Call me once you have a report. Have a safe flight back east."

"Thank you. We will."

Tomas gave the drone power, took it up to five hundred feet, and flew it in a westerly direction. Soon the dark shape of the Hollywood Reservoir appeared. He piloted the craft to the center of the water and cut its power. He watched the lake rapidly approach as the machine plummeted to its death. The image jumped from the impact, then went dark.

He drove the SUV to the intersection of Spring Oak and Park Oak. Draped in a towel, with her clothes concealing the shotgun, Ursula stepped out from a lush line of landscaping and got in.

She leaned over, gave him a kiss on the cheek, and fastened her seat belt.

And just like that, they were gone.

CHAPTER 10

Nathan and Harv were in the kitchen, chowing down on a pair of Angelica's famous bacon sandwiches, when Cantrell called.

"We know who attacked Genneken, and you're not going to like it. The Bustamonte twins."

Nathan watched Harv's eyes narrow. "Ursula and Tomas," he said quietly. "Did your guest disclose that?"

"Yes."

Harv said, "We thought they'd retired."

"It seems they've been reactivated. We think they're responsible for the recent string of assassinations I mentioned."

"How did you break your guest so quickly?" Harv asked.

"We didn't get too rough, if that's what you're asking. We gave him a sample of what he could expect over an extended period of time if he didn't cooperate. When he asked for other options, we gave him two choices: he could either spend the rest of his life in Guantánamo Bay surrounded by radical jihadists intent on killing every infidel they could get their hands on, or retire to Belize as a rich man with a new identity."

"Good call."

"It works in most cases when fanatical ideology isn't a factor. People don't like the concept of disappearing forever."

Nathan wanted to ask if the guy would end up at Gitmo anyway, but decided it was a foregone conclusion. Cold-blooded murderers deserved a needle, or worse. "You feel pretty good about the information he gave up?"

"The algorithm makes this kind of intel much easier to corroborate. Plus we got facial-recognition IDs on several of the dead gunmen. Two are Venezuelans here on work visas. Three are Venezuelan Americans with dual citizenship who've been in the US for a long time, but as far as our records show, they've never pulled anything like this. All are positively linked to the Bustamonte twins."

Nathan looked at Harv. "I'm impressed with how quickly your people moved."

"We're highly motivated. Once our guest started talking, we were able to run IDs and verify the info he gave us."

"Obviously the work-visa guys didn't bring duffle bags full of guns and tactical gear with them."

"No, they didn't. The twins have ties to organized crime here in the US. Here's where it gets interesting. Do you recall your Venezuelan rescue mission?"

Nathan did. Another instance of Harv and him being brought out of retirement for a CIA op. They'd rescued Linda's husband-to-be, Glen. She hadn't known Glen at the time—only that he was a US citizen being held against his will in Caracas by the Bustamontes. During the operation, Ursula Bustamonte had nearly killed Nathan; her bullet missed his heart by less than an inch.

Harv must've sensed his thoughts because his friend said, "I'm sure there's a point to all of this."

"We're 99 percent sure the twins are in Daniel Cornejo's employ again."

"And that's important because?" Nathan asked.

Harv jumped in. "Because Cornejo's the front-runner in Venezuela's special presidential election."

"I see you guys are up to speed on Latin American politics."

"That's Harv's thing, not mine."

"Harvey's correct. Short of a miracle, Cornejo's expected to defeat acting president Cadenas, who was President Garmendia's VP."

"I'm remembering something in the news," Nathan said. "Didn't Garmendia have a stroke or heart attack?"

"Stroke," Cantrell said. "The situation's quite controversial. The Venezuelan Constitution calls for a special election within thirty days upon the death or incapacitation of the president, but Garmendia's partially coherent. He can answer yes-and-no questions with hand gestures, but he can't talk and the doctors can't say with certainty he ever will again. It's a political mess. To make a long story short, the Supreme Court of Venezuela ruled that a special election is warranted and it's going to take place in ten days."

"And I'm assuming we don't want Cornejo to succeed," said Nathan.

"You assume correctly. Since Hugo Chavez's death, Venezuelan-US relations have remained strained, but they've warmed a little. Cadenas is considerably more pro-capitalist than Garmendia and he's promised to bring Venezuela back to economic health by repealing some of Garmendia's failed social-spending programs. It's more complicated than this, but in a nutshell, rationing, price-fixing, and over-taxation have decimated Venezuela's economy. To make matters worse, crude oil is near a fifteen-year low and it accounts for 96 percent of Venezuela's export income."

"How much of that 96 percent do we buy?" Nathan asked.

"Depending on who you talk to, about 40 percent."

He exchanged an incredulous glance with Harv. "That has to be tens of billions of dollars."

"It is. Again, depending on who you talk to, Venezuela's Orinoco Belt contains around three hundred to five hundred billion barrels of recoverable heavy crude. That means Venezuela has the largest reserves on the planet. Cornejo, on the other hand, is purely self-interested, a robber-baron type. He's perfectly positioned to see a huge windfall if he gets control of Venezuela's national petroleum company. He already owns the biggest oil-drilling company in South America. Nearly all of his competitors are dormant or out of business."

"His doing?" Nathan asked.

"Harv?" Cantrell obviously believed his friend knew the answer.

"More like natural selection. There's been too much supply versus demand for some time now, and the Russians and Saudis have no intention of curtailing their production. It's a giant squeeze play. It wouldn't break their hearts to see Venezuela removed from the competition."

"So much for OPEC unity," Nathan said dryly.

Harv continued, "The Venezuelans have no choice. They have to keep lowering their crude prices to compete. It makes a bad situation worse."

"That's exactly right," Cantrell said. "If the economic situation isn't remedied, Venezuela could find itself following in Greece's footsteps."

"How bad are things down there?" Nathan asked.

"If the murder rate per capita is any indicator," said Cantrell, "they're in a full-blown crisis. Percentage wise, it's ten times higher than ours. A murder is committed every twenty minutes."

"Incredible," Harv said. "I knew it was high, but that's crazy."

"Acting president Cadenas wants reform, but Cornejo's one of the richest men on the continent who can quite literally buy his presidency. Venezuela doesn't really have a pro-capitalism party. The socialists are just too well entrenched. We aren't going to interfere with Venezuela's internal politics, but we *are* going to find out why Cornejo hired the twins to carry out this recent string of assassinations and abductions."

"The simplest answer," Harv said, "is that Cornejo's tying up loose ends that could torpedo his bid for the presidency."

"That's our conclusion as well. We're working overtime to find links from other victims back to Cornejo. It's still unclear why his people attacked Genneken. The guy we interrogated wasn't leading the operation and didn't know. He said he was planning to meet Tomas at a rest stop along the I-5 corridor near Camp Pendleton."

"So they were heading toward Los Angeles after the attack?"

"It appears that way. Our prisoner was supposed to check in by 12:30 a.m."

"And since we drugged him . . ."

"That's right, he couldn't make the call. Things were fluid and I didn't consider it. A mistake on my part."

"Don't beat yourself up, Rebecca. We didn't think of it either. I think we can safely assume Tomas is long gone from the rest stop. At least we know he's in the area. And if he's in the area, it's a good bet his sister is too."

"I wonder what their next step would have been," said Harv. "Chances are they have a private jet waiting somewhere, especially if Cornejo's as rich as you say."

"We're checking the ATC logs of all the chartered and private jet flights over the last seven days. But we're also looking at Cornejo's US business ownership and real-estate holdings. It's possible the twins didn't plan to leave the country right away. Without knowing why Cornejo wanted to get his hands on Genneken, we can only speculate on his motive."

"I'm still not clear on something," said Nathan. "Why do we, the US, care if Cornejo becomes Venezuela's next president? I get that we don't want a crook running Venezuela who'd make the economic situation worse, but it sounds like something much bigger's going on."

"There *is* something bigger going on," she said.

Harv shifted in his chair; Nathan suspected his friend knew the answer.

"In two words," Cantrell said, "nuclear weapons. I can't say more than that, it's on a need-to-know basis."

"Okay, we won't ask."

"Presidential terms are six years and the First Amendment to their most recent constitution abolished term limits. If Cornejo wins, we're looking at an unpredictable situation for an indeterminate amount of time. He hates the US more than Chavez did."

"I didn't think that was possible," Nathan said.

"It definitely is."

Nathan took a deep breath and exhaled slowly. "So what are we supposed to do? Keep hanging tight here with Linda?"

"No, actually, you're going to pay a visit to an exotic car dealership in Santa Monica."

"Okay . . . ," said Nathan. "And we're doing this because Cornejo owns the dealership and you think it's a viable location to pick up Bustamonte's trail?"

"Yes. Cornejo did a good job hiding his title under a multi-tiered shell company, but my personal aide is quite resourceful. Cornejo's involved with many legitimate businesses in the US and Canada. Restaurants, nightclubs, car dealerships, real-estate groups, banks, you name it. Several are in the greater Los Angeles area. Most of them he owns outright; with others he has partners in the US. Almost all of his businesses are likely being used as fronts for his money-laundering operations to one degree or another. Santa Monica Exotics seems to be his flagship operation in North America. He spared no expense con- structing it—you'll know what I'm talking about when you see it. He gutted an older building and built the dealership from scratch. The ground floor is the dealership and he rents office space on the second and third floors. We've found that those tenant businesses fall under the same umbrella of shell companies as the dealership."

"So he's paying rent to himself," Harv said.

"At highly inflated rates. I wouldn't be surprised if these nebulous businesses received loans from the umbrella company that will never be paid back. It's classic laundering. The rent is seen as income, but the bogus loans are recorded as losses, hence no income is recognized and little or no tax is paid."

"How much money are we talking about?" Nathan asked.

"All told, hundreds of millions."

Nathan and Harv raised their eyebrows at one another.

"I want to know why Cornejo views Genneken as a threat. If she has dirt on him, find out what it is. And it's entirely possible she doesn't know what she knows, so to speak."

"And if she *has* dirt on him?" Harv asked.

"We make an anonymous call to the Venezuelan media. Needless to say, we're prohibited by law from domestic intelligence-gathering operations against US citizens, and we don't have any direct law-enforcement powers. But since Cornejo isn't a US citizen and it's clear he's behind the murder of Genneken's husband and her attempted kidnapping, he and the Bustamonte twins are fair game. The DNI's on board with that assessment and he wants regular updates on your progress."

"Wouldn't it be easier to just bring us out of retirement again?" Harv asked, somewhat humorously.

"What would be the point? You guys won't take any money."

"You're right, we wouldn't," Nathan said.

"Let's be clear. You two inserted yourselves by responding to Genneken's home invasion, and I'm glad you did. Nathan, based on your initial report after you arrived at her house, there were still gunmen around and Genneken wouldn't have been able to defend herself because of the Ketamine. You kept her from falling into the twins' hands."

"It was the right thing to do."

"That's what I love about you guys, and why you have personal access to me. You put yourselves at risk without any expectation of getting anything in return."

"What can we say? It's a character flaw."

"Hardly."

Cantrell never greased them; she didn't need to and it wasn't her style. They both appreciated the compliment for what it was.

"We're at your service, as always, but what do you want us to do with Linda while we're gone?"

"You'll be taking her with you. Keep her close at all times. I'm getting some assets on line in the LA area so be ready to move out on a moment's notice. After the Ketamine's fully out of her system, ask her about Cornejo. If she knows why he came after her, let me know right away. Once she's 100 percent, you three are going to wreak havoc on Cornejo's North American world, starting in Santa Monica. At the same time, we'll begin a series of hit-and-run actions against Cornejo's other business interests in LA, with the goal of flushing the Bustamonte twins into the open. We're tracking all their known aliases, but I figure we have zero chance of finding them unless we force them to fight back."

"So we're bait?"

"Bait is such a crude word. I'd prefer to think of you guys as the trap. Keep in mind we need the twins alive. Needless to say the clock is ticking toward the special election. In NFL lingo, we're running a hurry-up offense, not allowing the defense time to rest or change its personnel. We're hitting back, and hitting back hard. Cornejo sent a squad of mercenaries to capture Linda Genneken alive and render her. He's also responsible for one of the stars on our wall, and Ursula came within an eyelash of adding yours. Behind his 'man-of-the-people' veneer, he's the absolute worst a human being can be. Child trafficking is one of the many crimes he's associated with. His cartel buddies buy them from impoverished parents and sell them with no questions asked of the buyers."

Nathan shook his head and looked to Harv.

"Is Cornejo officially part of a Venezuelan cartel?" Harv asked.

"Not directly. He calls himself a successful businessman. We call him an organized crime boss. But he's too smart to get his hands dirty. Think of him like an underwriter. He hires others to do his dirty work for him. Look, if you guys want a pass on this, I'll understand with no questions asked, and no hard feelings. Flushing out the twins will be a difficult and risky assignment."

"We've done worse."

"Yes, you have."

"So why us? Why not use an FBI SWAT team or a joint terrorism task force?"

"Quite frankly, because they have to play by the rules."

Neither of them said anything.

"I'll share a personal belief with you," she said. "The more power a person has, the more accountable that person has to be. I trust you and Harv with the power you're being given, more so than my other teams."

"That's flattering, Rebecca, and we're honored, but again you really don't need us for this kind of thing."

"Who else can hear what I'm saying right now?"

"Just Harv. LG's awake, but she's still pretty groggy. She's in the other room."

"She's the main reason I chose you for the job. I'm sure you'll agree that given everything we know about the woman, there will be no stopping her after tonight. She'll go after the Bustamontes with or without our help. That's why I'm sending her with you. I don't want her doing it alone, and quite frankly, we need the twins alive."

Nathan looked at Harv. "That's our assessment as well. Changing the subject, we'll do our best to avoid crossing paths with law enforcement, but it's possible we could end up in custody. I trust that situation will be . . . appropriately handled?"

"Yes. If it happens, ask for a lawyer, and get word to me."

"Understood," Nathan said. "Regarding what to expect in Santa Monica . . ."

"The car dealership's pretty straightforward, but the second and third floors aren't. There could be cash, drugs, and guns. You name it. All the lifeblood of a crime family's operation. Don't worry about friend-lies. Everyone inside the structure should be considered fair game."

"So there are no undercovers?" Harv asked.

"Correct. I'm working on getting eyes on the building, but we won't be able to give you any direct support. DNI Benson said no boots on the ground except yours. Officially, we don't conduct 'domestic' ops like this."

"Understood."

"So, to review: Your job has three elements. Capture the Bustamonte twins so we can get dirt on Cornejo, determine why Cornejo wants Genneken, and find out how her personal information leaked. You may have to conduct field interrogations."

"We'll leave that to LG."

"I don't care *how* it gets done, only that it *gets* done. Let me be clear, I want both of them alive. I'm sending you our profiles on Tomas and Ursula; take a moment to look them over. I've got to run. Call or text me as needed."

Nathan was tempted to hang up first, but that would have been poor form. The line went dark.

"You look wiped," Harv said to Nathan. "I'll take first watch with Linda. You'd better get some rack time."

CHAPTER 11

The bamboo cage swings with a gust of wind, quietly creaking.

Twenty feet below, the ferns bend, then straighten.

Nathan can't believe he's still alive. How long now? Three days? He doesn't know, doesn't care.

No one's coming to his rescue.

They would've been here by now.

His emaciated skin hangs like a scarecrow's clothes. He can't weigh more than a hundred pounds.

The reddish glow on the horizon accents the color of his ruined flesh. Is it a sunrise or sunset? Doesn't matter.

Forcing him to stand, the custom-built cage fits like a glove. The agony in his legs and lower back defies understanding, defies description.

His arms are tied behind his back and secured to the bamboo struts. The rope binding his wrists isn't tight enough to cut off circulation, but he can't get any leverage to work his hands free.

It triggers a childhood memory of how helpless he'd felt at being buried up to his neck at the beach. It had been a dumb kid's game. His sixth-grade friend promised over and over he'd dig him out, but once Nathan became helpless, Marty Drugar thought it funny to walk away. Nathan didn't. He'd experienced his first true rage that sunny afternoon. Screaming to be let out, he remembered people staring and pointing, but no one came. His mom and dad couldn't rescue him; they'd taken a stroll down the beach. After the lifeguard dug him out with a shovel, he proceeded to beat the living tar out of Martin Drugar. He put the little punk in the hospital. Broken teeth. A busted nose. And five cracked ribs. Shrinks came next. All he could claim was that he'd warned Marty what he'd do if he left him there. A promise he'd kept. He remembered how good it had felt teaching that skinny little punk a lesson.

Time drifts again.

He opens his eyes to a dishwater gray jungle. Must've been a sunset, it's gotten darker.

Praying for death, he whispers it over and over like a mantra.

Could he already be dead? No, it wouldn't be like this.

The dryness in his mouth is beyond gruesome; it's become his worst enemy. He'd trade twenty more lashes for a drink of water. But no one's around to offer him either.

He hasn't seen Montez or his little runt assistant for a long time. Candlelight no longer fills the shack's windows at night.

He's totally alone, abandoned to a slow death.

The sense of desertion tears at his soul like a jackal stripping his bones.

This must be his penance for the lives he's taken.

What else could it be?

He never enjoyed killing, but he'd been exceptionally good at it.

Too good.

He should've felt worse than he did, maybe if he had . . . What goes around comes around? He'd never believed that stupid idiom until now.

Why has God discarded him? It's so cruel. He feels forsaken and curses God again, then regrets the thought. God isn't to blame, only himself. Deep in his soul, he knows the truth. Denying it changes nothing.

Another truth hammers him: slow starvation is the enemy of impulsive thought. Every decision he's ever made has been questioned—from childhood to the ugly here and now. If only he'd done this differently, or that differently, maybe he wouldn't have joined the Marines and become a sniper. And if he hadn't become a sniper, he wouldn't have been recruited by the CIA and he wouldn't be hanging here to die.

Would haves.

Could haves.

Should haves.

Circular arguments always ending in the same place. This wretched cage.

It's pointless to think about it, but his mind's stuck in a feedback loop.

At least he hadn't caved. His love of Harv had overpowered all else, including the instinct to save himself. Montez never got what he wanted—Harv's escape route.

Didn't that selfless act of bravery buy him a ticket to heaven?

He almost laughs at the absurdity.

No one buys tickets to heaven, they're offered freely. Besides, his pockets are empty. Another stupid thought. Montez had stripped him naked.

Another burst of rage erupts.

Over and over, he bangs his forehead against the bamboo, causing the cage to vibrate. Pain explodes from everywhere. His vision grays, then winks out.

Time drifts again.

A deep boom brings him to consciousness.

What's that sound?

He hopes it's a jet on a bombing run to level the camp and him with it.

Not a bomb.

Thunder.

He looks up and tries to focus.

Rain slaps his face, supplying precious water to his eyes. He opens his mouth and lets a few drops enter, but it's not nearly enough—an unkind tease.

Above his head, the dish-shaped ant barrier is tight where the rope passes through. It will act like a dam, preventing water from running down the rope and into his mouth.

The dish begins to fill. He can hear the sound of raindrops landing in the tiny pool.

He says a prayer to ease the cruelty of having water so close but so utterly unreachable. The dish continues to fill, then begins to lean. Farther and farther. It reaches the point of no return and flops to the side. A torrent falls—

Into his open mouth.

The stream bathes his tongue and teeth with something akin to pure ecstasy. Tears of joy flow. He can't believe it's really happening.

Then as quickly as the flow began, it ends.

The dish levels out.

The stream stops.

No! He needs more. That can't be all there is. *Please . . . More!*

He keeps his eyes on the dish. Then, like the dipping bird toy, the dish begins another cycle. It tips from the weight and another torrent falls into his mouth. Oh, dear Lord, thank you. Thank you, thank you.

The water is beyond anything he could've ever imagined.

Is this real? Could he be hallucinating? Somewhere in the back of his mind, he knows this will prolong his suffering, but he doesn't care.

Over and over, the dish fills, then tips. He's getting more water now than he's had over the previous three weeks. He knows he can't drink too much too fast, but it feels so good. He forces himself to slow down.

Swallowing mouthful after mouthful, he asks God for forgiveness.

The water has an acrid taste, but he doesn't care.

His flesh burns from being drenched, but he doesn't care.

His life has been extended, but he doesn't care.

Another boom shakes the cage, this time louder. What's that sound?

What's going on? Who's there?

Leave me alone! I'm getting water. LEAVE ME ALONE!

CHAPTER 12

"McBride!"

Where was he?

Reality imploded. *I'm not in the cage. I'm in my bedroom. On the floor again.*

He looked around.

LG stood in the open door, her horrified expression telling all.

"Are you okay?"

He nodded and wiped perspiration from his face.

"Harvey left me a note. It said he's outside with your dogs and some FBI agents. I didn't mean to intrude, but it sounded like you were in pain. I knocked, but you didn't answer."

He got up. "I'm sorry you had to see that."

"I'm glad I did. It reminds me of the pure hell you went through."

"It happened. It's over."

"Clearly not."

"The aftermath of burned toast. I've learned to deal with it."

"Where were you just then?"

"Hanging in the cage. It rained on the third day. I got water."

"Probably saved your life. Didn't Fontana find you on the fifth day?"

Not knowing how much she knew, he nodded. "I'll be right back, I'm really thirsty."

"Sit tight, Marine. I'll get it."

"Thanks, LG."

She grabbed his glass from the nightstand. "It's the least I can do." She stopped at the door and looked down at herself. "I'm going to need some clothes."

"Angelica will fix you up."

"Angelica?"

"She lives here. Takes care of the place for me."

"You have staff?"

"It's not like that."

"If you say so."

A moment later, she returned and he took a long swig. "I like your house."

"Thanks." He looked at the nightstand clock, 1:57 a.m. "How much do you remember?"

"I remember Glen charging down the stairs and tackling the gunman." Her expression changed. "He's dead, isn't he?" She turned away and wiped a tear.

"Yeah, he's gone. I'm so sorry. You told me what happened before you lost consciousness." He gave her a short recap.

"When I got tased, I remembered feeling so helpless and angry. I was worried they were going to render Glen."

"I didn't kill the guy who injected you."

"And you're telling me this because . . . Wait, I asked you to kill him?"

He nodded. "You were pretty woozy."

"I always thought it would be me, not Glen. You know what's amazing? He was worried about our dogs. He told me to get them out of the house."

110

"I'm really sorry, Linda. After Caracas, I'd only talked with Glen once, at your wedding. I liked him."

"He didn't have a mean bone in his body. When we saw a stray dog, he'd stop to help it, every time, even in the rain. He funded a massive endowment at Hillsdale College under its Frederick Douglass scholarship program. The interest from the endowment pays the tuition for twenty underprivileged kids every year." She wiped more tears.

He knew what she needed and keyed his radio. "Harv, you copy?"

"I'm outside. What's up?"

"I'm awake and Linda's up and around. Did you get her dogs from Cantrell's people?"

"Half an hour ago. Cantrell's people had to carry them down the bluff's stairs. Want me to bring them in?"

"Please."

"Be right there."

"Fontana's outside with Morgen and Elsa?"

"Harv thought you'd want to be with them when you woke up."

"When I knew you were coming, I thought about your dogs."

Nathan smiled. "Some might say they're more memorable than me."

Linda didn't return the emotion. He couldn't imagine what she felt.

"Linda, if you need some time . . . We don't have to talk about any of this right now."

She didn't say anything for a few seconds.

"I'm going after them," she said softly. "Please don't try to stop me."

"Just the opposite."

"I can't ask you guys to do that."

"You aren't asking, and the decision's already been made. You're coming with us."

"Cantrell?"

"Surveillance and reconnaissance. No boots but ours."

"I can live with that."

"It's not ideal, but it's all we get. How's your head. You got stuck with Ketamine."

"The K hole," she said slowly.

Just then, Harv entered the room with four large dogs in tow.

Linda got down on one knee and wrapped her German shepherds up in a hug.

Her body shuddered. Their tails wagged.

Watching the action, Grant and Sherman stood near Nathan's side, awaiting orders. Their intelligent gaze almost had him believing they understood the situation. In reality, they were probably thinking about their next meal, wondering if they'd have to share it with the newcomers.

"It's good to see you guys," Linda said through tears. She buried her face between them. "They're rescues," she said. "Ironic, isn't it?"

Nathan didn't say anything.

"We rescue Glen and then he ends up rescuing me." She wiped her face with both hands.

"Full circle," he said. "Your dogs are beautiful."

"We're volunteers for the German Shepherd Rescue of Orange County. We've had as many as six. Right now, we only have Morgen and Elsa. They're permanent. We adopted them a few years back."

"I like their tags," Harv said. "They remind me of the big cross on Mount Soledad."

"Glen had them custom-made a long time ago. The veterans' memorial up there was one of his favorite spots."

Nathan was impressed—he'd never seen such a thing. Each of her shepherds wore a thick, white cross dangling from its collar. They measured about two inches long by one inch across.

"Thanks again, you guys. For everything. If you hadn't shown up, I would've ended up in an interrogator's chair, or worse."

"You're welcome, but you did most of the work before we arrived. Do you have any idea what it's about?"

"No, but it has to be related to one of my old ops. What else could it be?" Linda paused, her eyes clouding. "Wait, I'm remembering something. It was just before the guy injected me. What was it he said? Shit, I can't remember, but it made my skin crawl."

Nathan waited, not wanting to break her concentration. It was best to let her work the memory forward. He watched her expression change.

"Little Peach," she said softly.

He exchanged a glance with Harv, but neither of them said anything.

"It's what Tomas Bustamonte liked to call me."

CHAPTER 13

Linda knew there were times when the truth shouldn't be withheld, this being one of them. She trusted these men with her life. They'd never judge her. They had, after all, shared their somewhat questionable evening in a Shanghai brothel. Somewhat? What they'd described could only be considered scandalous. They'd been young, horny Marines. What more needed to be said?

They'd moved to the kitchen, where McBride's housekeeper had brewed a pot of coffee while they awaited the go signal from Cantrell.

McBride asked, "Were you and Tomas—"

"Yes," she said quickly. "I'd gone undercover to get close to the Bustamontes in hopes of finding Glen. You guys knew that much."

McBride and Fontana nodded.

"Well . . . getting inside is never easy. Sometimes it requires . . . compromises. In this case, it meant earning Tomas Bustamonte's trust. Which meant . . ."

"We get it," said Fontana.

"It happened more than once. It had to. Before we rescued Glen. I never told him."

"No one's judging you, LG."

"Tomas's sister was furious when she found out he was sleeping with me. I heard them arguing the following morning. I got dressed and raced out of there. He tried to start it up again a few days later, but I told him in no uncertain terms it wasn't happening. He wasn't heartbroken, but he wasn't happy either. Ursula, though . . ." Linda shook her head at the bitter memory. "She confronted me about it, started a fistfight."

"Who won?" Fontana asked.

"Who do you think? And it felt great kicking her scrawny ass."

"Why do I get the feeling there's more to the story?" McBride asked.

"A few days later, she sucker punched me. I would've put her in a hospital, but Tomas stepped in."

"Lucky for her," Fontana said.

"Very. She had no accountability. None. She did whatever she wanted and never faced the consequences. I wanted to beat the living crap out of her to show her otherwise. She and her brother were responsible for untold kidnappings, human trafficking, torture, murder—you name it. If I learned one thing getting inside their organization, it was that Ursula was far more vicious than Tomas. The woman has no conscience. The amount of suffering those two have caused can't be easily quantified."

"I don't doubt it," McBride said. "We want them as badly as you do. But the question remains: why come after you now?"

"Does Cantrell have a working theory?"

"She thinks it's related to the special election in Venezuela."

"I'm familiar with it. Corn Hole's favored to win by a large margin."

"Corn Hole?" McBride asked.

"It's what the twins called him behind his back. Venezuela's favorite son—former attorney general, father of three, loving husband, wealthy industrialist, and closet crime boss. That guy scares me, no easy trick. Does Cantrell think the twins are working for him again?"

"Yes. Several of the dead gunmen at your house have been positively linked to them. And there have been other recent attacks and abductions in Latin America."

"Tomas and Ursula hated Cornejo. It got so bad that they talked about killing the guy. Why would they dive into that relationship again?"

"Simple," McBride said.

"Money," she said softly. "Cornejo offered them a contract they couldn't turn down . . . Cantrell's right. The hit on me's somehow related to the election."

"Is there any reason Cornejo might consider you a loose end?"

"No. We were never able to prove Cornejo was behind Glen's kidnapping. After we rescued Glen, the twins disappeared and the state department closed the case."

"No other outcome was possible," Fontana said. "Our rescue mission was never sanctioned by the Venezuelan government. As far as the US is concerned, it never took place."

She nodded. "Why attack me at my home? They could've grabbed me anywhere."

"The easiest answer is they wanted it done covertly. I'm assuming Glen worked out of your house?"

She nodded. "The kidnapping turned him into a recluse. He rarely left."

"I can't blame him. Your disappearance might've gone unnoticed for days, maybe longer."

No one spoke for a few seconds.

"I wish we'd killed the twins when we had the chance," she said.

Judging by his expression, Fontana agreed with her. "All we were authorized to do was rescue Glen. If they got killed during the process, no one would've questioned it, but taking them out wasn't our primary mission."

"It should've been," she said.

"Hindsight is always like that," said McBride. "We did as we were told. Once we had Glen, we got out of there in a hurry."

"A big hurry," Fontana added. "You took one through your vest. It's amazing you lived."

"I remember our Seahawk ride out to that Navy destroyer," she said. "Fontana never left your side."

"He's like that," McBride added. "My wound wasn't life threatening."

"The hell it wasn't," she said. "You were minutes from dying when we landed. You'd lost a lot of blood."

"I've got a lot to spare."

She didn't say anything, didn't trust herself to. Her hatred of Ursula was absolute. If she got an opportunity to kill that witch, she'd do it and make it look like self-defense.

"Whatever Cornejo's reason," McBride said, "we're also concerned there could be a leak on the Agency's end. It would explain how he found you. And if he managed to get your address, he could probably get Harv's and mine as well. He could come for any of us at any time. But before the special election seems the most likely."

"All the more reason to kill them all," Linda said. "And sooner than later."

"That's not our mission. Cantrell wants them alive."

"A pity." She watched the men exchange a glance. "If I'm going with you guys, I'll need my emergency duffle. No offense, McBride, but Angelica's clothes aren't the best of fits and I need my tactical gear." She told them where she kept it.

"I'll call Cantrell to arrange something." McBride softened his tone. "She wanted me to assure you that Glen would be taken care of."

She felt her expression go blank.

"We're really sorry," Fontana said.

"You did well, Linda. Not one in a million people would've survived that attack."

She nodded. "Where are we going?"

McBride relayed what they'd learned from Cantrell about Cornejo's business center in Santa Monica.

"I'd still like to get my bag right away."

"How about this?" said Fontana. "One of Cantrell's people can leave it at the base of the stairs below the bluff. We'll grab it before we head north."

"I must look terrible. That guy nailed me pretty good."

Nathan winked at her. "You look like you were engaged in a fight to the death. A fight you won." His phone went off. "Here we go . . ." He read the text. "Cantrell wants us on the move. Right away."

CHAPTER 14

To save time, all three of them went on LG's duffle-retrieval run. Since Harv's sedan was all shot up, Nathan suggested they use his second vehicle, a big four-door Lincoln MKZ that Angelica normally drove. Linda favored his 2010 Mustang, but it was a little small and Nathan thought it might draw more attention than they wanted. As usual, Harv did the driving.

Linda's tactical gear retrieved, they didn't talk much during their drive north to Santa Monica. Harv attempted some small talk, but it never got too far. The shock of the attack had worn off and Linda had withdrawn. Figuratively and literally, she'd been kicked in the stomach. It was best to give her some space.

Nathan used the downtime to read aloud the files Cantrell had sent. For years, until they retired, the twins had basically acted as hired muscle for the Caracas-based cartel Cornejo had been associated with. As Linda had said, the twins had committed every kind of crime during those years: Contract killing. Extortion. Racketeering. And worst of all, human trafficking in the slave trade—including children. He found it hard to disagree with LG's earlier assessment about just killing them. But like a good combat soldier, he'd follow Cantrell's orders. If she wanted them alive, they'd deliver them alive.

Per texted instructions from Cantrell, they made a brief stop at the Hawthorne Costco on Hindry Avenue in southwestern metro Los Angeles to pick up the encrypted radios they'd use for tonight's op. Cantrell had said the radios would be in an unlocked white sedan in the northeast corner of the Costco parking lot, facing Rosecrans. When he stepped out into the dark parking lot and grabbed the plastic grocery bag from the sedan, Nathan knew he was being watched, but resisted the urge to look around.

The bag contained four radios and an eight-by-ten aerial photograph. Written on the back of the photo was information about the radios. They were UHF, ultrahigh frequency, and they'd work well inside buildings. All they had to do was turn them on. Locked to a preset frequency, each radio came with a wireless, wraparound earpiece and boom-mike combo. The spare radio had the same capability. Nathan noticed there was no LCD or other type of screen that would produce light. The instruction sheet also indicated they could be set for auto-voice activation or manual, and they had battery lives of six hours.

The center of the aerial photo showed their target building, outlined by highlighter pen. Santa Monica Exotics occupied the northwest corner of a city block. An alley ran along the building's eastern side, intersecting another alley that ran behind the building to the south. A large street—Olympic Boulevard—fronted the dealership, while the smaller Stewart Street bordered the building to the west. Several hundred yards south of the dealership, Stewart Street crossed a local light-rail line.

"The surrounding buildings don't look like apartments or condos. The roofs and shapes are wrong for residential."

"It's probably a mix of commercial and light manufacturing," Harv said. "It's been a long time since I was on that stretch of Olympic, if ever."

"Me too. LG?"

She shook her head.

Nathan relayed the additional info written on the back of the photo. Harv, Linda, and he would be designated as Kilo unit, the military and aviation phonetic word for the letter K. Nathan would be Kilo One, Harv Kilo Two, and Linda Kilo Three.

They didn't know the CIA surveillance team's code designator yet but would get it when they made contact. Nathan suspected they'd be talking with one of the CIA's elite Special Activities Division teams, which meant that they'd be all business. No lighthearted banter would be exchanged or wanted, despite this being a fairly light task for such a team. Before Harv and he had retired from CIA duty, they'd done reconnaissance and surveillance many times—a mostly tedious and boring assignment.

They took a few more minutes to study the photo before heading back to the freeway.

Their drive fell into silence again until, after a few miles, Nathan said, "We're about ten minutes out. Let's take a few minutes and go over some hand signals." Everyone knew radios can fail, become damaged, or get dislodged, and there could be situations where whispering might not be possible. LG seemed okay reviewing the gestures and didn't seem the slightest bit indignant, which probably meant she needed the refresher course.

A mile and a half away, Harv checked the time. 4:20 a.m. "Traffic should be nonexistent," he said.

"We'll cruise past our target once, then turn on our radios and make contact with Cantrell's team. She knows we're approaching the dealership; she's tracking my phone. Harv, you look for cameras along the glass front. LG, you look down the alley to the south. I'll be looking for people sitting in cars or anything else that looks out of place."

"Looks out of place?" LG echoed. "Care to elaborate on that?"

Her tone made Nathan uneasy, so he said nothing.

"Nate doesn't know what will look out of place, but he'll know it when he sees it."

"Chances are, nothing will look out of place," she said. "We'll cruise past a well-lighted showroom packed with vehicles few people can afford—present company excluded."

"That includes you, LG," he said.

Harv stepped in. "Let's just wait and see what we see. The nav says it's the next corner. There's someone behind me about fifty yards back. I'm going to pull over to the curb and act like I'm on my phone. His headlights are gonna nail us. It might be best if you guys duck down. A car with one occupant at this hour is far less suspicious, especially to a cop."

Nathan complied, but it was a tight fit. He had to lean sideways toward Harv's lap. "If you grab my ears, I'll kill you slowly."

"You mean that's not normal behavior for you two?"

Nathan didn't respond, but found himself smiling at the crass comment. He watched the headlight intrusion grow and with it, his unease. Given all the tactical gear in the car, there'd be no explaining it. The interior of his sedan brightened to the bursting point, then faded.

"There's another car coming," Harv said, "but he's pretty far back. We're rolling."

The showroom looked exactly like LG had predicted. A few windows glowed on the second and third floors, but they weren't bright. Nathan saw an issue right away; they all did. Santa Monica Exotics had a glass façade along the sidewalk, but six-foot-high accordion-like security bars sat behind the glass. If things got heavy once they were inside, they'd be able to break the windows and exit out to either street, but they'd have to scramble over the bars first.

All of SME's classics were inside the building. Just as the aerial photo showed, intersecting alleys separated the dealership from its fellow businesses to the south and east. A sign tagged SME's eastern neighbor as Matthew's Heating and Air Conditioning Supply. Some kind of light industrial building sat opposite the south alley.

Nathan was no engineer, but figured the dealership's huge interior floor-to-ceiling truss just behind the security bars made up for the loss in shear strength from the glass façade. The place had the feel of a modern airport concourse. He admired the architecture, then withdrew the thought. This obscene display of wealth was the result of Cornejo's blood money.

Maybe I'll burn it down, he thought, but finding the sprinkler system's shutoff valve could take time, a luxury they likely wouldn't have. And there was a risk a fire could spread to the neighboring buildings. Maybe a few dozen whacks with lug wrenches were in order.

He hadn't seen any video cameras on the interior, but several exterior cameras were mounted above the glass front, including a camera overlooking the entrance to the alley. He felt confident there'd be a camera overlooking the other alley's entrance as well.

"What do you think, Harv? If we had to, could we grapple across from that building to the east?"

"Hard to say without getting a look. We may not have to. Cantrell's team may have already done the scouting. Let's hope they found a hole in the surveillance. Even if we can't be identified, we still have to avoid being seen on camera."

LG spoke up. "Can we all agree that if anyone sees three people wearing black clothing, ski masks, and goggles stalking their building, they won't ignore it?"

"You have a gift for understatement," Nathan said. "When was the last time you shimmied across a rope line?"

"Well, let me think . . . I don't have one set up in my backyard."

Her sarcasm had returned in force.

"I'm sure it will come back to you."

"Nate, she's got a low-grade concussion. Hanging upside down from a rope isn't such a good idea."

"I can handle it."

"Harv's right; besides, we don't need to make this decision right now."

"I said I can handle it," she said more forcefully.

"And I said we don't have to decide this right now."

"Who put you in charge? Last I looked, I outranked you."

"Same old LG."

"What's that supposed to mean?"

"It means you haven't changed."

"And you have?"

"For the worse, I'm afraid."

"Ah, guys, if I can jump in," Harv said. "I really think we should stay focused."

"If you don't mind, I'd like to finish our argument first," she said.

Nathan took a deep breath. There'd been a time in his life when he would've lashed out, but calmness won the moment. LG's husband had been murdered and that earned her some latitude. *Some,* but within limits. He fully expected Harv to intervene and that's exactly what happened.

"Linda, with all due respect, you can't command this mission. You're too close to it. If we were still active, you'd be sidelined. I'm not saying you can't handle command calls, but it's more complex than that. Split-second decisions may have to be made and those decisions have to be completely objective."

She didn't say anything.

"We haven't worked with you in many years and we're about to go on a combat mission full of unknown variables. Cantrell got a positive nod from DNI Benson to include you because of our involvement. She trusts us and Benson trusts her. You know how the intelligence community works. It's no small thing she did. She's on the hook if we screw this up. We're not trying to pick on you, but you need to understand that none of us would be here if it weren't for Nathan."

"Sorry, McBride. I guess I'm a little on edge."

"Forget it. We're in this together."

Harv turned onto a side street and pulled to the curb. "Let's change clothes and do a final equipment check before we power our radios."

Nathan always felt butterflies just prior to a mission. He'd long ago learned not to fight the feeling. It reminded him that the slightest mistake could prove fatal.

Because they didn't want to look like special forces on the drive up, they'd worn civilian attire. Each of them now changed into their black tactical clothing, donned their ballistic vests, waist packs, and night-vision visors. Once they were safely inside the building, they'd put on their ski masks and tinted goggles. Each of their waist packs held a thermal imager, a suppressed pistol with a grip-activated laser sight, extra ammo, duct tape, and various other items they might need.

Nathan broke the silence. "Are you good, LG?"

"I was just venting."

"Hey, it's allowed."

"To answer your question, I haven't flipped my switch yet, but I will when the time comes."

"Fair enough." Nathan knew exactly what she meant because he and Harv used the same mental technique. Even though LG said she was okay, Nathan needed confirmation. "How's your concussion?"

"I'm feeling some mild symptoms, mostly in the form of a headache. My vision's good and I'm not feeling any unsteadiness from the Special K. If I felt the slightest bit impaired, I'd tell you guys."

If she'd said anything less, Nathan would've left her in the car. There was no way she could've sustained the kind of head trauma she had and have zero symptoms.

"Did I pass your test?"

"Knowing it was a test prejudices the result, but, yeah, you passed."

"And if I hadn't?"

"You'd sit this out."

"That would be . . . unsatisfying."

"Better to be unsatisfied than dead."

"Amen to that," Harv said.

"Well, now that we have the small talk out of the way, can we get in there and kick some asses?"

Nathan smiled and looked at Harv. "I think that could be arranged. Let's hope Cantrell's team found a hole in the video surveillance. We'll know within the next thirty seconds when we make contact." The tingling in his stomach intensified. "You feeling it, LG?"

"Oh, yeah. Despite my earlier indiscretion, it's good to be working with you guys again."

"Likewise."

"Rules of engagement?" she asked.

"Deadly force only if warranted, but no one hesitates. We shoot first and ask questions later. No friendlies are expected inside. If Tomas and Ursula are in there, we take them alive, but not at all costs. One more thing. No summary executions."

"That's directed at me," she said.

"Yes."

"You're in command."

"I need more than that, LG."

"No summary executions," she said.

"Thank you. And no names. We use our Kilo designators." When they turned on their radios, Nathan imagined a computer screen coming to life with three reds dots plotted on a map.

"This is Kilo One, with Kilos Two and Three. Radio check. How do you copy?"

"Five by five, Kilo One."

Nathan was a little surprised by the digitally altered voice coming through his earpiece. It seemed Cantrell's SAD team was taking no chances. Nothing more would be said until Nathan recited the phrase Cantrell had given him.

"It's an intrepid night," he said.

"Kilo One authenticated. This is Delta Lead. Welcome to the neighborhood."

"Thank you, Delta Lead. Kilo Two, Kilo Three, radio checks, please."

The surveillance team confirmed Harv and LG were loud and clear. Nathan also heard them perfectly. Both LG and Harv issued a thumbs-up.

Delta Lead continued, *"All assets are in place and online. We have you east of the target building. Turn right at the next corner, proceed two blocks south, and turn right again. Proceed east on Olympic, roll past the target building, and enter the parking lot for Matthew's Heating and Air Conditioning. Park at the southeast corner of the building. We'll lose sight of you once you turn into the driveway. Initiate contact once you're parked and we'll update you on all activity we've monitored to date."*

Nathan copied the transmission. It only took thirty seconds for Harv to park and Nathan to make the radio call.

The surveillance team said that activity had been light since Santa Monica Exotics closed for business at 1800. Nathan was informed the surveillance team hadn't entered the building, but a walking reconnaissance along the glass façade had been conducted. They gave Nathan the basic layout of the showroom floor, including the location of an elevator on the east wall. The sales offices were on the south wall.

No vehicles had entered either alley and aside from some occasional pedestrian traffic along the sidewalk, nothing significant had happened. Then, starting at 2200 and lasting until 2230, five men carrying briefcases had entered SME through the fire exit door in the east alley. Once inside the showroom floor, they turned left and headed toward the elevator. Half an hour after that, a pizza delivery occurred at the same fire exit door. Delta Lead gave them a secure website link to look at the video clips of the five men entering the building. Nathan used his iPad and held it so LG and Harv could see it. Each clip took about ten seconds and showed each man press a sequence of numbers into a keypunch above the door handle and go inside.

Tomas Bustamonte wasn't one of the men entering the building.

"They don't look like muscle," Harv said. "They look like businessmen."

"We concur," the metallic voice said.

"I also didn't see a security keypad inside the corridor."

"Again, we concur. For reference purposes, we'll designate the alleys as east alley and south alley respectively. Olympic Boulevard borders SME to the north and Stewart Street borders SME to the west. We've studied the video extensively and can't determine if any of the men who entered the building wore firearms with 100 percent certainty. We think it's a possibility with the smaller, heavyset man, third to enter the building. There's a slight bulge on the right under his coat that's consistent with a hip holster. Based on the way the pizza boxes were carefully unpacked from their thermal sleeves and the manner in which the boxes were handed off, we believe it was a legitimate pizza delivery. The man accepting the pizzas wasn't one of the men who entered with briefcases. We weren't able to track the first briefcase-carrying man, but we sent an asset to street level and successfully tracked the others. They all turned left and walked along the east wall toward the elevator in the southeast corner. Three of the last four used the elevator. One of them used a keypunch and opened a door next to the elevator and went through. We didn't see the sequence he entered. We believe it's a stairwell, but we don't have confirmation. If the door does access a stairwell, then it's reasonable to assume the elevator also requires a keycard or combination to access the upper floors."

"I agree," Nathan said. "It's probably the same sequence as the fire exit door. Do you have ears inside the building?"

There was a slight pause. *"Negative."*

The delay in Delta Lead's response spoke volumes. Cantrell had assembled this team on the spur of the moment and they'd probably been diverted from their current assignment to do this mundane job. It was time for a warm thank-you, which Nathan gave them.

"Appreciated, Kilo One. Proceed on foot westbound into the south alley. Follow the wall of Matthew's over to a Dumpster and use it to access the fire exit stairs. Do not deploy the spring-loaded extension—bypass it. Ascend to rooftop, stay low, and traverse to the midpoint of its west-facing parapet.

We'll be standing by until you reach that location. Police and first-responder frequencies are being monitored. We'll come up on the net should the need arise. Confirm instructions."

"Confirmed." Nathan didn't need to ask why they were being routed that way. It avoided the security cameras eying both mouths of the alleys.

He put a forefinger to his lips, reminding Harv and LG that their radios were in voice-activation mode. If any of them spoke, Cantrell's SAD team would pick it up.

He noticed the wall-mounted security light on the corner of Matthew's was broken, as was the public streetlight a few yards away. *So much for no boots on the ground,* Nathan thought. Unsurprisingly, no broken glass littered the ground.

Nathan took a quick glance down the south alley toward SME. All quiet. Trash was scarce, but some painted-over graffiti marred the walls. They saw the Dumpster right away. Nathan knew it had recently been moved. Twenty feet away, he saw the stain on the asphalt outlining where it used to be. It now sat directly underneath the fire exit stairs. LG went first and Nathan studied her movements. Like a gymnast, she hoisted herself onto the platform and grunted in pain. Her ribs had to hurt like hell. The metal framework offered a barely audible creak as she climbed. Harv went next.

When he reached the roof, Harv and LG were crouched, waiting. Although there weren't any buildings in the immediate area taller than this one, he felt naked up here.

"We have you, Kilo team. Locate the coiled rope at the west parapet and lower yourselves down directly below that spot. Avoid dislodging the wad of gum to your left as you descend."

"Camera?" Nathan asked.

"Affirmative. Once in the east alley, cross over to the fire exit door of SME. Enter push-button code of one-three-six-four-seven-nine. We'll come up on the net if anything changes out here. Maintain open frequency and

return verbal copies if possible, single clicks if not. We won't respond to your traffic unless you specify 'Delta Lead.' Good hunting, Kilo One."

Nathan thanked them again.

Harv pointed to the coiled rope and grappling hook. It seemed the surveillance team had tossed it up here sometime earlier this evening, presumably when they planted the gum camera on the wall.

Crouching, they hustled over to the west parapet where Harv inspected the rope's connection to the hook. Since they wouldn't need rappelling gear for such a short distance, the rope was knotted every eighteen inches or so.

Less than a minute later, all three of them stood on the ground in the east alley.

He mouthed the words *You okay?* to LG and got a nod.

Nathan pulled a thin ski mask over his face and put on his goggles. Harv and LG followed suit.

Nathan turned, issued a thumbs-up to the camera, and received a click from Delta Lead.

He pulled his suppressed Sig, reached for the keypunch, and entered the code.

CHAPTER 15

The lock clicked and Nathan cracked the door enough to peer inside.

A dark, empty hall greeted him. Twenty feet distant, a bright line of light emanated from under a closed door—Nathan knew it came from the showroom.

He scanned the corridor for cameras and saw none. Not taking his eyes from the closed door ahead, he gave Harv a hand signal to check six high.

He sensed Harv lean into the corridor to take a look. "No camera," Harv whispered.

Nathan stepped to the side, allowing Harv and LG to enter.

"Go ahead and close the door," he said in a low voice. "We're going to hold position for two minutes. If we tripped an alarm, we might be bugging out in a big hurry. Kilo team, observe radio silence. Delta Lead exempted. We're in listening mode."

Time slowed to a crawl as their eyes adjusted to the dark. They heard nothing, then the sound of wastewater moving through a pipe.

The gurgling behind the wall reached a peak, then went silent. Everyone knew what had just happened.

He looked at his watch and let the final fifteen seconds wind down. The lack of activity suggested no one knew they were here. The flushing toilet seemed to confirm it. Who would use a bathroom if an alarm had been triggered?

"Besides the door leading to the showroom, we've got two doors to check on the left. Kilo Three, you're on my six. Lineup formation." Normally he'd ask Harv to cover him, but he wanted LG involved.

LG stepped forward, put a hand on Nathan's back, and gave him a nudge—the signal she was ready to go. Moving down the corridor like a single unit, they stopped at the first door. Nathan put everyone on hold again and listened for sound.

Nothing.

The lack of visible hinges indicated the door would swing away from him. He turned the knob and slowly pushed. A pitch-black room loomed. The smell of cleaning chemicals wafted. Not wanting to deploy his NV scope yet, he grabbed a small penlight from his waist pack and confirmed this was a janitor's closet, a big one. Everything needed to clean the building and detail the cars was neatly arranged in here.

The next door was a bathroom. Nathan had hoped it would be a stairwell. No such luck. That meant they had to enter the showroom, and it looked like a supernova loomed behind the door. "Kilo Two, check for seams along the walls. Let's make sure there aren't any hidden doors."

Harv reported finding no seams.

"Kilo Two, you're on the exit door. I'm going to take a look in the showroom. Kilo Three, you're still with me."

The door was unlocked and Nathan cracked it less than an inch. Squinting, he surveyed the room. A large open space full of classic cars loomed. It looked to be about seventy-five feet deep and a hundred and fifty feet long. Identical to the floor-to-ceiling truss along the glass front, a second truss bisected the showroom along its short axis, but stopped short of the exterior walls to allow the cars to move across the room. The trusses were painted bright red. Again, he marveled at the engineering but hated what this place represented.

Most of the cars were European from the mid- to late-twentieth century—lots of color and chrome. They were arranged in three rows along the long axis of the showroom. Just as Delta Lead had indicated, sales offices lined the south wall. He couldn't see the elevator, but he *did* see two cameras overlooking the center of the showroom. They hung above the glass façade on the opposite side of the room. The closest row of vehicles sat ten feet away. He gave a brief description of what he saw to Harv and LG.

An idea came to him.

"Kilo team, if we stay low, I think we can avoid the cameras on the far side of the room, but I need to see what's on the wall above this door. If there are motion sensors, they were probably turned off for the guys with the briefcases. They might've been reactivated. The cameras are likely in continuous operation, shooting stills every few seconds until activated into video mode."

Harv said, "Look for a security keypad next to the door."

"I will. Delta Lead, do you still have eyes on the showroom floor?"

"Affirm. We'll take a look for a keypad. Stand by, we're repositioning our street asset to a different vantage point."

Nathan opened the door ultra-slowly until he could fit his hand through. He pulled a mirror from his waist pack and used it to scan the wall above his head and on either side of the door. As far as he could see, there were no cameras, motion detectors, or a keypad. It made sense, especially if illegal activity were taking place. Cameras and criminals didn't mix well.

"I'm taking a better look." He opened the door wider and peered in the direction the men with the briefcases had gone. He knew the elevator was down there, but he couldn't see it. The walls were adorned with huge photographs of classic cars, just like the models in the showroom. Each car had a generous amount of space surrounding it to allow customers ample room to circle their potential wares.

Nathan pulled back into the exit corridor. "What are the odds that someone's monitoring live feeds on a bank of TVs? Either in this building or somewhere else?"

"I'd say slim to none," Harv offered. "This isn't a Vegas casino. If this is a criminal enterprise, as our friend suspects, those men with briefcases won't want to be recorded. I seriously doubt they're here to conduct legitimate business, unless they're doing it in a different time zone."

"Kilo team, our street asset is back online. We located two keypunches. One is next to the elevator, the other's next to the door near the elevator, presumably to unlock access to a stairwell. Other than those, we aren't detecting any other security keypads."

"Copy, Delta Lead. I'm going to walk over to the elevators and see what happens."

"We'll be monitoring your progress. We have eyes on the elevator's lights. It's currently on the third floor; if it moves we'll let you know."

Nathan turned toward Harv and Linda. "I might be coming back in a big hurry so be ready to engage." He sensed LG liked that idea. "If this place erupts with blaring alarms, we'll have to assume the Santa Monica Police Department will be dispatched. No doubt, the security company relays triggered alarms to the police. Here goes . . ."

Feeling like a party crasher, he stepped into the showroom floor, took a few steps to his left, and stopped. If motion sensors were present and active, they should've picked him up and triggered the alarm system. It didn't make sense for a place like this to employ silent alarms.

So far, so good. Willing himself to be invisible, he began a normal walk toward the southeast corner. As a Marine scout sniper and CIA special-operations-group officer, Nathan had survived by being stealthy. This felt like anti-stealth.

Since no additional lights came on, or any security sirens blared, he began to believe the system was in standby mode. Again, it made sense. Nathan doubted those briefcases held—

"Kilo One, you've got company. The elevator's on the way down."

The icy calmness of the metallic voice sent a shiver across Nathan's chest.

Decision time. Fight or flee?

"Kilos Two and Three, hold position and stand by."

He diverted to his right and ducked behind a classic Bentley, his mind working overtime. How many people did an average elevator hold? Ten? Fifteen? In a building this size, he doubted there would be that many. It probably held five to seven. Would they burst out with guns drawn? And why use the elevator? Why not the stairs? The elevator gave their approach away. Something felt wrong. Could the elevator simply be returning to the ground floor after a pre-programmed delay? If so, its doors wouldn't open. The elevator would simply go into standby mode.

The truth was almost upon him.

He watched the lighted numbers change from three to two. He didn't think it would stop there and it didn't.

Number two went dark and number one came to life.

He'd have to hold fire until he was certain Tomas or Ursula weren't present, but if multiple gun-toting thugs spilled into the showroom, he'd start shooting.

"Kilo team, five seconds."

Despite the tension, a smile touched his lips. Screw Cornejo and his billions.

This place belonged to a first-class turd. Nathan didn't care about the Venezuelan election, the price of crude oil, or entitlement spending.

All he cared about was right here and right now.

He left his laser dark and increased pressure on the trigger.

The elevator issued a pleasant chime and its single door slid open.

A man exited and turned right. Nathan recognized him as the third man the surveillance team had recorded entering the fire exit door: Bravo Three. He was empty-handed.

It was clear this guy had no clue Nathan was in the room. The man walked straight toward the exit corridor where LG and Harv were holed up. Was he leaving?

Decision time again.

For several tactical reasons, Nathan chose to let Harv and LG deal with this.

"Bravo Three's heading for your location. Close the door quietly and back up a few feet. He's empty-handed. No visible weapons. Copy?"

"Affirm," came Harv's whisper in his earpiece. *"We're ready."*

"We need intel."

"Understood."

"Delta Lead, maintain eyes on elevator. I'll be returning to the exit corridor."

"Copy."

"Kilo Two, five seconds."

Dressed in a white dress shirt, nice slacks, and wing tips, it looked like this guy could buy any car in this room. Lots of gold adorned his fingers and neck. Latino and slightly overweight, he appeared to be in his mid-fifties. He didn't look formidable, but looks could be deceiving. Nathan saw an expensive watch and a wedding ring. *Does your wife know where you are?*

The man looked at the cars as he walked. Nathan couldn't blame him, it was hard not to.

Bravo Three reached for the knob and, without hesitating, stepped into the corridor.

Nathan heard an inhalation, a rustle of clothes, then a grunt of pain.

Harv's low voice came next. *"We aren't going to hurt you if you cooperate. Please nod your head if you understand what I just said."* They'd once made a mistake in a situation nearly identical to this one. They'd captured a man who hadn't spoken a word of English. Assumption tended to be the mother of all screw-ups.

Nathan walked at a medium pace toward the door as Harv wasted no time questioning their captive.

"*Were you planning to leave or come back?*"

"*Who are you?*" the man asked. "*Do you know who owns this place?*"

Halfway to the exit door, Nathan heard a louder grunt.

"*We're asking the questions. You have three seconds before I dislocate your shoulder. Answering my questions will be much more difficult after that.*"

"*My car! I'm just going out to my car.*"

Nathan entered the exit corridor and left the door partially open.

Upon seeing Nathan's sheer size and bulk, the man's mouth dropped slightly, but he recovered.

"Why were you going out to your car?" Harv asked.

"Cubans, I forgot the Cubans."

"Cigars."

"Good ones. You can have 'em."

"So if we escorted you out there, we'd find cigars?"

"Yeah, man, I swear."

"What was in your briefcase?"

The man closed his mouth.

"We saw you carry it in here. What was in it?" Harv asked again.

Again, the man didn't answer.

"Torque his shoulder out of the socket," Nathan said. "Not too rough, we don't want him passing out."

Keeping the guy's arm pinned behind his back, Harv began applying upward pressure.

The man's face contorted. "Wait! It's cash. We all bring cash for the game."

"What game?"

"Texas hold 'em."

"Is Tomas Bustamonte up there?"

"You mean Mr. B? I didn't know his first name. Everyone just calls him Mr. B. He got a call and had to leave the table."

"How long ago did he get the call?"

"I don't know, maybe a minute ago. He asked me to get the Cubans but I had to take a leak first."

"You said you forgot them."

"I did, I mean, he wanted to get them after the hand—"

Nathan's earpiece came to life. "Okay, okay. Now, shut up. Repeat, Delta Lead."

"We've got activity. Two SUVs just turned into the east alley from Olympic and the elevator's on the move, it's going up."

"What are the SUVs doing? Are they stopping?"

"Affirmative . . . Six armed men just got out and they're heading for the door. You're blown."

"You two, take cover behind the cars. Close the door behind you."

"Nate—"

"Go!" Nathan said. He belted the gambler's jaw, instantly dropping the guy. Two seconds later, he heard the keypunch being stabbed as Harv and LG disappeared into the showroom. Leaving the unconscious man in the hall, he ducked into the pitch-black bathroom as the door to the alley swung open.

CHAPTER 16

Had he been fast enough? He wasn't sure. He wanted to close and lock the door, but it was too late. He lowered his safety goggles to his neck, pivoted his NV scope down in front of his eye, and powered it.

"Delta Lead, report," he whispered.

"The first gunman is looking through the door. He just gestured for two of the men to circle the building in opposite directions. They're in motion. The first of two gunmen is now entering the corridor; the other two are waiting in the alley. They're carrying suppressed Mac-10s with fifty-round mags or better."

"Do they have night vision?"

"Negative."

"Going silent."

His radio clicked.

Harv's going to kill me for doing this, he thought. *If I live through it . . .*

He listened for sound but heard nothing except Harv and Linda working out their positioning in the showroom.

Nathan's mind kicked into high gear. He possessed an uncanny ability to size up tactical situations. Within two seconds, he'd weighed the positives and negatives.

Negatives: These newcomers weren't loud and sloppy. They possessed formidable firepower. He was outnumbered four to one. And he was effectively trapped inside a small room with no exit.

Positives: He had night vision. They didn't know he was in this room—and they'd never expect anyone to be stupid enough to trap himself in a small room with no exit. They'd also be momentarily distracted by the unconscious man in the hall, and they'd be confined in a tight, narrow space.

No problem. He owned this.

He heard slow, steady footfalls, then a door being opened. His night-vision scope automatically dimmed at the sudden surge of light as the gunman flipped the switch inside the janitor's closet. A second later, the light winked out.

His door would be next.

He needed an update from Delta Lead but didn't want to risk being overheard, even whispering. *Come on, Harv. Now would be a good time.*

Right on cue, Harv's voice came through his ear speaker. *"Delta Lead, report."*

Nathan cranked the radio's volume to its lowest setting.

"Two have entered the corridor, two have circled the building in opposite directions, and the other two are watching the door from the cover of their SUVs."

Nathan knew he was facing two immediate threats rather than four. He liked those odds a lot better, and it changed how he'd deal with it. Waiting like a trapdoor spider, he watched the bathroom door for movement.

His wait wasn't long.

In slow motion, it began easing toward his face.

***

Harvey didn't like leaving Nathan behind but didn't question his orders.

Dividing their forces held some risk, but at times like this, his trust in Nate's tactical decisions was absolute. Inside the showroom, he told LG to go right while he went left, toward the elevator.

Playing a hunch, he had LG relocate to a position directly in front of the door so she could fire down the length of the corridor. He knew Nate had copied his transmission. "Kilo One, confirm you're in the bathroom."

Harvey heard Nate's click.

He'd listened to the radio traffic between Delta Lead and Nate and knew he needed to become Nate's voice. "Delta Lead, report."

The answer confirmed what he suspected. Two of the gunmen remained outside in the alley.

"The elevator's going up."

"Copy, Delta Lead. Kilo Three, stay here and cover the exit corridor. I'm relocating to a position closer to the elevator."

The third-floor light was now illuminated. It wouldn't be long before the elevator started back down.

Delta Lead hadn't reported seeing anyone enter the building prior to the briefcase crew, but Harvey knew there was at least one additional man in the building—the guy who'd accepted the pizzas. Regardless, this situation smelled like a trap. It was entirely possible someone in Bustamonte's employ had seen the three of them move across the neighboring building's roof and descend into the alley. Cantrell didn't have the resources to put eyes on the entire neighborhood, especially on such short notice.

None of that mattered right now. His job was to cover Nate's blind side, basically everything inside this showroom.

He hurried toward the elevator, weaving his way through the maze of automobiles. He'd made it about halfway when Delta Lead gave them another update.

One of the gunmen who'd separated from the group would soon be in a position where he could see inside the showroom from Olympic. The other gunman who'd circled the building in the opposite direction had a substantially longer distance to cover before he'd reach the main entrance on the west side.

He whispered to LG, "We're in a shoot-to-kill situation unless it's one of the twins. No wounding shots. Copy?"

"Loud and clear."

"Do you have eyes on the Olympic gunman yet?"

"Negative."

"From this point on, stay low and remain focused on the exit corridor."

"I'm on it."

"Delta Lead, you're our eyes on the Olympic gunman."

"We've got him. Ten seconds."

Harvey watched the lights above the elevator change from three to two.

He pictured Nate alone in that pitch-black corridor, facing multiple gunmen armed with some of the most proven machine pistols ever made. Harv knew the Mac-10 well; he had one in his private collection.

Number two went dark.

Number one illuminated.

With a telling chime, the elevator announced its arrival.

***

Nathan watched the door move toward him. There was something menacing about a slowly moving door with an enemy combatant behind it.

He flipped his mental switch, severing all doubt.

Bullets were going to fly.

People were going to die.

He placed his boot where it would block the door from opening more than eight inches.

The door struck his foot.

As predicted, the gunman retracted the door and tried again, this time with more force. Again, it struck his foot.

Nathan's night-vision scope gave him a good view of the intruder's reflection in the mirror.

Exactly like LG's attackers, the man wore digital camo and body armor, but armed with a menacing Mac-10 instead of a TASER.

Radio traffic between Delta Lead and Harv buzzed in his ear.

"The elevator's on the move."

"Copy, Delta Lead," Harv said. *"Kilo Three, stay here and cover the exit corridor. I'm relocating to a position closer to the elevator."*

In his mind, he saw Harv weaving between the cars, heading for the elevator.

Delta Lead's voice cut in. *"Kilo Three. That gunman's five seconds from reaching the glass along Olympic."*

Nathan took slow, shallow breaths, calming his mind.

It was all about timing. *Perfect timing,* he silently added.

The door retracted again. Knowing the obstruction caused some puzzlement, he moved his foot back six inches.

When the door struck his foot a third time, he started a mental countdown.

The gunman's expression changed to irritation and Nathan knew what was coming.

Like a snake moving down a gopher hole, a hand extended through the opening.

Three.

The hand swept up and down on the wall—

Two.

143

And stopped at the switch.

One.

Putting his full weight behind the move, he shouldered the door shut and felt bone snap.

A howl of pain erupted, but Nathan kept the man's arm pinned. "Kilo Three, shoot through the door. Now!"

Nathan yanked the door open, kicked his assailant into the corridor, and thrust himself backward.

The showroom door erupted in a horizontal hail of splinters.

Several of LG's rounds pounded the gunman's vest before he fell against the wall. The man grunted and tried to bring his Mac-10 to bear on the bathroom, but one of LG's rounds struck the outside of his shoulder, missing the ballistic vest.

Fountains of light now gushed through the perforated showroom door and Nathan could see the man still trying to bring his weapon up.

Staying within the safety of the bathroom, he painted the gunman's face with his laser and fired.

A green hole replaced the green dot.

"Kilo Three, cease fire, cease fire!"

Any of LG's bullets that hadn't struck the first gunman had forced the second gunman to duck for cover.

When the barrage ended, he pivoted into the corridor in a crouch, lined up on the remaining man, who sat on the floor applying pressure to a leg wound. With his free hand, the man tried to bring his weapon up. Nathan drilled him in the forehead.

It wasn't pretty.

The guy began convulsing, then fell over and continued to jerk around like a tortured earthworm. Not all head shots resulted in a quick death. He'd seen this before.

Nathan ended it with a bullet under the man's chin.

Three rounds fired, thirteen left in the magazine.

He couldn't afford to feel badly right now. *Them or us,* he reminded himself.

After advancing to the door, which was propped open with a spare Mac-10 magazine, he flattened himself against the wall. Whoever remained out there had to know what was going on. Several of LG's rounds had struck the exit door but hadn't passed through.

Delta Lead said, *"The two gunmen in the alley are moving toward the door."*

Before Nathan could click his radio, Harv said, *"Kilo Three, incoming!"*

***

Harvey heard Nate's order for LG to shoot through the showroom door and knew it would draw the attention of the gunman along Olympic Boulevard. It put LG at risk, but she'd deliver the suppression fire with no questions asked. Thankfully, Nate didn't need a prolonged salvo. He called for an immediate cease-fire and LG's pistol went silent.

Sure enough, as soon as she opened fire, the gunman on Olympic did the same thing.

"Kilo Three, incoming!"

The guy discharged his suppressed weapon through the glass, sweeping it back and forth like a firefighter.

The result was chaotic.

Like a crystalline waterfall, a downpour of glass fell into the showroom.

Windshields shattered, sheet metal tore, and tires flattened.

Some of the slugs skipped off the granite floor and slammed into the offices on the far side of the room.

Harvey slid sideways to get behind the rear tire of a Jaguar. "Kilo Three, suppression fire on Olympic!"

He listened to LG's shots change tone as she fired toward the shooter. The barrage from the street ended. Either she'd scored a hit or the gunman was changing magazines.

He had his answer.

Another salvo tore through the room and the mayhem began anew.

The sound was surreal.

The suppressed Mac-10 couldn't be heard over the banging, clanging, and breaking glass, but it looked like invisible demons were unleashing Hell's wrath upon the vehicles.

He broke the side window of an Aston Martin and lined up on the elevator. It took all the control he had to keep his attention focused away from the shooter on Olympic, but he couldn't allow anyone to flank them along the rear wall of the showroom.

The elevator doors opened.

Nothing happened.

No one came out.

Someone could be hiding in there, so he maintained his position.

A bullet whizzed past his feet to the right. *Shit!*

"Kilo Three, status?" he whispered.

"He keeps ducking behind the corner. I can't get a clear shot."

"Keep firing."

"Kilo team, the other gunman just turned onto Stewart Street. He'll be in a position to shoot into the showroom near the main entrance in five seconds."

Harvey copied the transmission.

The second barrage from LG's gunman went silent.

Delta Lead said, *"Good shooting, Kilo Three. You winged him. He's limping back to the east alley."*

The stairwell door next to the elevator burst open and three men carrying pistols fanned out in different directions. Unless they'd changed clothes, these weren't the men who'd entered the building with briefcases. These guys were dressed exactly like the mercenaries who'd attacked LG a few hours ago.

Harvey reported the new threat to everyone and lined up on the first gunman. He scored a head shot, but the other two hit the deck and disappeared below the cars. He moved to his right a few feet.

Good thing he did.

Both gunmen opened fire.

Several slugs careened off the floor where he'd just stood.

"Kilo team, we recommend you shoot the overheads and switch to night vision."

He wasted no time taking out the overhead spots. Harvey concentrated on his half of the showroom while LG broke the others. Within six seconds, they'd engulfed themselves in darkness.

Advantage good guys.

"Switching to NV," Harvey whispered. "I'm moving toward the rear wall. Kilo Three, maintain eyes on the exit corridor. Be prepared to give Kilo One more cover fire. Delta Lead, what're the gunmen in the east alley doing?"

***

Nathan didn't like the delay in action and needed an update.

Harv came through again. After giving instructions to LG, Harv asked about the gunmen in the alley.

"They're standing on either side of the door."

Nathan didn't know if their Mac-10s were 9mm or 45ACP, but he was fairly certain the bullets wouldn't penetrate this steel-clad door. If they did, they wouldn't have much energy left. At least he hoped not.

"Kilo One, the man Kilo Three wounded just limped into the east alley. One of your gunmen is running over to him. Now would be a good time to slam open the door and catch the remaining gunman on the right side."

Without answering Delta Lead's transmission, he stepped back and kicked the door with all his strength.

The door accelerated around its radius and hammered the gunman. Needing eyes on the two remaining threats, Nathan peered around the jamb toward Olympic.

Caught in the open, the gunman running toward his wounded comrade stopped, focused on the exit door, then made the decision to abandon his humanitarian mission. He ran past his wounded comrade toward the mouth of the alley at Olympic.

So much for loyalty, thought Nathan.

The guy was savvy enough to weave back and forth, creating a difficult target.

Nathan used the door's frame to steady his aim. Not wanting to risk a head shot, he painted his laser on the gunman's back, adjusted it slightly lower, and fired three shots just below the guy's ballistic vest.

Ten rounds left.

The man shuddered from being struck at least once, but managed to stay on his feet. Limping as fast as he could, the gunman continued his retreat toward Olympic.

Nathan checked the gunman who'd taken the impact from the door and saw the guy on his hands and knees—his Mac-10 a few feet away. Blood flowing from his nose, he looked up with a resigned expression. Even though this man wouldn't have shown Nathan the same mercy, he made a split-second decision to spare him from the underworld, though he might need a cane for the rest of life. Nathan shot both of the guy's shins, stepped into the alley, and kicked his weapon under the parked SUVs.

Although hobbled, the man LG had wounded brought his Mac-10 to bear. Nathan darted back into the exit corridor just as the guy fired. The subsonic bullets missed him, but the man he'd spared wasn't as fortunate. Multiple slugs pounded him. It wasn't pretty and he averted his eyes.

When the salvo ended, Nathan peered around the corner and saw the shooter frantically attempting to change magazines. He again used the jamb to steady his aim and drilled the gunman's face. Nathan lined up again on the guy limping toward Olympic. He couldn't allow him to reach the mouth of the alley and disappear.

Nathan aimed at the man's butt and fired three quick, but controlled rounds.

The projectiles found their mark.

The gunman tumbled.

With only four rounds left in the magazine, he took a few seconds to reload. His shot count jumped back up to sixteen rounds. One in the pipe, fifteen in the mag.

Nathan looked at the man he'd hammered with the door. Moaning in agony, the guy was a bloody mess. Half of his face was shredded and his neck spurted from a torn artery. He'd be dead soon. In an act of mercy, Nathan shot him through the temple.

"Kilo One, incoming!"

He took a backward step into the exit corridor as another salvo of bullets shrieked and howled down the alley.

The faceless man shuddered as more slugs plowed into him. Farther down the alley to the south, the Mercedes shuttle and Dumpsters took impacts. Metal thumped and glass shattered.

When the barrage ended, Nathan leaned out of the door and began a rapid-fire salvo of his own, firing several rounds per second at the remaining gunman. He purposely aimed low, skipping the bullets off the concrete. Some of the slugs might strike the guy's vest, or miss altogether, but he needed to keep the last gunman from reloading.

In an aggressive move, he left the safety of the exit corridor and charged down the alley, firing as he ran.

At this distance, he didn't try for a head shot, but concentrated his bullets center-mass, all at the same spot. He didn't see the impacts, but he could hear them thumping the guy's vest. Although they wouldn't penetrate the body armor, their kinetic energy was delivering a beating.

"Kilo One, a car's approaching from the east in a big hurry. ETA twenty seconds. It's not a cop. Recommend you drag that gunman deeper into the alley."

Nathan copied the transmission and kept charging.

As he closed the distance, he adjusted his aim to the man's head and ended the dispute.

Eight rounds left in the current magazine.

The score in the alley? Three to zip, good guys.

He kept telling himself he wasn't taking lives indiscriminately. This was a live-or-die fight. He didn't feel good about killing, but didn't feel terrible either. His situation reflected what it often did: the real world.

The bleed headlight grew brighter and he sprinted the remaining distance. "Delta Lead?"

"Ten seconds."

He hooked his fingers under the dead man's vest at the shoulder and hauled the body deeper into the alley. Willing himself to be invisible, he flattened himself against the wall of Matthew's Heating and Air Conditioning.

He heard the vehicle's tire sounds getting louder and louder as the bluish-white light reached a peak. To his relief, the vehicle sped past the mouth of the alley at twice the speed limit.

"Stand by, Kilo One. That driver just hit the brakes."

CHAPTER 17

Harvey heard Nate's query to Delta Lead, *"What's that vehicle doing?"*

"It's turning right at the next block. We'll monitor and let you know if it circles back."

Delta Lead suggested Nate drag all the dead gunmen into the exit corridor and Nate copied the request.

Harvey's NV was a little too bright, so he adjusted it down a bit. Being able to see in the dark against an opponent not equally equipped made for a huge advantage.

Staying low, he eased along the length of the Jaguar, then hustled across a gap between the next row of cars and kept moving toward the showroom's east wall.

He peered around the trunk of a car he didn't recognize and saw a gunman crouched near the rear bumper of a Rolls-Royce thirty feet away.

An image of shooting fish in a barrel flashed through his mind, but he shelved it.

He painted the gunman's ear with the laser and sent a bullet.

His brain scrambled, the man slumped to the granite floor and lay still.

The other gunman was somewhere near the offices toward the main entrance. Again staying low, he used the cover of the cars to work his way toward the elevator.

"Kilo Three, maintain position to support Kilo One."

"I'm secure out here," Nate said.

"Kilo Three, move toward the interior truss and try to get eyes on the gunman outside the main entrance. Delta Lead, is he still out there?"

"Affirmative. Target is looking through the glass near the corner of the building just shy of the main entrance. He doesn't appear to be in radio contact with any of the other gunmen."

"I can't see the gunman near the main entrance," LG said. *"I'm adjusting my position for a better angle."*

"I don't have eyes on the last man inside the showroom, but I think he's somewhere near the offices. Delta Lead, does your ground-level asset still have eyes in here?"

"Affirmative."

"Maintain continuous eyes on the elevator and stairwell door."

***

Grateful for his gloves, Nathan hauled all the dead gunmen into the exit corridor. There wasn't anything he could do about the snail-trails of blood. In the dim light of the alley, he doubted anyone driving along Olympic would see the smears. But if anyone turned into the alley, they couldn't miss them. Based on everything that had happened tonight, he didn't discount the arrival of more mercenaries. Thankfully, all the gunfire had been suppressed and the neighborhood fell into silence again.

"Kilo One, status?" Delta Lead asked.

"Available," Nathan said.

"Suggest you circle the building via the south alley and engage the gunman at the main entrance."

"On my way."

"There's no police radio traffic specific to this location yet. The dark showroom helps, harder to see the broken—"

Delta Lead stopped mid-sentence, then continued:

"We've got activity on the roof. A man just climbed out of a hatch. He's running toward the west side of the building. He's in civilian garb and we spotted a handgun tucked into his waistband."

"Everyone copy that traffic?" Nathan asked.

Harv and LG confirmed they had.

"What's he doing?"

"He's talking to the guy down below at the main entrance."

"Is there any way down from there?" Nathan asked.

"Negative. Check that, he's climbing down the decorative lattice."

"Kilo Three, backtrack through the exit corridor and circle the building on the Olympic side."

"On my way," LG said.

Nathan ran past the shuttle and Dumpster and stopped at the intersection of the alleys. He peered down the south alley toward Stewart Street.

All quiet.

Halfway down the alley—next to the roll-up door the dealership used to get the exotic cars in and out of the showroom—some large recycling bins offered minimal cover. If he got caught out in the open, he'd have little chance against a fully automatic Mac-10. The slugs might cut through the plastic bins and their contents.

"Delta Lead, how far away is the entrance to the dealership from the corner of the south alley and Stewart Street?"

"About twenty yards. We lost sight of the gunman. We believe he's inside the entry alcove."

"Kilo Two, can you pop off a few shots at the gunman outside the main entrance and pin him down? I'm going to advance down the alley."

"I've still got a live one in here," Harv said, *"but I can send a few shots through the windows. The falling glass will definitely distract him."*

"Stand by to shoot on my mark."

Delta Lead cut in. *"The man on the roof is about halfway down the wall; if he hangs from the bottom of the grid, he can drop the last eight feet to the sidewalk. He appears to be in good physical shape. He's descending that latticework with ease."*

"I'm at the corner of Olympic," LG reported.

"Let me know when you're at the corner of Olympic and Stewart."

"I'll be in position in ten seconds."

Nathan decided it didn't make sense to have LG exposed along Olympic Boulevard. She'd be much better deployed covering his advance down the south alley. "Kilo Three, turn around and hustle over to my position at the intersection of the alleys. Let me know when you have eyes on me. Copy?"

"Affirm," she said. *"On my way."*

"Kilo Two, are you all set?"

"Yes."

Nathan heard LG's footfalls as she sprinted toward his position.

"I've got eyes on you," LG said.

When she arrived, Nathan noticed she wasn't the slightest bit winded. He gave her a nod. "Okay, Kilo Two, on the count of three, send two shots through the glass near the main entrance."

"Kilo team, the man from the roof's on the ground . . . he's running south along Stewart Street. He'll be at the south alley's mouth in a few seconds. Be prepared to engage him if he turns your direction."

Nathan copied and decided to hold position. The runner would either enter the alley or keep running along the sidewalk. He'd have his answer soon enough.

Nathan felt confident the runner was Tomas Bustamonte, given that his gambling cohort called him Mr. B, but fleeing the scene didn't fit the CIA's profile on him. Everything in Tomas's file suggested he'd rather fight than flee. He knew profiles could be, and often were, wrong. Either way, Nathan didn't intend to let him get away.

When he saw Bustamonte dart across the alley's mouth, Nathan stayed in the east alley and began a full sprint, paralleling Bustamonte's course.

While running, he said, "Kilo Three, regroup with Kilo Two inside the dealership. Clear the building floor by floor. We need to know if Ursula's in there. Delta Lead, let me know when you lose sight of the rabbit. I'm going to try to catch him at the Expo rail line. If I move out of radio range, I'll turn on my cell and mute it. Everyone copy?"

Everyone did and Harv added, *"Proceed with extreme caution, Kilo One."*

"I've got this," Nathan said, pumping his arms to generate more speed. If he could reach the end of the alley in time, he might get a glimpse of Bustamonte before he arrived at the Expo rail line.

"Delta Lead, is the rabbit still running?"

"Affirmative, but we just lost sight of him. I recommend you scale the fence at the end of the east alley and cross the tracks. The runner isn't aware of your pursuit."

"Will do. I thought I saw a huge recycling center bordering the Expo line. Concur?"

"Affirmative. He might try to disappear in there."

"Do you know if the recycling center conducts night operations?"

"Negative."

Nathan was almost to the fence when he heard Harv's or LG's handgun pop several times.

"Kilo One, do you need Kilo Three's assistance?" Harv asked.

"Negative," Nathan said. "Be prepared to bug out in a hurry if Delta Lead reports the police being dispatched."

"All quiet so far," Delta Lead replied.

For how long? Nathan wondered. Although all the gunfire had been suppressed, sooner or later, someone was going to notice the broken windows or the dark showroom, putting them out of business. And as LG had put it, that would be unsatisfying. He wanted Tomas and Ursula to experience the CIA's tender loving care. A lengthy stay at Guantánamo Bay would fit the bill. Ursula had come within an eyelash of ending his life and he'd had a lot of time to think about it while recovering in San Diego's naval hospital. LG was right: the woman had the emotional quotient of a copperhead and he hoped she was still in the building.

Nathan reached the end of the east alley and looked toward Stewart Street. He caught a glimpse of Bustamonte darting across the rail line. Directly ahead, Nathan saw he'd have no issue getting over the fence protecting the tracks. The problem was, he'd be in plain sight as soon as he did that. For now, Bustamonte wasn't running at full speed, but that would change if he saw someone chasing him. Although Nathan wasn't the fastest person for short bursts of speed, few people could outlast him in a prolonged chase.

Nathan waited a few more seconds, then hopped the fence. The sound of crunching gravel concerned him as he angled across the tracks, but it couldn't be helped. Nathan knew he'd lose sight of Bustamonte in a few seconds because a block wall separated the recycling center from the Expo line and it extended all the way to Stewart Street where it turned the corner. He'd need to reacquire visual contact quickly. When Bustamonte disappeared behind the wall's corner, Nathan made an all-out burst of speed to follow.

He didn't like the illumination coming from streetlights, but there was nothing he could do about it. He stopped short of the corner, peered down Stewart Street, and saw his mark still running along the sidewalk. Given the sizable distance between them, Nathan had no choice. He took off in pursuit, but stayed in the street next to the parked cars. If Bustamonte looked back, he'd have a fighting chance to avoid being seen by ducking.

As predicted, Bustamonte veered to the left, heading for the recycling center's wall. Nathan watched the guy scale the eight-foot barrier and disappear over the top.

That's a good trick, he thought, *and Bustamonte made it look easy.*

Would his prey keep running deeper into the facility, or try to hide and wait the situation out? If Bustamonte had a car parked at the dealership, he wouldn't likely circle back to get it. At least not tonight. Like Nathan, he'd expect the police to be dispatched—along with a helicopter—and it would definitely search the entire neighborhood with one of those super-bright spotlights. If Nathan were in Bustamonte's shoes, he'd put several miles between himself and the car dealership, call a cab, and come back for his ride later.

Nathan ran several yards past the location where Bustamonte had gone over, then hoisted himself up for a glance. Seeing no sign of his mark, he scaled the wall, dropped into the recycling center, and immediately liked the increased darkness. Apparently, recyclables weren't high on thieves' bucket lists.

He deployed his night-vision scope and scanned the yard, confident that the dark would prevent Bustamonte from seeing him.

Familiar with the recycling center's layout from his review of the satellite photo, he knew where the prominent buildings were located. As always, everything looked different from ground level. The wall bordering the Expo line held garage-sized, three-walled bins for holding various types of recyclables. Parked between the bins and the buildings, recycling trucks formed a long row.

If Nathan were the runner, he would've headed toward the large buildings to the southeast. They offered the most cover. There were security lights mounted on the walls, but they weren't bright and most of them were burned out or turned off to save energy.

Nathan estimated he'd scaled the fence approximately ten seconds after Bustamonte. That put his mark at least fifty yards distant in any given direction, assuming the guy had kept running at a medium pace and hadn't stopped to hide somewhere.

Rather than randomly take off in the wrong direction, Nathan stayed put. With only eight rounds left in his pistol, he decided to reload. The closest building was at least 250 feet away and he now believed his prey hadn't run that direction. Off to his right, several front-end loaders sat dormant against the wall, providing a good place to hide.

If he fired a few shots under the loaders, it might flush Bustamonte out.

He was two seconds from pulling the trigger when motion caught his eye.

Got you.

Bustamonte stepped out from the closest three-sided bin, looked around, and began a jog toward the main building.

Using the line of recycling trucks for cover, Nathan took off in pursuit.

"Delta Lead, do you still copy?"

"Affirmative, Kilo One. Status?"

"I'm inside the recycling center, half a click south of SME. Pursuing the runner in a southerly direction."

"We're still all quiet here. No fire or police traffic."

Nathan listened to Harv and LG exchange radio traffic and wasn't worried. Harv was a capable operative, and he'd conducted these kinds of ops many times. The wild card was LG, but under Harv's leadership, she'd be okay.

Bustamonte reached the corner of the main building and Nathan lost sight of him again. He flipped his NV up and made a full sprint over to the building. He stopped short of the corner and took a quick look to make sure Bustamonte hadn't stopped. He hadn't. Nathan arrived in time to see Bustamonte disappear around a far corner. Nathan began running again. Just ahead, a large roll-up door hung open and a good amount of light spilled out. Could somebody be in there at this early hour? Given the open door, it seemed likely. If no one were in there, that door ought to be closed and locked.

Hustling past the large opening, he glanced inside. An incredible sight greeted him. Workers standing along an elevated conveyor belt were sorting various types of recyclables and tossing them into large bins. A smaller front-end loader worked the backside of the bins, scooping up the various plastic bottles, aluminum cans, glass, paper, and cardboard. There had to be thirty or forty workers stationed along the conveyor belt, half of them women. They were too engrossed in their work to notice Nathan sprint past the twenty-foot-wide opening. It was also noisy in there; most of the workers wore ear protection in addition to masks over their mouths.

Nathan continued to the corner of the building and took a quick look. Parked cars obscured his line of sight to the far end of the building, so he moved into the parking lot's aisle for a better look.

He spotted Bustamonte just as he cut around the far side of the building, heading back to the north, toward the Expo rail line. That surprised Nathan. He'd expected his prey to bolt through the open gate onto the street along the south property line. Maybe Bustamonte didn't like all the light out there. Nathan played another hunch. Rather than follow the same path, he backtracked, ran across the opening, and stopped at the corner.

Sure enough, Bustamonte appeared at the far side of the building and made a beeline for the middle section of the bins along the wall bordering the Expo line.

It was time to end this pursuit. He had a clear shot without risking a stray bullet hurting anyone. Nathan brought his Sig up, activated the laser, and painted Bustamonte's hip. His mark must've seen the red dot because he glanced over his shoulder, saw Nathan, and doubled his speed.

The laser sight gave Nathan an advantage, but because he had to aim out in front of his mark, it took his beam off-target.

Doing his best to estimate a twenty-four-inch lead, Nathan popped off three shots.

All missed.

Because his rounds didn't make supersonic *crack*s, Bustamonte had no clue how close he'd come to being drilled.

The man bolted through the line of recycle trucks and Nathan lost sight of him again.

Nathan didn't beat himself up for missing. It was a low-odds attempt, but worth a try. The man had to be at least a football field away. At a full sprint, that was a ten-second lead. Nathan couldn't let it grow any bigger.

He heard the diesel engine just in time.

***

Harvey felt some concern about his friend being on his own in a foot chase against Bustamonte but, mano a mano, few people in the world stood a snowball's chance against Nathan McBride. Right now, he had to concentrate on ending the threat inside this dealership. If Ursula was upstairs, she posed a serious threat. People with little or no emotion were totally unpredictable. And with her résumé? Lethal.

His immediate vulnerability came from the remaining gunman who'd gone to ground somewhere. Harvey got low and looked underneath the cars but didn't see the guy's feet. He'd either ducked into one of the offices, climbed into one of the cars, or concealed his feet behind a tire. Given the options, Harvey put his money on the offices.

"Kilo Three, do you have eyes on me?" Harv whispered.

"Affirm."

"Stand by to advance. I'm going to flush out our last gunman. Be ready to put suppression fire on the gunman outside the main entrance."

His radio clicked.

Starting at the east end, near the elevator, Harvey began firing rounds through the glass windows of each office. One by one, the windows shattered and fell.

Halfway through his salvo, the gunman bolted from the office closest to the elevator, firing as he ran.

The gunman on Stewart Street must've seen his comrade's predicament because he fired his Mac-10 through the glass. Once again, huge cascades of glass fell.

Crouching, Harv yelled, "Kilo Three, get down!"

Chaos erupted again as dozens of bullets slammed into metal, glass, leather, fiberglass, and wood.

None of the rounds came close to him, but LG was in the line of fire. *"I'm okay,"* LG said.

Harv ran in a crouch along the aisle between the cars toward the offices. He knew the remaining gunman inside the showroom intended to climb the security bars and flee the scene. Unfortunately, as long as that guy outside kept spraying bullets, he wouldn't be able to get a bead on his target.

"Kilo Three, give me suppression fire at the main entrance. Don't try to be precise, just pound the area." He heard LG copy his request over the banging metal and breaking glass.

He heard the claps of her pistol begin a steady rhythm.

More waterfalls of glass fell along the street as some of her bullets found the floor-to-ceiling windows.

The salvo from the exterior gunman went silent.

"Keep firing. He's probably reloading." Harv straightened up enough to see over the tops of the cars and fired a few rounds in the general direction where he thought the other gunman was hiding between the cars near the offices.

Movement outside the entrance caught his eye.

The gunman jerked, as though stung by a hornet. He grabbed his neck and crumpled to the ground.

"Great shooting," Harv whispered. "Hold your fire. Copy?"

Since the showroom had gone silent again, she clicked her acknowledgment.

Reminding himself it was dark in here and the remaining gunman didn't have night vision, Harvey charged the offices, firing periodically as he ran. He purposely aimed low, skipping his rounds off the floor. He couldn't do anything about the glass shards crunching under his boots, and the sound echoed through the showroom, making it hard to pinpoint the source.

Harvey reached the edge of the cars at the south end of the showroom. Tempered glass from the broken office windows covered the granite floor like translucent carpet.

There was no sign of the interior gunman.

"Delta Lead, do you have eyes on the last gunman in here?"

"Negative."

Harvey ducked low and looked for the man's boots.

Nothing.

In a whisper, Harv said, "Kilo Three. Eyes on me." He knew the last gunman couldn't leave without scaling the bars.

In the green image of his NV scope, Harv watched her come up from a crouch. She too had her device pivoted down to her eye. He gave her a hand gesture like that of a quarterback calling for a huddle.

"Copy," she whispered. *"On my way."*

He didn't like leaving the exit corridor unguarded, but Delta Lead had the outside of the building covered. If any new threats arrived, he'd send LG back.

The eastern side of the showroom didn't have any broken glass on the floor and LG was able to make a silent approach. Most of the damaged cars were toward the center of the showroom. Harv reloaded his Sig and moved east to meet her.

She arrived a few seconds later.

"I think the last gunman ducked into one of the offices again. I need you to cover the elevator and stairwell door while I flush him out."

"Shoot to kill?" she asked.

"Yes."

Harv gave her shoulder a squeeze and eased toward the offices, keeping layers of cars between himself and the gunman.

He stopped about fifty feet short of the offices and began walking his shots along the three-foot half-walls below the broken windows.

It worked.

With his Mac-10 slung over his shoulder, the last gunman made a mad dash for the security bars at the entrance.

Harv yelled at him to stop, but the man kept running.

When the guy reached the security bars and started to climb, Harv shot him in the ass twice—once for each cheek.

This turd would've killed me without a second thought, Harv told himself. *And nearly did.* He ran toward the entrance, careful not to slip on all the glass shards.

The guy fell to the floor and tried to unsling his weapon.

"Don't do it," he said in English. "It's over. Don't make me kill you." Even if this guy didn't speak English, the message couldn't be mistaken.

With two bullets lodged in his butt, the gunman couldn't sit so he plopped over onto his side and extended his arms above his head.

Harv kept his laser painted on the gunman's head as he approached. *"Habla inglés?"*

"Poquito."

In Spanish, Harv asked if there were more gunmen in the building. The man said no, and Harv believed him. The tone of urgency in his quick answer rang true.

It was a good thing LG had suggested they bring disposable cuffs, because they came in handy right now.

The man grunted as Harv secured his arms behind his back. Harv searched the guy, found a knife, a cell phone, and a wallet. All three items went into his waist pack. Harv could've dragged the guy through the glass, but kicked it aside as he pulled the man into the closest office.

He used a second set of plastic cuffs to secure the man to the leg of a heavy granite-topped desk. Harv tested its weight and could barely lift it. Confident the wounded man wouldn't be able to get free, he returned to LG's position.

"Delta Lead, all threats on the showroom floor are neutralized. I left one alive in the office closest to the entrance."

"Copy, Kilo Two. We recommend you climb the security bars and drag the dead gunman on Stewart Street around the corner into the south alley. He's in plain sight. No vehicles are approaching, so you've got a good window if you go over the bars quickly. No police-radio traffic yet."

Harvey wasted no time scrambling up and over the security measures. He grabbed the dead man by the collar and hauled him along the sidewalk to the corner of the building. Halfway down the south alley, he saw some recycling bins and dragged the body over to them.

Harvey reentered the showroom and met up with LG near the elevator.

"We'll leapfrog up the stairwell. Let's turn our NVs off; the stairwell's bound to be brightly lit. How's your ammo?"

"I've got two full magazines and two partials."

He reached into his waist pack and produced a box of fifty rounds. "Let's top off our partials. We have no idea what we'll be facing up there." As he pressed the bullets into the magazines, he said, "Kilo One, status? Ignore if engaged."

"You're partially broken . . . I'm in the recycling center, still in pursuit."

"Delta Lead?" Harv asked.

"All quiet."

With LG in tow, Harvey approached the stairwell door.

He turned, received a nod, and entered the same numbers into the keypunch.

CHAPTER 18

A loader came roaring out of the twenty-foot opening, forcing Nathan to pivot around the corner. He flattened himself against the wall as the vehicle sped past, mere feet away. He took off behind the loader and followed it over to the line of trucks. The loader kept going and dumped its load of clear glass into a recycle bin.

The sound was incredible as thousands of bottles clinked, clanged, and shattered.

He eased between the trucks and saw Bustamonte heading for the northeast corner of the property. Beyond the wall, the Expo line would provide darker cover than the street to the south. That could be the reason Bustamonte chose to run this direction. He could also be trying to retrieve his car before the cops arrived. In any case, Nathan knew the guy planned to hop the wall.

Not wasting any time, the loader's operator executed a Y-turn, drove back through the line of trucks, and disappeared the way it had come. Nathan pivoted his NV down, and began a full sprint as Bustamonte climbed atop a huge stack of cardboard bales and disappeared over the wall.

"Delta Lead, do you still copy?"

"Affirm. We can still read you."

"I'm about to leave the recycling center. I think my mark is running along the Expo line. I'm in pursuit. He knows I'm on his tail."

"Copy, Kilo One. Good hunting."

Nathan knew it could become a long run down the tracks. There was no denying Bustamonte was faster than he was. The real question became, how long could the guy keep it up?

First things first. Right now Nathan had to get up and over the block wall to reacquire his prey. He angled to his right and climbed atop the same stack of bales. Problem was, he'd make himself a juicy target if Bustamonte hadn't fled down the tracks. Running atop the cardboard, Nathan played the odds, believing Bustamonte wouldn't stop and try to ambush him. When he reached the wall, he looked east down the Expo's barren line of tracks and saw no sign of his mark. A scan in the other direction revealed Bustamonte sprinting back toward Stewart Street, where they'd entered the recycling center. Good news and bad news.

The good news: He wasn't going to be ambushed.

The bad: Bustamonte had an appallingly long lead.

Nathan wasted no time.

He lowered himself into the easement, then took off again in pursuit, running down the middle of the left-hand track. He wasn't worried about a train showing up at this hour, as this was a local commuter line, not an Amtrak or freight route. Bustamonte kept looking over his shoulder, which caused him to nearly lose his balance and fall.

Less than half a click ahead, Nathan saw the Stewart Street crossing.

He estimated he trailed Bustamonte by ten to fifteen seconds.

Would Bustamonte keep following the tracks, or turn right toward the dealership?

He felt some relief when Bustamonte went straight through the street crossing. The guy obviously believed he could outrun Nathan, his first tactical error. When Nathan reached the crossing, he glanced both ways before hustling across.

Bustamonte kept looking back. Perhaps he was hoping Nathan would give up and call off the chase. *Sorry, pal, that's not happening. You've got a date with Cantrell's people and I don't want to deprive you of the experience.*

It didn't look like the man intended to hop the fence and find cover in the buildings lining the left side of the tracks. The right side was a major street with a landscaping strip in the middle. Olympic Boulevard. He'd seen its proximity to the Expo line on the aerial. He estimated the next intersection lay some five hundred yards ahead. As he settled into a sustainable pace, Nathan made up a running-cadence song, a trick he'd learned in the Marine Corps.

I am going to catch that man, he's not going to foil my plan.
If I fall and tumble down, I'll get up without a frown.

He silently chanted the lines over and over, saying a word every other stride. The last time he did something like this, he was in Nicaragua, running up a steep dirt road after a formidable enemy.

If he could close the distance to fifty yards, he might stop, take a knee, and attempt a wounding shot. Bustamonte wasn't wearing a vest so anything above the waist was potentially fatal. For now, his best bet lay in outlasting the man in a prolonged footrace.

Every so often, Nathan passed an upright metal cabinet of some sort, probably an electrical or other underground conduit access point for the rail system. He tried not to become distracted, concentrating instead on breathing, taking a full breath every fourth stride and a full exhalation four strides later. Creating consistent breath-to-stride pace was key to maintaining a prolonged effort.

He heard another transmission from Harv and LG, but some of it was broken and unreadable. Nathan figured in another half mile or so, he'd be completely out of range. He still had his cell phone, which reminded him to turn it on. He reached into his waist pack and held the power button for several seconds. Its glow wasn't a concern now; Bustamonte didn't have night vision. He also made sure it was set to silent mode.

Somewhere off to the south, he heard the rumble of a diesel engine, but he couldn't see the source. Other than the slipstream of cars on I-10, the neighborhood remained quiet. A few gang tags were present here and there, but it didn't look like the neighborhood had been infested, which meant gunshots would be immediately reported.

From what Nathan could determine, there were no residences in the immediate area, but there were bound to be some people in these larger buildings, and he couldn't discount the possibility of a security patrol, either on foot or in a vehicle.

He continued to sing the marching song. He liked the way the Marines did things—time-tested methods of creating warriors. His blood pumped, his lungs heaved, and his muscles burned, all feelings he loved. This was now a battle of wills and Nathan intended to get under Bustamonte's skin and whittle away at the man's will to resist.

His prey appeared to be fumbling with something. Perhaps he'd forgotten to load his handgun, or was checking to make sure its safety was off. If the guy turned to shoot, Nathan wouldn't hesitate to return fire, but he'd keep his shots low. Whatever Bustamonte had been doing, he finished and returned his focus on running again.

The next intersection lay just ahead.

Nathan had detected a pattern in the man's routine. Every five seconds or so, Bustamonte turned to check on his pursuer.

Nathan timed his move perfectly. He waited until Bustamonte was fifty or sixty yards from the crossing and slowed to a stop, then, keeping his head just high enough to watch his target's reaction, he bent over, put his hands on his knees, and acted as if he were totally winded. He wanted Bustamonte to continue straight and not leave the tracks.

Come on, Boosty, look back . . .

Any second now . . .

Like clockwork, the man looked over his shoulder. When he saw Nathan's staged pose, he slowed to a medium-paced jog, passed over the next intersecting street, and kept following the tracks.

Perfect.

Nathan resumed his pursuit.

The next time Bustamonte looked back, Nathan sensed the man's primal panic.

This pursuit wasn't over; it had begun anew.

How do you like me now? Thought you were going to outrun me? Well, think again.

Nathan had reserve energy to spare.

After another hundred yards or so, one thing had become clear: Bustamonte was proving to be a worthy prey. Nathan hadn't been able to close the distance. Every time he sped up, the guy matched his speed. For the first time during this foot chase, Nathan experienced a small pang of doubt. He didn't want to risk an all-out burst of speed. If it didn't work, he'd be spent and lose the contest.

Over the next five hundred yards or so, the Expo line gradually gained elevation as it passed over Olympic Boulevard. It forced Bustamonte to remain inside the right-of-way because of the vertical drop-offs on both sides. At the highest point of the overpass, Bustamonte fumbled with his gun again and Nathan fully expected a handgun fight, but it never came.

The only thing Bustamonte did with any predictability was look over his shoulder.

Another street crossing lay ahead. If Bustamonte left the tracks, Nathan might lose him. The right-of-way had narrowed, with buildings lining both sides. If his mark made a left or right turn up there, Nathan would lose sight of him and he didn't know what the surrounding area looked like. The aerial photo hadn't extended this far away from the dealership.

He heard it then.

It came out of nowhere.

The high-pitched whine of an approaching car.

CHAPTER 19

Three thousand miles away, Rebecca Cantrell picked up her hard line and punched a number from memory. She stared into the foul weather beyond her windows, insulated from the wind and rain. Insulated, she knew, in more than one way. She longed for the world outside this sterile environment.

DNI Scott Benson could see her caller ID so she didn't need to identify herself.

"They've engaged," she said.

"I hope you're right about this, Rebecca. I'm still uncomfortable turning McBride loose, US soil or not."

Rebecca didn't interrupt. She sensed a CYA lecture coming from her old friend.

"Your boys have important friends in every branch of government, I get that, but that leverage doesn't extend to the failure point. At some point, I'll have to brief the president and I'd prefer to have this wrapped up by then. Give me your gut: what are the chances McBride and Fontana will succeed?"

"Fifty-fifty."

"Fifty-fifty . . ."

"I won't blow smoke, Scott, but remember, they have a proven history with us. The Beaumont security teams don't have half their experience."

"I understand, but this has serious blowback potential—engaging on American soil to interfere with a foreign election."

"We aren't doing that. An operation to protect our citizens can't be seen as interfering in Venezuela's politics. Facial-recognition identified three of Genneken's assailants as being from a sophisticated LA gang, more like a crime family, with links to the Bustamonte twins."

"Bustamonte . . . Why is that name familiar?"

"Before Genneken became station chief, she was part of a secret operation we carried out against a Caracas-based cartel engaged in money-laundering in Iran and North Korea. Cornejo was linked to the cartel, though never officially. Ursula and Tomas Bustamonte looked after his interests in the organization. Anyway, after the Bustamontes kidnapped a US citizen, we sent in Genneken to infiltrate the group. She wanted McBride and Fontana for the op, so we asked them to come out of retirement. They got the American out alive, but barely. He was in pretty bad shape. Some months later, he and Genneken ended up seeing one another, and eventually got married. He was killed during the assault tonight."

"I'm sorry to hear that, but it raises a critical question. Do we have any idea how Cornejo or the Bustamontes found Genneken?"

"If you're asking whether we have an in-house security breach, I don't think so."

"What about Genneken herself?"

"I've considered that, and I can't discount the possibility, but I think she's clean."

"Let's hope so," Benson said.

"Could she have dirt on Cornejo? Yes. Could she be blackmailing him? Again, yes. I can't rule those possibilities out with absolute certainty. But she doesn't need the money. Her husband makes—made—about a million per month as an investment consultant."

"Not too shabby, but some people can never have enough."

"I'm not taking anything for granted." Rebecca let a few seconds pass. "Although the rescue never became public, it infuriated Cornejo, who was Venezuela's attorney general at the time, corrupt to the core."

"If I'm remembering things correctly, one of your Special Activities Division officers was killed in Caracas just prior to the rescue."

She closed her eyes and tried to vanquish the man's face. It didn't happen. "He made it into the Agency on my endorsement."

"I'm sorry, Rebecca. It never gets easier."

"No. It still hurts. Pretty much every day."

"I'd worry about you if it didn't."

"McBride took a bullet to the chest during the op, which nearly added another star to our wall."

"I hear you, Rebecca, and I want you to continue personally handling this one."

"I will."

"You've got Beaumont Specialists engaged in other locations tonight, correct?"

"Yes. I told McBride and Fontana we'd be conducting other ops against Cornejo's LA assets, but they have no idea we're using contractors."

"I don't think they'd care," Benson said. "Does Vincent Beaumont know who his team's supporting?"

"Yes, and he was more than willing to help."

"It seems we aren't the only ones who owe McBride a few favors."

Cantrell leaned back in her chair and pivoted toward her muted bank of televisions, all set to different news channels. "I believe the Bustamonte twins will try to flee the country today. We're attempting to grab them before they succeed. If we can get one or both of them alive, I'm hoping we'll get what we need."

Benson didn't respond. He didn't need to. Though neither of them wanted the CIA to be seen as interfering with the Venezuelan presidential succession, doing so ranked high on the administration's list of foreign-policy goals. It wasn't simply a matter of ideology. Cornejo had long-held business connections with Iran, forged and strengthened during the years in which Iran had suffered nearly universal trade sanctions because of its nuclear ambitions. Recent intel from Venezuela revealed that Cornejo-owned companies were working to procure the type of centrifuges Iran needed in order to refine uranium into weapons-grade material. If Cornejo became president of Venezuela, then Venezuela itself would almost surely be going into the nuclear-weapon production business with Iran. In return, Venezuela would receive much-needed cash for its coffers. Or at least Cornejo would.

"We go way back, Rebecca, so I'm going to give you some latitude on this. Conduct this operation as you see fit, keep me informed, and pull the plug if it gets out of hand. I'll leave the definition up to you."

"McBride knows the score. If he screws this up, it's on my watch."

"Conversely, if he succeeds, it's another medal on your chest."

"I have no political aspirations."

"I didn't mean to suggest you did."

"You didn't. Truthfully, this job has taken a chunk out of me. I can only imagine being in your shoes."

"You've heard the prayer about being able to change what we can, accept what we can't, and know the difference?"

"Yes."

"It's absolutely true. Most people have the luxury of keeping their worlds small, we don't."

"My personal feelings aside, we can't let Daniel Cornejo become Venezuela's next president."

ANDREW PETERSON

"On that we're in total agreement. So how much time do we give McBride to get containment?"

"I would think if we don't have the Bustamonte twins in custody in the next forty-eight hours, we pursue other options."

"Keep me informed, I've got to take another call. No goodbyes."

The call ended. It's what Benson always said before hanging up. *No goodbyes.* Obviously, the director of National Intelligence was superstitious too.

Her thoughts returned to Nathan.

Every time she talked to him, it could be the last.

CHAPTER 20

Harvey felt LG's hand on his shoulder along with a nudge, a signal she was ready to go. He cracked the door a few inches and peered inside.

A bright stairwell greeted him. No surprises there.

Once inside, he put her on hold and listened for sound.

Nothing.

He looked up the narrow gap between the rails to verify the stairwell went up to the third floor. It did.

"We're moving. Stop at the landing and cover my advance to the second floor."

She started up.

"Stop!" Harvey whispered.

LG froze in place.

"Your footsteps."

"Shit," she said. "Sorry."

"It's okay." He smiled and gave her a nod to continue. He wouldn't beat her up over it. It had been years since LG had conducted this kind of op. Her steps hadn't been overly loud, but in the absolute silence of this stairwell, they were definitely detectable. It was a mistake she wouldn't make again.

On the second floor, they found a dimly lit hallway that ran the entire length of the building.

Barring some secret hiding spot, the entire second floor looked vacant. All of the offices lining the hallway were unlocked and none of the "offices" held more than superficial furniture. No computers, personal pictures, or anything else indicating these spaces were being used, or ever had been.

Clearly, Cantrell had it right. This entire building was nothing more than a money-laundering mechanism. A sweet setup, really. Harvey wondered how many buildings like this Cornejo owned.

Halfway down the hall, they located a break room.

Several cups of coffee sat on one of the small round tables. He felt one. "Warm?" she asked.

He nodded.

An open pizza box, paper plates, and napkins lay on the counter next to the sink.

Since Delta Lead hadn't reported seeing anyone but the briefcase crew enter the building, the gunmen who'd stormed out of the stairwell had been here first, which meant they were probably personal security. He had to wonder what kind of activity needed that level of firepower. A simple poker game? The man they'd questioned said they'd all brought cash. Perhaps that was reason enough.

There was no sign of a card game on this floor, so it had to be upstairs. He gave Delta Lead an update and said they were ascending to the third floor.

***

Nathan didn't see any headlight intrusion, but a vehicle definitely raced toward the crossing.

Who'd be speeding through this neighborhood with their headlights off?

Knowing it might cost him his prey but save his life, he made a split-second decision to end his pursuit and find cover. The problem was, there wasn't anything available except a power pole supporting the overhead electric line for the trains.

He sprinted to its metal form.

Good thing he did.

A white lowrider stopped in the middle of the railroad tracks directly in front of him. Its windows tinted black, it looked like a gangbanger's ride. The only thing missing was obnoxious, thumping music.

Four armed men scrambled out of the far side and used it for cover. He wasn't sure, but it looked like they carried compact Kalashnikovs. If this metal pole didn't stop bullets, this could be a very short fight.

With no other place to go, he'd have to engage.

Using the side of the pole to steady his aim, he painted the laser on the biggest gunman, and squeezed off a round.

The man's head jerked from the impact.

The remaining men dropped out of sight as he fired three shots through the lowrider's windows.

He'd lost sight of Bustamonte, who'd either kept running down the tracks or joined his friends at the car.

It hit him suddenly, like an open-handed slap. Bustamonte hadn't been fumbling with a gun; he'd been making calls. To make matters worse, the man clearly had been baiting him—likely the whole time—buying time for these guys to arrive at this exact location.

As pissed off as he was, he couldn't let his temper get the best of him.

He adjusted his aim lower and pounded the vehicle's doors, hoping to nail at least one more gunman. He fired the last five rounds of the magazine underneath the chassis.

In ideal conditions, with a magazine pocket on a holster, Nathan could reload his weapon inside of two seconds. But having to grab loose magazines from his waist pack added costly seconds to the process.

And the result was hellish.

At the same time he saw their flash suppressors ignite, a staccato roar of automatic fire reverberated off every hard surface within half a mile.

Completely pinned, Nathan tried to make his massive six-foot-five-inch hulk skinnier.

It didn't work.

Despite being seasoned in combat, he found the hail of lead stretching his ability to remain calm. He was reminded of a scene in *True Lies*, in which Tom Arnold had used a streetlight to hide from automatic gunfire. Fortunately, this pole was considerably wider.

Amid the racket of rifle fire, deformed slugs screamed and howled as they ricocheted off the gravel.

Some of the bullets found the metal pole.

The moment of truth arrived.

The post vibrated from the impacts.

But no holes appeared.

He thanked the city of Santa Monica, ejected the empty magazine, and inserted a full one.

The roar of automatic fire ended, only to begin again.

If the cops weren't already on the way, they soon would be and Nathan couldn't be here when they arrived.

The mayhem continued as one gunman fired while the others reloaded.

The longer this went on, the more likely Bustamonte would escape and one of those AK rounds would find his flesh.

All he needed was a short break to return fire on the lowrider.

In situations like this, Nathan's mind didn't flash with childhood memories, reflect on regrets, or seek solace in self-pity: it shifted into high gear and analyzed every available option.

Ignoring the vibrating steel and the tortured gravel erupting all around him, he recognized an opportunity.

A control box sat ahead and to his right. He'd seen it when he'd ducked behind this power pole.

If he moved straight back by ten feet or so, he might have a chance.

The move would be risky. These guys seemed to have an unlimited supply of ammo. They'd switched to shorter bursts, but the barrage remained nonstop.

The decision made, he eased back from the pole.

The sensation of backing away from such a narrow source of protection felt insane.

Bullets continued to whiz past on either side of him.

Fighting every instinct he had, he kept stepping backward.

Crap! Something sliced his shin. A chunk of granite or a copper jacket fragment, not a bullet. The force of the impact hadn't been severe, but it was going to leak.

He put it out of mind and concentrated on moving in a straight line. An inch of lateral movement would be disastrous.

He hated having his eyes exposed, but there was nothing he could do about it. He couldn't wear protective goggles and use the NV at the same time.

A little farther . . .

There.

The control box came into his line of sight and the angle looked pretty damned close.

He painted the face of the cabinet with his laser and fired three controlled shots.

The barrage from the white lowrider ended.

It worked!

His slugs had ricocheted off the cabinet and struck the car, forcing the gunmen to duck for cover.

Wasting no time, Nathan charged forward to the pole again and used its form to steady his pistol. He took careful aim at an exposed pair of feet.

The bullet found its target and the man fell, exposing his entire body under the vehicle. Nathan wasted no time sending two more bullets under the lowrider.

Now wasn't the time to show clemency.

He initiated another continuous barrage, firing a bullet every second, punching a dozen more holes in the lowrider. With a little luck, maybe he could get one of them to—

Run.

Just like that guy.

One of them bolted for the safety of the building to the north.

Based on the man's size and clothing, Nathan felt confident it wasn't Bustamonte.

He used the brief lull in the action to reload his handgun.

And brief it was.

The man who'd fled the vehicle reappeared at the corner of the building and opened fire with his AK.

All of the bullets missed high, a common mistake with Kalashnikovs. When the barrage went silent, he painted the man's face and pulled the trigger.

The guy performed a flawless face-plant onto the concrete.

By Nathan's count, that left one man—not including Bustamonte—still crouched behind the vehicle.

He needed an alternative to hiding behind this pole.

Once a Marine, always a Marine, he thought. *Here goes.* He stepped out from his cover and charged the lowrider, firing as he ran.

His aggression took the last gangbanger by surprise.

The guy left the cover of the lowrider and sprinted in the opposite direction from his fallen comrade.

Nathan stopped, took a knee, and steadied his aim. He only had time for a single shot.

In desperation, the man discharged his AK with one hand as he fled, but none of his rounds came close.

Nathan dropped him with a precisely fired round. The bullet must've severed his spinal cord because the gunman's legs quit working, but not his upper half. He tried to reload his AK, but fumbled with the magazine.

Nathan squinted, and sent a bullet into the man's head.

The next thing he heard were deep, throaty booms of a large-caliber handgun.

CHAPTER 21

At the top of the stairwell, Harvey turned to LG and whispered, "Same thing as before. We'll clear the hall room by room."

Harvey cracked the door and saw an empty corridor. No cameras were visible.

"Stay here and leave the door open a few inches. You should be able to hear if anyone enters the stairwell. You've got my six."

LG nodded.

As below, the office doors weren't locked but, unlike the second floor, these rooms didn't even contain furniture. The men's restroom was on the left side and he stepped inside. Sitting in the middle of the floor, a six-foot A-frame ladder sat directly below an open roof hatch. He reported his find to Delta Lead, returned to the hallway, and continued checking doors. Near the halfway point of the corridor, he heard something.

A man's laughter from somewhere ahead, probably the next door on the right.

Who would be laughing at a time like this?

Gun up, he approached the door and heard jazz music emanating from within.

A thin line of light spilled under the sill.

He leaned in and placed an ear on its surface. More laughter erupted and he pulled back.

Incredible. Either that was a recording, or whoever was inside had no clue what had happened below. Granted, all the weapons were suppressed and the sound of breaking glass hadn't been all that loud. If illegal activity were taking place in there, it made sense to have the room somewhat soundproofed.

Clearly, then, someone had tipped off Bustamonte by phone. He'd obviously abandoned the other poker players, leaving them behind as sacrifices. Pretty cold-blooded.

Just above the doorknob, there was a slot for a cardkey, like hotels used.

Moving slowly, he tried the knob.

Locked.

Harvey was tempted to kick it open, but knocking might be a better approach. Better yet, the man they'd intercepted probably had a cardkey to get back in.

He whispered into his boom mike, "Kilo Three, double-time down to the exit corridor and check the briefcase guy we intercepted. Search him for a cardkey, like hotels use. I'll maintain position here. Don't worry about being stealthy, just get down there and back as fast as you can."

"On my way."

He admired how LG never questioned orders or hesitated. Despite being recently traumatized and years into retirement, she'd proven herself to be a valuable asset. Her gaffe on the stairs had been her only tactical mistake. Not bad at all . . .

His thoughts went out to Nate, and he hoped his friend wouldn't get too reckless in his pursuit. *Reckless?* he mused.

"I found a cardkey in the guy's shirt pocket," LG said. *"On my way back up."*

He clicked his radio.

Twenty seconds later, LG showed up and *quietly* hustled down the hall to his position.

"We're going to rush into this room simultaneously. I'll tell everyone to freeze and show me their hands. If anyone makes a threatening or sudden move, they get a bullet. I seriously doubt Tomas would've abandoned his sister, but we need to be certain she's not in there. If you see a woman, use nonlethal force on her."

"I'll do my best."

Knowing Delta Lead could hear every word he said, Harvey chose his words carefully. "Kilo Three, do not use deadly force on any females in the room."

"Understood," she said.

He slipped the cardkey into the slot and lifted it out quickly.

The lock mechanism clicked and the tiny light blinked green.

***

Bustamonte's handgun reports echoed off the buildings. Nathan had no idea where the bullets had gone, but the gravel didn't erupt.

Caught in no-man's-land, Nathan sprinted for the control box.

Problem was, he couldn't see the source of the shots. The muzzle flashes had come from somewhere on the far side of the lowrider, he knew that much.

The hand cannon's staccato booms ended at eight shots. Nathan logged the info.

Seeing no movement at the lowrider, he ran in a crouch to its punctured form and used the front end for cover, keeping his feet protected by the wheel.

He looked along the tracks and caught a lucky break: a glint of light next to a Expo line power pole. There and gone.

There it was again.

Whoever hid behind the pole was sloppy, exposing his hands as he reloaded the weapon. Bustamonte?

Nathan had his answer.

His prey stepped out from the pole and fired three more shots. The bullets slammed into the lowrider, making it vibrate.

He peered over the hood, saw Bustamonte hop the rail line's fence and run away, heading west again.

Your little surprise party failed, Boosty. The next time you pull your phone, you're getting a bullet in the ass.

This was the closest Nathan had been during the chase and he didn't intend to allow the gap to grow bigger. He estimated less than one hundred feet separated them.

Nathan took off in pursuit, angling across the intersection. He saw headlights down the street, but they were distant. Not a factor.

Time to get serious.

Based on the eight shots and deep booms, he was fairly sure Bustamonte had a 1911 in .45 ACP. Heavy bullets, probably 230-grain full-metal jackets with a muzzle velocity of 850 feet per second. Subsonic, but packing lots of energy. The high-gloss nickel plating on Boosty's gun might look impressive at indoor shooting ranges, but in a combat situation, it might as well glow in the dark.

This time, immediately after Boosty finished looking over his shoulder, Nathan stopped running, carefully raised his Sig, and squeezed off a shot, purposely aiming below the belt.

His target jerked.

Looking like half of a two-man potato sack race, Bustamonte limped around the corner of an industrial building.

Nathan initiated a burst of speed and reached the corner about five seconds later.

He stopped short and took a quick look.

The bullet arrived simultaneously with the flash, but Nathan had already pulled his head back. The slug slammed the corner and knocked a chunk of concrete free. Another crackling boom echoed around the neighborhood.

Nathan figured they had to be at least a mile from the dealership at this point. He hoped the police would converge to this area, buying time for Harv and LG to clear the dealership.

"Give it up, Bustamonte!" Nathan yelled. "Stop running or I'll drop you."

He stole another look and saw his prey limping through the landscaping strip next to the building.

He's persistent, I'll give him that.

Gun up, Nathan pivoted around the corner and eased along the wall. If Bustamonte turned to shoot again, Nathan might have to kill him. The separation was inside seventy-five feet and it wasn't dark enough to remain unseen. The streetlights looked like small suns in Nathan's NV. He was tempted to shoot them but decided to conserve his ammo. Based on everything he'd seen tonight, he couldn't discount the arrival of more mercenaries or gangbangers.

He took advantage of a waist-high hedge and ran in a crouch. At this point in the game, Nathan needed to maintain continuous eyes on his prey. If Bustamonte tried to duck around the corner of the building up ahead, Nathan would drill him before he got there, then do his best to stop the bleeding.

He decided it was unwise to advance this close to the wall. If his mark managed to turn and shoot, the bullet could skip off the wall and find him.

Nathan stayed in the shadows of some trees and diverted over to the street where a smattering of cars were parallel parked. He stepped off the curb, entered the street, and used the line of cars to advance.

When he looked along the building, Bustamonte was gone.

The guy couldn't have reached the far corner of the building in the time it took Nathan to divert over here. No possible way. Bustamonte could barely walk, let alone run.

His prey must be hiding in the landscaping. There were several hedges growing perpendicular to the street.

Nathan darted to the next parked car and stayed low. Wounded men can, and often do, act recklessly. Losing eyes on Bustamonte didn't spell disaster, but it put him at considerably more risk. Nathan didn't think he'd been seen, but he wasn't certain. Even for the best marksman, an iron-sighted pistol shot in low light was a tough assignment.

A single boom announced Bustamonte was still in the fight.

Nathan ducked when the rear window of the vehicle exploded. A second shot broke more glass.

Time to relocate.

In a crouch, he paralleled the street and found cover behind the next vehicle, a pickup truck. Although his NV worked great, it was a line-of-sight visual device and Bustamonte still couldn't be seen.

Nathan pulled the thermal imager from his waist pack, powered it on, and gave the landscaping a quick scan.

Got you.

The device picked up Bustamonte's heat signature easily. Glowing like a ghost, his prey lay in hiding behind the second perpendicular hedge.

"Give it up, Bustamonte. It's over!" He fired a suppressed shot over Bustamonte's head, which whistled off the wall beyond. "That's a warning shot. The next one won't be."

In response, the man fired twice more, the slugs pounding the pickup's bed. Apparently, Bustamonte had tracked his relocation.

Have it your way.

Making good on his word, Nathan fired into Bustamonte's thigh.

What happened next could only be described as berserk.

His prey came up from the hedge and hobbled toward the truck, firing as he came. The bullets thumped and clanged into the sheet metal, forcing Nathan to duck for cover.

Screw this, he thought. *Cantrell's not getting a live prisoner after all.*

The wail of an approaching siren, coupled with the suicidal charge of an utter nutcase, became the deciding factors.

He fired three rounds into the center of Bustamonte's chest.

The result was immediate.

Bustamonte collapsed to the grass and rolled onto his back. In a pitiful display, the man tried to sit up, but couldn't.

Nathan sprinted over and kicked the pistol from Bustamonte's hand. As suspected, it was a nickel-plated 1911.

What the hell . . . ?

This man wasn't Tomas Bustamonte.

CHAPTER 22

"I'll take the left," Harvey whispered. "Clear your right corner as we enter."

In a fluid movement, he opened the door and rushed inside. Scanning the room from left to right, he focused on a scene few people ever saw.

Seated around an oval table, four men looked at him with shocked expressions—all but one. His expression reflected anger, not fear. Harvey zeroed in on him.

"Hands where I can see them!" he yelled.

Angry Face either didn't speak English, or was trying to be a hero because he dropped his right hand below the table.

Harvey nailed him in the middle of the chest with two quick shots.

The expended brass clinked away on the stone floor.

Angry Face became Pain Face.

The man opened his mouth, but nothing came out except a strained *uhhhh* sound. Whatever discomfort Pain Face felt would soon end.

Harvey spoke calmly. "Anyone else?"

Wisely, the others remained frozen. The room smelled of cigar smoke and alcohol. Lots of it.

Huge stacks of bundled bills dominated the gap between the players. He estimated each pile contained at least a hundred thousand dollars; all he saw were fifties and hundreds, no tens or twenties. There could be half a million dollars in front of him. Just like the man they'd questioned in the exit corridor had indicated, these men were engaged in a high-stakes game of Texas hold 'em and the flop had been dealt.

Two empty chairs stood away from the table, but only one of them had cards in front of it. He looked at LG, pointed to his eyes, then pointed to the closed door on the far side of the room.

The mortally wounded man slumped forward onto the table. Harvey hadn't wanted to shoot anyone, but when the guy dropped his hand out of sight, it was lights out; no other outcome was possible.

"I want nods from everyone. Do you speak English?"

Everyone did.

The guy sitting to the right of the dead man looked at the huge piles of cash on the table and pursed his lips. He obviously thought this was a robbery.

Harvey pointed his pistol at the guy. "Who else is up here?"

"No one!"

Keeping his pistol aimed at the man, he eased across the room to a spot where he could shoot directly through the closed door where LG now stood.

"If anyone's behind that door, you'd better tell me right now."

"It's just a bathroom, no one's in there."

"Check it," he said to LG.

She moved to the edge of the jamb, crouched, and turned the handle. In a quick motion, she sprang up and disappeared inside. "Clear," she called out.

"I'll be asking some questions and I expect truthful and immediate answers. Is the price of noncompliance clear to everyone?"

More nods.

"We aren't here to rob you; all we want is information." The men seemed to relax a little at hearing that. "There were two other men at this table. One of them left around five minutes ago and the other left around two minutes ago. Who left two minutes ago?"

Pursed Lips nearly stuttered when he spoke. "Mr. B. He said he'd be right back, he had to take a call."

"He left the room after answering his phone?"

"Yeah."

"Did he say anything about coming back?"

"He didn't take his money." The guy looked at the other men. "We just assumed he'd be back."

"He's not coming back," Harvey said. "Neither will the first guy who left. What does B stand for? Bustamonte?" Harvey watched the man closely. He could usually tell when someone lied to him.

"We don't know, we just call him Mr. B."

"Is there a woman up here?"

"No."

"If you're lying . . ."

"I'm not, I swear!"

"All right. Nobody makes a sound. If I hear a mouse chew cheese, somebody dies."

Harvey used the silent interval to listen for sound, heard nothing.

Now that the initial urgency was over, he could see this was a very plush room. It looked a lot like his office at First Security, Inc., only bigger and with nicer furnishings. Looking around, there had to be two hundred grand in art and furniture alone. The floor was intricately laid marble, granite, and travertine. The walls were clad with beautiful zebra wood paneling. The only current source of light in the room was a crystal chandelier directly above the table. Huge glass windows overlooked the street.

He'd seen something similar in the Gaslamp Quarter of downtown San Diego a while ago. But this place was far more lavish.

Harvey considered his options. Although they'd inflicted a lot of damage on Cornejo's operation, they didn't have their objectives: the twins. Nate had moved out of radio range, so Harv had no way to know if Tomas Bustamonte was in custody. He didn't want to risk calling his friend for an update. He was sure Nate had silenced his phone, but even a vibration at the wrong time could distract him enough to be fatal.

Interrogating these men might yield something useful if they had time.

There were two cell phones on the table, which meant there were two cell phones missing.

The man with the largest pile of money didn't have one in front of him.

"I'm going to collect everyone's phones and wallets. You." He waved his pistol toward the guy with the most cash. "Stand up slowly and take three steps back from the table. Everyone else, place your hands flat and don't move."

Keeping his hands about shoulder height, the man complied. Harv saw the outline of a phone in the guy's pocket.

He looked at LG. "Right front."

She stepped forward, liberated it, and tucked it into her waist pack.

LG didn't need to be told what to do next; she yanked the dead man from the table, toppling his chair in the process. Harv was a little surprised at her strength. The guy had to weigh close to two hundred pounds, but she dragged him across the floor easily. She frisked him, found his phone and wallet, and stashed them in her waist pack. She also found the compact revolver he'd been attempting to use.

"Kilo team, you've got company. A sedan just unloaded four men armed with AKs at the main entrance. We couldn't see the sedan approach on Stewart Street. They look like gangbangers. They're climbing the security bars."

"Copy, Delta Lead, we're on the move." There were times to fight, and times to flee, and this was the latter. Harvey didn't want to get trapped up here and have to shoot his way out of this building, night-vision advantage or not. Taking out all the overhead fluorescents in the hallways couldn't be done easily.

He looked at the men. "Pack up your cash and wait thirty seconds before leaving."

"Kilo team, another vehicle is speeding down Olympic toward this location. The four gunmen are heading for the stairwell."

Outside the gambling room, he fired three shots through the door in a direction he knew wouldn't hit anyone. That ought to make the poker players think twice about following too quickly. He whispered for LG to shadow him, sprinted down the hall to the men's restroom, and ducked inside.

"Up you go," he said. "I'm right behind you."

LG wasted no time scrambling up the ladder.

Harvey was quite literally on her heels, his face inches from her very fine-looking . . .

"Don't even think about it," she said.

"The thought never crossed my mind."

"Of course not."

Once he grabbed the rim of the opening, he hooked his boot under the top step of the ladder and brought it up with him.

He told LG to reach down and hold the ladder while he folded it. It wouldn't fit through the opening otherwise. After pulling the ladder up to the roof, he closed the hatch. The damned thing made a loud *clunk* as it locked. There was no going back at this point; the hatch could only be opened from the inside.

"We've got eyes on you, Kilo team. Good thinking. The second vehicle is turning into the east alley. You've got a brief window to descend the latticework."

Rather than click his radio or reply, Harvey issued a wave.

"It's possible those gamblers know about the roof hatch," LG said.

"Even if they do, there's no way they can jump up and grab it, not in the shape they're in. The rim's nine or ten feet above the floor. I'm not worried. We'll be long gone by then. I'm sure Delta Lead will let us know if anyone follows us up here."

"Copy that, Kilo Two."

At the west side of the building, they looked over the edge at the latticework. He didn't think it looked all that inviting. In fact, it looked like a five-hundred-foot vertical cliff.

"We don't need to rush this," he said.

"I'm okay. I did a little rock climbing in college."

"I'm assuming you don't mean those wimpy artificial walls?"

"Grand Tetons."

"Why am I not surprised. An athletic sorority girl like you? A rock climber? I can totally see it."

"I'll take that as a compliment."

He grinned. "You know what *tétons* means in French?"

"Good grief, is that all you guys ever think about?"

"Pretty much."

"If you two don't mind the interruption, one of the two gunmen from the car in the east alley's on the move. He's circling the building to the south. We think he's heading for the main entrance. The other guy's running toward Olympic. Looks like they're bracketing the building."

Throwing caution aside, they made the descent. If they got caught on these pipes, they'd be toast. The first part was a little tricky because the top of the latticework ended three feet below the parapet. Fortunately, the pipes were a few inches out from the wall, which allowed them to get good footholds and handholds. Once they got the hang of it, it wasn't tough going.

"The four gunmen who entered the showroom are now heading up the stairwell. The gunman running toward Olympic stopped. He's checking out the blood trails."

"Kilo Three, cover my six." He dropped the last eight feet to the sidewalk and sprinted to the corner of the building to get eyes into the south alley.

Holding his assault rifle in one hand, a young man ran directly toward him.

He maintained position, peering around the corner with one eye.

When his opponent closed to ten yards, he stepped out and fired two center-mass shots.

The gunman spun, tumbled, and lay still.

Harvey motioned LG over. "We're going to find out how fast you can run. We're making an all-out sprint to the Expo rail line. We'll turn east from there and come back for Nate's Lincoln. I don't want it around when the cops arrive."

They took off.

"Delta Lead, how long before that other guy clears the corner of Olympic onto Stewart?"

"Ten seconds; we recommend you hide between the parked cars."

"Affirm, we'll do that, but I want to put more distance between us and the dealership. Give me a five-second warning."

"Copy, but don't cut it too close . . . Stand by . . . Now! Get cover."

They cut to the right and crouched between some sort of small import and an SUV. He lifted his head high enough to see the gunman turn the corner and race down the sidewalk toward the main entrance.

"Follow my lead," Harvey said. "He doesn't know we're here. If he heads into the south alley to check his downed man, we'll take off again and stay in the street. The line of parked cars will give us some cover."

"Kilo team, we'll lose sight of the gunman if he does that. We won't be able to warn you before he reappears."

"Short of slaughtering him, we're low on options." Harvey didn't like killing needlessly. It wasn't his thing, or Nate's.

"Understood. You've got eyes on him?"

"Yes." As the gunman closed the distance, Harvey saw how he was dressed.

LG must've come to the same conclusion because she whispered, "Gangbanger."

"Yep. It explains why there are so many of them."

"Why don't we just shoot him?"

"No need."

"If you say so."

Sure enough, the gunman stopped at the corner and looked into the alley. Harvey listened while the guy called the dead man's name and got no response.

When the gunman entered the south alley, he said, "We're moving." They resumed their sprint toward the Expo line. Harvey thought it would take the guy at least ten seconds to check his downed colleague and return to Stewart Street. "Stand by, Kilo Three, we're taking cover again."

For the second time, they crouched between parked cars.

Waiting for the gunman to reappear, Harvey thought about LG's comment, knowing Delta Lead had heard it. He understood her indifference about killing these men because he felt it too. But Cantrell was right. The more power a person had, the more accountable they had to be. Could he have justified shooting the other gangbanger? Absolutely. Would he have to answer for it? No. In the wrong hands, that level of power became intoxicating, even addictive. Nate and he had experienced it firsthand as a sniper team. It turned his stomach thinking about it. Just because this guy was a worthless criminal today, it didn't mean he'd always be that way. It wasn't his role to play God. People could, and did, turn their lives around. As much as Hollywood lionized it, there was no glory in the business of killing—just ask any combat soldier with a conscience.

They waited a full thirty seconds for the gunman to return. When he didn't, they resumed their sprint south.

In the distance from their right, deep booms of gunfire rang out.
Nate!

***

This wasn't the man who'd kidnapped LG's husband in Caracas. It was
also clear this man was younger than Tomas by at least ten years.

"You're not Tomas Bustamonte," Nathan said. "Who are you?"

The man coughed up blood and grimaced. "Brother."

"You're Tomas and Ursula's brother?"

The man nodded.

"Why did you make me shoot you? You could've given up."

"No . . . she'd kill me."

Nathan put a hand on the man's shoulder. "What's your name?"

"A-Ashton." The man shivered.

"Where is she? Where's Ursula?" It was worth a try.

"Mounnnn—"

The man's eyes became unfocused, then lifeless. Their brother had
effectively committed suicide rather than face Ursula's wrath. The word
chilling came to mind.

The wail of a second siren penetrated the neighborhood.

Nathan searched the man, found a wallet, a cell phone, and some
keys. Without examining them, he put the items in his waist pack,
then used his phone to take a picture of Ashton's face. After checking
the picture for clarity, he stowed the 1911, grabbed Ashton's collar, and
dragged him over to the hedge paralleling the building.

He hefted the body over the hedge and placed it where it couldn't
be seen from the street. A quick scan with the TI confirmed no one
was around. He returned to the vehicle with the broken windows and
picked up his expended brass. Using his ski mask, he did his best to
sweep the broken glass under the car. He couldn't get all of it, but took
care of the biggest pieces.

Time to go.

He wanted to run, but if anyone happened to see him, it would bring the police into this area. The first officers to arrive should be tied up at the lowrider. At a brisk pace, he walked south, back toward the Expo line.

The approaching sirens made him extremely uneasy.

Although tempted to circle back and get within radio range, he decided that was the wrong direction to go. Once Harv left the dealership, his friend would make contact via cell. Speaking of, he needed to call Cantrell using the encrypted phone.

She answered on the fourth ring. "I've got you over a click away from the dealership."

"Any word from Harv and LG?"

"Not yet. It's my next call. What's your situation?"

Being as brief and concise as possible, Nathan recounted the foot chase, the gunfight with the gangbangers, and the final shootout with Ashton Bustamonte several blocks away.

Cantrell said, "It's surprising to learn that Tomas and Ursula had a younger brother. There's nothing in their files about him. I'll have our people look into it. He might have lived in the area."

"Maybe we can use this to bait the twins."

"It's a possibility."

"You wanted us to disrupt Cornejo's dealership—consider the mission accomplished. The showroom is absolutely trashed. Multiple fatalities. If Tomas and Ursula weren't in the dealership, it's safe to assume they know about the attack. Or will shortly."

"I'm counting on it," she said.

"I've got Ashton's cell phone, but I haven't looked at it yet. I wouldn't be surprised to see recent texts or calls to Tomas or Ursula."

"Clear the immediate area first. I'll be in touch."

The call ended.

Nathan angled across the Expo tracks and looked at the intersection with the shot-up lowrider.

Nothing had changed.

Seeing the carnage in retrospect felt wholly different, a harsh reminder of how deadly he still was.

He pulled off his NV visor and goggles and stashed them in his waist pack. There was nothing he could do about his black tactical clothing but duck into the shadows should a police cruiser arrive.

Avoiding streets, he made his way south toward I-10. Every twenty yards or so, he formulated a new escape plan, by looking for shadowy places, walls, or parked vehicles to hide behind.

He now counted at least four sirens coming from every direction. To err on the safe side, he decided to put more distance between himself and the Expo crossing.

A few dogs around the neighborhood answered the sirens, but he didn't notice any lights coming on; this wasn't an area where sirens were uncommon, but the automatic gunfire was.

At the next intersection, he turned south and resumed his trek toward I-10. He found an alley with parked cars and settled in for the wait.

How many men had he killed tonight? He leaned his head against the wall and tried to block the thought pattern.

It didn't work.

Nine. Nine men. It didn't matter if they were "all bad." The number was sobering and the day was just beginning. Them or him. As true as that was, it didn't make it any easier. Although their operation had disrupted Cornejo's empire, and possibly yielded a means of finding the twins, it had come at a high price. Making matters worse, the convergence of cops into the area meant Harv and LG had to abandon the dealership or risk being trapped inside. Despite what he'd told Cantrell, it was hard to think of their mission as a success.

He checked his phone to make sure it was still set to vibrate. It was fairly dark in this alley, so he donned his NV visor but left it pivoted up.

Nathan's respite was short lived.

Coming from his right, he heard running footsteps, at least three or four strong.

Had Cornejo's goons tracked him? No way. He'd made sure he wasn't followed. He took a deep breath, reached into his waist pack, and grabbed the butt of his Sig. He now wished he'd chosen a tighter gap between the parked cars.

It only took a few seconds to realize the footsteps were getting louder. Who in the hell was running around out here, especially now? They seemed to be running toward the action, not away from it. It had to be street punks. He'd seen some tagging in the area. With a little luck, they'd race past without seeing him.

Willing himself to be invisible, he held perfectly still. Two young men ran past his position, followed by a third who—

Turned his head.

Crap. Nathan knew he'd been seen.

The kids' footsteps stopped.

A head slowly appeared around the edge of a parked car to his left.

"Hey, someone's in the alley."

"Who is it?"

"How'm I supposed to know? Just some dude sitting between the cars."

Nathan evaluated the kid who'd found him. African American. Athletic shoes. Pants halfway down his scrawny ass. Black tank top. Purple headband. Definitely the look of a gangbanger. Possibly even armed and dangerous.

"Spooner, come check this clown out."

Nathan couldn't believe his luck. What were the odds? Not that bad, given the automatic gunfire and police activity. Maybe these three were planning to check out the action. If they'd arrived at the intersection where he'd engaged the lowrider before the police, they would've scored some fully automatic Kalashnikovs. Not a bad night's haul.

The first two kids came back, both apparently Hispanic.

"What the fuck you doing in our alley?" the biggest kid asked.

"Just chilling for the night," Nathan said.

"Well, you picked the wrong place, old man."

Old man? He felt his blood pressure increase. *Well, relatively speaking,* he supposed. None of these kids could be more than eighteen years old.

"That's a nice night-vision rig. We'll give you five bucks for it."

"Add three zeroes and it's yours."

"It's already ours. What else you got?"

"Anger-management issues," Nathan said.

"Say what?"

"I'll speak slowly and use small words. I. Get. Mad."

The youngest kid said, "Come on, Spooner, let's leave this guy alone. He ain't hurting nothing."

"He's in our alley and he ain't paid the rent."

"Here's the deal," Nathan said. "I'm giving you five seconds to walk away. After that, I *will* hurt you. I'm in no mood to deal with a bunch of worthless street rats."

"Spooner, let's go, man. This guy's nuts."

"Fuck him. I'm going to teach his white ass a lesson." Spooner pulled a compact semi-auto from his pocket.

Before the kid could point it at him, Nathan had his pistol out of the waist pack.

He fired a single round, driving a bullet through the kid's bicep. The kid's gun clacked on the asphalt.

The kid on Nathan's right reached into his sweatshirt pocket, presumably to pull a gun.

Without taking his eyes from Spooner, Nathan shot the second kid in the shoulder, then sprang to his feet, dropped the first kid with an elbow to the jaw and swept his foot, toppling the second kid. He followed up with a blow to the side of the second kid's head, driving his face into the asphalt. Dazed, the second kid didn't resist as Nathan checked the pocket and removed the gun. He stashed the weapon alongside Ashton's 1911.

Everything had happened inside five seconds.

The youngest kid backed away with his hands up.

He waved his Sig. "Have a seat against the wall and put your hands on top of your head."

The kid obeyed. "Are you going to kill me?"

"Do I have a reason to kill you?"

He shook his head. "I didn't want this fight."

Nathan kept his Sig pointed at the trio and picked up the other handgun.

He addressed the first kid he'd shot. "In a few more seconds, the adrenaline rush will wear off and you'll experience an intense stinging ache. The stinging is from your torn flesh, the ache is from your shattered humerus bone. Don't worry, I purposely missed the brachial artery." He looked at the other kid. "You'll be okay too. I avoided the clavicle and scapula."

The kid who'd drawn on him was holding his upper arm, trying to look tough. But the pain and fear in his eyes alleged otherwise.

"Let me give you three a little advice. Never pick a fight with someone you aren't 100 percent sure you can beat. You assumed I'd cave and not fight back. Bad assumption."

None of them said anything.

"Your phones and wallets, hand them over. Slowly. Any quick movements will result in more flesh wounds."

The two kids with bullet wounds had some trouble, but they managed to comply.

"Are they passcode-locked?"

They looked at each other, then nodded.

"Give me the codes."

They reluctantly did, and Nathan verified each code worked, then wrote their passcodes down in the notes section of his own phone.

Although sirens still wailed in the distance, his suppressed shots hadn't been loud. The police had no reason to converge on this location.

"Now I know who you guys are and where you live. Here's the deal; if you give me your word you'll listen to what I have to say, I won't kill you." He didn't intend to terminate them, but he wanted them to believe otherwise.

Again, they looked at each other with confused expressions.

"Do I have your word? I need to hear everyone say it. Raise a hand, and repeat after me: 'I give you my word I'll listen.'"

When they didn't say anything, Nathan skipped a bullet off the ground next to the biggest kid. Across the alley, the bullet plowed into the concrete block wall and zinged away.

"Repeat after me: 'I give you my word I'll listen.'"

They all said it.

"Thank you. You're getting a second chance tonight, something you may not have received from anyone else. It's just you, me, and the alley. You understand I could kill you right now and get away with it?"

They nodded tightly.

"All the police activity you're hearing? It's because of me. If you know a crew that drives a white lowrider with blacked-out windows, you won't be seeing them ever again."

"What happened to your face?" the youngest one asked.

"I'll leave that to your imagination. Now, listen up. This path you're on has two outcomes. Your death or your imprisonment. Sooner or later, one of those two things is gonna happen. It doesn't matter what led to your involvement with a gang in the first place. Maybe you're bored or want easy money. Maybe your parents are dirtbags or absent, or maybe you're just pissed off at the world in general. All of that's just an excuse for bad behavior. What matters are the choices you make. And you *do* have choices. Are you guys in high school?"

"We don't go."

"The way you save your lives is to go back to class and get part-time jobs after school. If you do that, the leaders of your gang will let you out. It's not something they tell you, but I happen to know for a fact it's true. They may try to convince you not to do it, but they won't force you to stay in the gang. Especially at your age. You've taken bullets. They're your badges of honor. Use them to turn your lives around."

"Like you care," the youngest one said.

"You're alive, aren't you? Now, as far as I'm concerned, our deal is confirmed. You listened. I didn't kill you. One more thing. I want you to think about attending church this coming Sunday. Don't worry: it doesn't cost anything. Giving is optional. I'll bet there's one within easy walking distance. Think you can do that?"

More tight nods, but he gave that suggestion low odds. He knew they wanted to bug out.

"All gunshot wounds are reported to the police. What are you going to tell them?"

"We got nailed in a drive-by. We didn't see nothing."

"Don't try to tough it out. Tiny pieces of clothing in your wounds can fester and cause life-threatening infections. Get patched up at a hospital and take the antibiotics the doctor prescribes for you." He waved his pistol. "Now get out of *my* alley before I change my mind."

Looking like a band of refugees, they shuffled away.

Nathan went the opposite direction and watched them from the shadow of a rusting van. The youngest one looked over his shoulder. If he were a betting man, he'd put money on that kid.

CHAPTER 23

Cantrell shook her head in amazement. Although Nathan's radio couldn't pick up Delta Lead's transmissions, the reverse wasn't true. Delta had a powerful receiving antenna that picked up every word he'd said. She'd listened to the exchange via an encrypted cell-phone link.

She'd always believed McBride had a good heart, despite the living hell he'd gone through at the hands of a sadistic madman. How many people would have any shred of humanity left after that?

Part of her wished he'd killed the young thugs. They had it coming *and* countless taxpayer dollars would've been saved. She didn't think of herself as indifferent, but she hated gangbangers with a passion. She'd been fifteen or sixteen when she'd taken a beating from three girls who'd been associated with a street gang. Apparently, she'd looked at Vanessa's "boyfriend" wrong so they'd ambushed her on her way home from school. The beating hadn't been nearly as vicious as the obscene and hate-filled racial slurs they'd spewed. Something had snapped in her that day, and she'd known she would devote the rest of her life to fighting back against bullies and thugs.

The story didn't end there. A week later, she'd sneaked out of her bedroom window and ridden her bike over to Vanessa's house. Staying in the shadows, she'd dragged a garden hose out to the curb and inserted the nozzle into Vanessa's pimped-out Camry. It took a few attempts to get it positioned on top of the dashboard because the side window wasn't cracked more than an inch.

Satisfied with the location of the nozzle, she'd returned to the faucet and slowly cranked the valve about a quarter of the way so the nozzle wouldn't jet off the dashboard. A return trip to the Camry confirmed everything was good. Riding home, she'd felt justice had been served. Witnessing the meltdown at school the following day had been nothing short of glorious.

Now that she had a complete update from Delta, she called the encrypted phone.

"Are LG and Harv okay?" he asked immediately.

"They're fine but the twins weren't in the building."

"I thought I'd chased Tomas Bustamonte out of there, but he turned out to be—"

"Tomas's brother. I heard."

Nathan paused, and Cantrell knew he was absorbing the fact that she'd also listened in on his interchange with the gang kids.

"Square one?" he asked.

"Not exactly. We're working the problem."

"What's my best ETA on a pickup?"

"Five minutes, give or take. Harvey and Genneken should be back at their vehicle inside two minutes. The FBI's going to take the lead on the ensuing investigation at Santa Monica Exotics and DNI Benson will be personally involved. He's already called Director Lansing."

"What about Ashton Bustamonte?"

"I'm hoping Delta can recover the body before the police find it."

"I doubt anyone saw the action." Nathan described the exact location of Ashton's body. "I'm sending you the photo of him now."

"I'll look for it," she said. "Hang on, Nathan. I've got to take Delta's call. I'll be right back. Stay on the line."

***

Cantrell's call went silent and Nathan found himself thinking about the street kids. He'd spared them a meaningless death. Perhaps it was his faith, or something else, but there'd been intelligence in the youngest kid's eyes—a willingness to listen. Despite how society defined them—and how he'd initially seen them—they weren't just stupid punks. Misguided, yes. But not stupid. Nathan never judged people by the color of their skin, only by their actions. Perhaps they'd be able to do the same thing.

He found another place to hide in the loading dock of a medium-sized building and sat atop the stairs. Something LG had said kept floating around in his head. No, it was something her husband had said, about their German shepherds. He remembered now. Glen had been concerned about the dogs. He'd asked her to get them out of the house. Nathan hadn't thought it all that unusual—many people thought of their pets as children. He would've had the same concern, given similar circumstances. Leaving Grant and Sherman at the mercy of armed intruders wouldn't sit well with him. Although tactically trained, they'd have no chance against bullets.

Cantrell came back on. "About that pickup: Work your way over to the Twentieth Street on-ramp to the westbound I-10. Find a place to hide and wait for Harvey and Genneken. I'm sending them to the same spot. If a helicopter shows up, use the overpass for cover. Where are the keys to your car?"

"On top of the right front tire."

"A member of Delta will drive it to your location, followed by a second vehicle. He'll flash the high beams three times, pull to the curb, and get out. Put everything you collected on the shoulder of the road.

Do not approach your car until he's collected everything and returned to the other vehicle. Once Delta leaves, get in your car and wait for Harvey and Genneken to arrive."

"What happened to surveillance only?" he asked.

"It's been temporarily suspended, unless you'd prefer to walk out of the area."

He smiled. "Negative on that. While I have you, I'm going to try Bustamonte's phone."

"If it's passcode-locked, don't attempt to unlock it."

"I won't . . . It's not locked."

"Is it an iPhone?"

"Six plus. Exactly like mine, but everything's in Spanish."

"Good thing you're fluent."

"Good thing."

"Check the passcode settings."

He was already doing it, knowing the iOS program could be set for a delayed lock. If it was, they'd be out of business if he didn't keep the phone constantly active. He opened the settings and navigated to the screen.

"It's asking for a passcode to continue, which probably means it's using a passcode."

"The iOS program has multiple delay options."

"Yeah, it does. Hang on, I'm checking mine . . . One minute, five minutes, fifteen minutes, one hour, and four hours."

"You'll have to keep after it so it doesn't lock. I think we can safely assume it's not set for immediately or one minute. It's probably set for five or fifteen minutes."

Nathan realized there was another way, but it held some risk. "At a full sprint, I'm only about two minutes from Bustamonte's body."

"His fingerprint," she said.

"Yeah, that's what I'm thinking. Hang on, let me check something first." On his own phone, he navigated to the Touch ID and Passcode screen. The phone asked for his six-digit passcode to continue. He tried using his fingerprint to get past this screen, but it didn't work. The phone wouldn't respond. "It won't accept a fingerprint to get past the passcode screen. I just tried it on my own phone."

"Me too."

"We've got three attempts to unlock it. It wouldn't hurt to try the code from the door at Santa Monica Exotics."

"Okay, give it a try," she said.

Nathan had a good memory when it came to numbers and sequences. He didn't have a mathematical mind, but he remembered patterns. And the punch-key code they'd used to gain access into the showroom had a pattern. One-three-six-four-seven-nine. He tried it and the phone told him: *1 Failed Passcode Attempt.*

"It didn't work. We've got one more free try. Any ideas?"

"Not really. It could be anything."

"I'm going to try the numerical pattern in reverse."

"If that doesn't work, don't try a third time. Just keep the phone active so it doesn't lock."

Nathan ran the pattern the other direction. Three-one-four-six-nine-seven. "We're in! We didn't need this break, but it sure makes our job easier."

"Good work. See if he's been in touch with his siblings, and take a few minutes to review the way he texts. Punctuation, lack of caps, emojicons, favorite words, et cetera . . . If Tomas or Ursula send a text, we want the response to look as normal as possible."

"I'll do that."

"Keep Bustamonte's phone, but turn everything else over to Delta Lead. Call me right away if the phone receives a text. Obviously, you can't answer any calls."

"No problem. Do you want the street kids' phones as well?"

"Yes. They might contain something we can use, especially if they're connected to the gangbangers who attacked you."

Each of the kids' phones had a different protective case so he told her which passcode went with each phone.

"Got it," she said.

"I haven't thanked you for helping us, Rebecca. We're grateful for the support."

"Even though we don't have the twins in custody, we've got some valuable intel. Ashton's phone may lead us to them."

Nathan wouldn't mention the body count getting to this point. She knew how he felt about it.

"By the way," she continued, "about those kids in the alley?"

Nathan didn't know what her reaction would be. Would she reprimand him, or compliment him?

"Admirable, Mr. McBride. Quite admirable. Who knows? Maybe one of those kids will go on to become president. I might also win the lottery, but you can't win if you don't play."

"I'm glad you approve. Seriously, though, thanks again for the support. It certainly made the operation a whole lot easier."

"From what Delta reported, your operation was anything *but* easy. Keep your head down. We'll talk again soon."

***

Harvey and LG were still on foot, but he knew returning to Matthew's Heating and Air Conditioning kept growing less and less likely. From the sound of things, every cop in LA was converging. He also heard the blat-like horn of a fire engine. Firefighters were often the first to arrive at emergencies.

Delta Lead's voice broke in. *"Kilo Two, turn on your cell, initiate contact with Kilo One. Rendezvous with him at the westbound I-10 on-ramp at Twentieth Street. Power off your radios. We'll bring your vehicle to you. We know where the keys are."*

"Copy, Delta Lead. Thanks for your help tonight."

His radio clicked in response. He wished he could thank them in person, but knew it would never happen. He and LG turned off their radios.

"You did well back there," Harvey said.

"Hey, the plumbing may be old, but it still flows."

He half-laughed. They needed the stress relief.

The 20th Street on-ramp seemed a smart place to meet. There'd presumably be an overpass nearby to help elude overhead surveillance. He kept looking behind for a tail, but no one followed them.

"At least McBride's okay," LG said. "I had a bad visual when I heard the gunfire."

"You and me both."

"Does he ever talk about Nicaragua?"

"Not really. He's put it behind him. Why do you ask?"

"I saw him come out of a nightmare. How can he put what happened behind him with dreams like that?"

"You have to understand who he is. He's forgiven Montez."

"No way."

"That surprises you?"

"Uh, yeah."

"Forgiving Montez is for Nathan's benefit."

"I'd never be able to do it."

"In a nutshell, Nathan feels gratitude, not entitlement."

"Gratitude? For being nearly tortured to death?"

"For surviving it. No amount of money or reparation could ever make Nate whole after what he went through. Not then, not now. Forgiveness doesn't require reparation. No one owes him anything."

"He really feels that way?"

"Absolutely. We both do. Nate is one of the most generous people I know. He's given millions over the years to church missions and military charities."

"How rich is he, if you don't mind me asking?"

"We share our wealth. We're equal partners in our security business and financial investments. He doesn't really care about money. I handle all of it."

"I think what you guys share is beyond special and that level of trust is rare, but you dodged my question."

"Let's just say it's in the mid-eight-digit range."

She whistled softly. "And he doesn't care about money? What about his house in La Jolla?"

"It's more of an investment than anything else. He prefers to live in his Clairemont home. It's tiny in comparison. I bought the lot on Mount Soledad for him right after we retired."

"I understand why McBride got out, but why did you? You could've stayed in."

"Nate was in bad shape, physically and mentally."

"You gave up your career to help him." It wasn't a question.

"He once told me he would've killed himself had I not been there."

"I envy you guys, being that close. How long has he been with Holly?"

"A few years now."

"What's she like?"

"A lot like you, actually. Except for the hair."

"Hey, what's wrong with my hair?"

"Nothing. I have to admit, it's an alluring look."

"You really think so?"

"Absolutely."

"Glen liked it . . . I still can't believe he's dead."

"You got kicked in the teeth, but you did well tonight."

"I think I'm more angry than sad."

"It's normal to be angry; don't worry about it too much. If you're still angry a few months from now, start worrying."

"Is it iniquitous to want Ursula dead for murdering Glen?"

"Iniquitous? No. She's a wicked person and the world won't miss her."

"In the dealership, I felt . . . I guess I don't know what I felt."

"It's okay, LG. Your emotions are in turmoil. We've both been in the company shrink's office. Work through it. Don't force your feelings; they have to play out over time."

"Do you feel bad about killing the man at the poker table?"

"Yes."

"Even though he would've killed us, given the chance?"

"Again, yes. At the moment of truth, when it's kill or be killed, there isn't time to debate ethics."

They walked in silence for a spell.

"Are you okay?" he asked.

"Yeah, I'm just really conflicted right now."

"Welcome to our world. Nate and I fight a constant battle of good versus evil. And not just externally."

"Yeah," she said. "I got that impression."

***

One of the confiscated phones in Nathan's waist pack came to life with a single ding. He found the phone with the lit screen and was glad to see it was Ashton's.

The small bubble notification said it was from Tomas Bustamonte. In Spanish it read:

```
what the fuck is going on down there?
```

He was tempted to respond but knew he should call Cantrell first. He couldn't take too long, though. Tomas would expect an answer within sixty seconds or so.

Nathan dictated a text to Cantrell using his encrypted phone:

```
Call me ASAP Thomas just texted ash tons
phone.
```

He didn't bother correcting the misspellings and tapped Send.

The image of a cell-phone addict invaded his thoughts. Now wasn't the time to have his head bowed in phone prayer, though it made for natural enough cover, he supposed. He glanced up and looked around, clearing his immediate area. He was almost to a point where he'd need to turn east toward 20th. If he kept going straight, he'd run into the freeway's fence. He couldn't see the source, but a wailing cruiser approached from the right and it was definitely on the freeway.

Since an on-ramp existed at 20th, there might be an off-ramp too. In which case that cop is going to come screaming down the street. Sure enough, the source of the siren slowed its lateral movement, then began to grow in volume.

He stayed in the alley and peered around the corner of a building. No more than a hundred feet away, a CHP cruiser howled across the intersection and disappeared from sight. Like a passing train's, its high-pitched shriek changed tone as it headed north. Once it reached the lowrider, the state trooper would have to secure the scene and wouldn't be able to leave until backup arrived.

His phone vibrated with Cantrell's call.

No more than twenty seconds had gone by since Ashton's phone had received the text.

"I just got a text from Tomas."

"What's it say?"

He read it to her. "We'll figure out how to answer it, but a state trooper just sped past my position and he'll arrive at some bodies in a few seconds. Tell Delta they'll need to approach Ashton's location from the north and avoid the Expo crossing at Twentieth Street."

"I've got them on hold. Be right back."

Again, his phone went silent.

When she came back on, he read aloud the last five texts between Ashton and Tomas—a series of boring messages until tonight, when Tomas had warned Ashton to flee the dealership immediately—through the roof exit, if possible.

"Send this: 'the place is trashed I'm on foot and I can't get back to my car, what do you want me to do?'"

One of the things he liked about Cantrell? The woman's decisiveness. There was no hesitation or delay in her response.

"Okay, hang on, I'm going to use the dictation feature." He touched the little microphone icon, heard the tone, and dictated the message in Spanish. "I guess we're going to experience a moment of truth here. We should be thankful he didn't call."

"If he doesn't like our response, he might very well do that."

Ashton's phone chimed. "Here we go. It says: 'get your ass up to ACH I don't care if you have to take a two hour cab ride.'"

"Send this as a response," she said. "'Be there as soon as I can cops are everywhere.'"

Nathan dictated the text and sent it.

"Does ACH mean anything to you?" Cantrell asked.

"No, I can't think of anything off the top of my head. It could be anything. The name of a business or restaurant, or someone's house. Anything."

Another chime sounded off and he translated the message for her.

```
We leave today. I'm suspending operations.
There've been attacks on corn hole's
properties all over the place. We'll be home
by midnight.
```

"Pure gold," she said. "Send this: 'on my way.'"

"Doing it now." He typed the short message.

"We'll get to work with the info on our end. Put me on hold, and conference Harvey into the call. His end won't be secure, so no names."

He dialed Harv's number, realizing his friend would see *unknown* or *blocked*.

Come on, Harv! Answer. Put two and two together.

Nathan heard a click, then sirens blaring in the background, but no one spoke. "It's me," he said.

"It's damned good to hear your voice," Harv said.

"Likewise. Hang on, I'm on hold with our friend on the Potomac. Your end of this call isn't secure, so let's avoid using her name. I'm going to conference you in."

Nathan merged the calls and asked if Harv was still there.

He was.

Without using names, Cantrell filled Harvey in on Nathan's gunning down of Ashton Bustamonte and the texts that Nathan had exchanged—as "Ashton"—with Tomas.

"You've lived your whole life in Southern California," Nathan said to Harv. "What do the initials ACH mean to you?"

"The only thing I can think of that makes any sense is the Angeles Crest Highway. When we were kids, we would go up there for skiing trips and we always called it ACH."

"Where's the Angeles Crest Highway?" Cantrell asked.

"It winds its way up to the San Gabriel Mountains just north of the Los Angeles basin. Once it leaves the valley, there's not a lot of development along the route. I'm remembering some restaurants and roadside businesses, but nothing major. The time frame is right. From this area, it's probably two hours, plus or minus."

"That's good enough," she said. "Echo Four, disconnect and call Echo Five back in two minutes."

There was no sound as Harv left the call.

"Okay, Nathan, we're on this. We'll see if we can find something up there in Cornejo's real-estate portfolio. What do you guys have with you, armament-wise?"

"We've got my Remington 700 sniper rifle, along with an M1A and M4, both equipped with powered scopes. I brought three .40 caliber Sigs, but they're not suppressed. We also brought our ghillie suits. We didn't know where or if we'd need them, so we brought both desert and woodland colors."

"Once Harvey and Genneken get there, jump onto the freeway and stage a few miles away. We're giving the next phase of your operation high priority. I'll get back to you quickly."

"We're here for you, Rebecca." Nathan tried to put a positive tone in his voice, but so many people had died tonight already and, from the sound of things, the count would only increase.

"Use the downtime to question Genneken again. I want to know why Cornejo ordered the assault on her. He obviously thinks she's got something on him. Find out what it is."

"We'll try again, but she's already told us she doesn't know anything."

"Keep after it."

The call went dark.

Nathan sprinted across a street with a landscaping strip and realized it was Olympic. He could hear the freeway directly ahead.

Right on cue, his phone vibrated.

"I've got you on speaker," Harv said.

"We're on an open cell line, so let's not use our Potomac friend's name. I'm not worried about our names, but let's avoid using hers. When was the last time you were up the Angeles Crest Highway?" he asked.

"It's been years."

"LG?"

"I've never been up there."

"Good place for the twins to hide out?" Nathan asked.

"Sure, I suppose," Harv said. "I'd feel a whole lot better if we could review some satellite images before we go charging into another . . . situation."

"Me too. Good thing we took the mountain-warfare training course at Pickel Meadows. There could be snow up there. Probably is."

"Need I remind you of how long ago that was?"

"I think pterodactyls were flying."

"We don't have cold-weather gear and all the stores are closed. Too bad we can't stop at a sporting-goods place or a ski shop and pick up some white outfits."

Maybe we can, Nathan thought. "What's your ETA to the on-ramp?"

"We're in an alley heading your way. Without running, I'm guessing five or six minutes, assuming we don't have to evade any police cruisers."

"Well, somebody *did* shoot at me with fully automatic Kalashnikovs in the heart of Santa Monica. I suppose that warrants some sort of response. What'd you find upstairs in the dealership?"

"The other four members of the briefcase crew were inside a really plush suite on the third floor. Remember that pimped-out place in the Gaslamp? This one was bigger and better. We totally surprised them in the middle of their poker game. They had no clue anything had happened down below. Ashton left them there after taking a call." Harv recounted the arrival of more armed men and their hasty retreat from the building.

"Casualties?"

"One of the briefcase crew made a move for a gun, a fatal mistake. The other three became quite complacent after that."

"I found the text where Tomas told Ashton to skedaddle and not look back. Ashton didn't bother to tell his fellow gamblers about our raid."

"Sounds like he's as cold as his brother," Harv said.

"The clock's ticking. Tomas will be expecting his brother to arrive within the time frame given."

"It's a curvy mountain road. It might take longer than two hours. I suppose it depends how far up the property is."

"At least we won't have to fight rush-hour traffic."

"We could be facing more mercenaries where the twins are holed up. On second thought, if the twins think their hiding place is secure, we could be looking at fairly even odds."

"That raises a question. If they thought Santa Monica Exotics wasn't discoverable, why'd they have all the firepower standing by?"

"You mean inside or the extra firepower that showed up?"

"I don't know," Nathan said. "Both, I guess."

"The inside muscle makes sense. They had a boatload of cash. They must have known the raid on LG failed and they definitely know about the other raids our Potomac friend's been unleashing tonight. They could've anticipated an attack at the dealership and called in reinforcements. The timing smelled like an ambush. The gunmen could've been staged, ready to attack on a moment's notice."

"That makes the most sense."

"If our friend can't find anything on ACH, we might be out of business."

"Have faith, old friend," said Nathan. "Plus, her people are going to examine the contents of Ashton's wallet. It might have something useful."

"Good deal. Oh, for the record, I should say I'm fully comfortable in combat with LG."

"Thank you," she said in the background.

"Coming from you, that's high praise." He knew Harv's comment wasn't meant to patronize her. She didn't need it. Still, he sensed a coiled rattlesnake. He supposed he'd feel the same way. If someone murdered Harv and he knew who did it, they'd be marked for death.

LG spoke up again. "There's going to be fresh snow up there for sure. The weather we've been getting over the last few days covered all of Southern California."

"Unless we can get our hands on some cold-weather gear," Harv said, "we're looking at limited time in the elements."

"Nothing's open at this hour, unfortunately."

"Since when has that ever stopped you guys?" said LG.

"Are we talking about what I think we're talking about?"

"We're facing a national-security threat," Nathan said. "I think we can bend the rules a little bit and liberate some cold-weather clothing."

"You mean steal it," said Harv.

"Steal is such a harsh word. I prefer to think of it as . . . appropriating. What do you think?" he asked LG.

"I think boosting some clothes is the least of our worries."

"We'll leave an anonymous envelope of cash. Is that better?"

"Marginally," said Harv.

"Hey, I've got to go, my Lincoln just arrived, and I need to leave the confiscated stuff for Delta. I'll see you guys in a few minutes."

After the exchange, Nathan got into his car and found a note on the seat: *Vincent Beaumont sends his regards. I trust you'll keep our involvement confidential.*

He smiled. It had been Beaumont Specialists Inc. watching their backs. Outstanding. BSI's private military contractors regularly worked for the CIA. He'd have to send a case of wine to Vincent when this was over.

He called Harv back.

"We're almost there," said Harv. "We can see the on-ramp."

"My car's fifty feet around the corner."

"Glad to hear it. We can't get out of here soon enough."

"Amen to that."

CHAPTER 24

After a brief stop at a twenty-four-hour convenience store for a bath-room break, food, and hydration, Harv got them back on the highway.

They drove in silence for a few minutes. Nathan liked that LG didn't fill in the silent moments with meaningless banter.

"How're the ribs?" Nathan asked LG.

"Now that the action's over, I'm noticing them more."

"Adrenaline does that. Headache?"

"A little. When we were shooting it out in the showroom, I felt . . . I don't know . . . disembodied. Almost like I was acting in a play. It didn't seem real."

"Happens to Harv and me too."

She didn't respond.

"Anything more come to you about Cornejo? The kind of threat you pose to his presidency?"

"Nothing. I know there was a large reward on my head right after we rescued Glen, but it was purely for revenge's sake."

Harv looked in the rearview mirror. "Reward? Really?"

"Yeah. Kind of scary, actually. It was a million bucks dead and two million alive."

"Interesting," said Nathan. "I guess we have to consider the possibility that Cornejo reinstituted the bounty along with his other purges, and the twins are trying to collect it. Two million in cash is a strong motivator."

Linda said, "Man . . . I hadn't realized how hungry I was."

"In the Marines, we had an adage: Sleep when you can. It's also true for food. We should change back into our civilian clothes. Harv can change once we're parked somewhere."

"At least I've got some privacy back here," LG said. "I know how damned horny you grunts are."

He smiled at the slang term. "Don't worry, LG. We already saw everything during your rescue."

"And . . . ?"

"Let's just say it was truly memorable. I was especially impressed with your—"

Nathan's encrypted phone saved the day. He answered Cantrell's call.

"No hit on any property yet, but let's stick with the plan for now."

"Looks like we may be heading into some snow up there." Nathan told her they planned to liberate some ski clothing.

"Hold off doing that. I'll have Delta take care of it. I'm assuming you'll need one set of XXL, one set of XL, and one set of small?"

"That'll work. In white, or very light gray, preferably."

"You got it. Delta will make cell-phone contact with you within the next twenty minutes or so. We're tracking your location, so they'll rendezvous with you once they've got the ski clothing."

"Sounds good."

"Put me on speaker."

Nathan did.

"I want you three to know that DNI Benson is very appreciative of your efforts." Cantrell paused and no one interrupted her. "Linda, earlier this morning, I asked Nathan if you were able to remember anything that Cornejo might consider a threat, but I don't want you to feel overly pressured over it. DNI Benson asked if you could be holding something back and I told him no. I just want you to know my trust in you is absolute."

"Thank you, Director. The DNI would be remiss if he didn't consider the possibility of subterfuge on my part. I'm willing to come in at any time. Just give the order."

"That won't be necessary. I'll call once we've analyzed the contents of Ashton's wallet."

Nathan watched the call go abruptly dark. He was actually getting used to it. Maybe he'd develop the same technique with Harv. What's the point in saying goodbye, when the conversation's over? It's over.

"The good news is," Nathan said, "we don't have to break into a retailer to get our snow clothes. Delta's going to handle it." He thought for a moment. "Something just hit me. We need a taxi. Tomas will be expecting his brother to arrive in one."

"LAX isn't too far away," Harv suggested.

"Let's try something else first. LG, see if you can locate a big hotel somewhere along our route over to ACH, maybe in the downtown area. Harv, where does the highway start?"

"I'm pretty sure it's off the Foothill Freeway west of Pasadena. I'm checking."

"Once we find a hotel, we'll call and ask if there's a cab waiting. Maybe Delta can meet us there."

"About the twins, I have an idea," said LG. "You could send a text to Tomas saying you don't think it's wise to have the taxi take you all the way. Tomas might suggest a meeting spot."

He thought for a moment. "That's a brilliant idea, but let's give Cantrell more time. We'll use it as a fallback plan."

"Actually," Harv said, "it'll still work even if Cantrell finds the location. It might give us a better chance of taking the twins by surprise."

"I like it," he said. "LG, did you find a hotel?"

"Yes. The Ritz Carlton downtown. It's right next to the Staples Center off the 110. There should be lots of cabs around."

"I know where it is," Harv said. "I attended a huge private-security convention there a few years back."

"Good. I'll text Cantrell and let her know where we're going so she can pass it along to Delta."

***

Right after they arrived at the Ritz, Nathan received a call from Delta. Their smash-and-grab at a sporting-goods store had gone down without a hitch and they'd be arriving at the hotel within five minutes. The delivery would be handled the same way as the radios. Nathan was told to look for Delta's vehicle in an urgent-care parking lot across the street. He said he'd leave the rest of the confiscated phones and wallets from Santa Monica Exotics on the passenger seat. He thanked them again for their help.

He called Cantrell, who still hadn't located any Cornejo holdings in the San Gabriel Mountains. She thought LG's idea was tactically sound and gave them the green light to give it a try. She also agreed with the need for a taxi.

"We'll keep digging," she said. "Let me know how Tomas responds."

"Will do."

"Hopefully we'll find your destination while you're on the road."

"I'll text you after we hear back from Tomas."

Several taxis were staged near the Ritz's entrance. A valet approached and asked if they were checking in. Nathan said they were just dropping someone off but they needed to make a quick call first. With a pleasant smile, she told them to take their time, it wasn't busy.

"Okay, LG. We're going with your idea."

He dictated a message in Spanish:

```
on my way
```

Nathan found himself holding his breath and tried his best to hide it. Even though Harv was in the process of changing clothes, it didn't work—there was little his friend missed.

Harv said, "Don't worry, it's gonna work."

A long half minute later, Ashton's phone dinged.

"Here we go."

```
where are you?
```

Nathan sent:

```
Just passing downtown. It took forever to
get a taxi
```

The response was:

```
just get up here ASAP. Don't drive up to the
cabin. We'll meet you in the west parking lot
of the ski resort. Text me from the Cajon
Junction.
```

Nathan sent back a simple okay.

"We're in business. LG, you're on the ski-resort reference. Harv, does that ring any bells for you?"

"No, it's been decades since I was up there."

"No worries. Find out where Cajon Junction is."

"I think it's on the Fifteen, but I'll verify it."

"I'll update Cantrell while you guys are doing that." Nathan started a text, then decided to call.

"What's up? I only have a minute."

"A minute's all I need. Tomas wants to meet us—Ashton—at the west parking lot of a ski resort up there. He obviously doesn't want the cabbie to know where they are. We're at the Ritz Carlton, about to get a taxi. Delta will be here any minute with our cold-weather gear."

"Great news. And now for the not so great news, this isn't easy for me to say—"

Nathan saved her the trouble. "Delta's not coming up the mountain with us."

"No, they aren't."

"DNI Benson?"

"I spoke to him a few minutes ago and gave him a complete update. He didn't insist I pull the plug, but he strongly . . . suggested it. The escalation at the dealership that spilled onto the street wasn't your fault, but it's exactly what he wanted to avoid. Having said all of this, it's my decision, and my decision alone, to pull Delta and our other teams."

"Thank you for being honest, Rebecca."

"You deserve nothing less."

"We'll grab the twins when they show up to pick up their brother."

"It may not be both of them."

"If that's the case, we'll deal with it."

"The situation permitting, I want an update from the ski resort. I'll call if we find any Cornejo properties up there."

The call ended.

"Sounds like we're on our own," Harv said. "Did Benson pull the plug?"

"Cantrell."

"We knew it could happen. Besides, for Delta to be effective, they'd have to arrive well in advance to reconnoiter and set up their surveillance assets and there's no time for that. And since they can't directly support us . . ."

He finished Harv's sentence. "Their presence won't do us much good. LG, what'd you find?"

"It looks like . . . there're only two ski areas along ACH: Mount Waterman and Mountain High. I'm checking them out."

"We're looking for a 'west' parking lot. That should narrow it down."

LG nodded. "The Mount Waterman website says it's closed, didn't get enough snow from this latest storm . . . I'm checking Mountain High."

Nathan felt the pangs of pressure and took a deep breath. Patience, he told himself. They'd have an answer soon enough.

"Cajon Junction is the intersection of Highway 138 and the Fifteen," Harv said. "From what I can see on the map, it's the east terminus of ACH."

"Got it," LG said. "Mountain High's the place. East and west parking lots, and it's open for business, I mean, not now, but it will be later this morning . . . It says they can make snow. Probably why they're open and Mount Waterman isn't."

"Where's the nearest town up there?"

"Wrightwood," Harv said. "It's a few miles east of the resort. I'm looking at it on the Google Earth app."

"What's the fastest way over to the Fifteen?"

"The Ten. It runs into the Fifteen just past Ontario Airport."

"We've got enough to get moving."

"From our current location," said LG, "it's a little over eighty miles to the ski resort."

"Good to know."

After formulating their plan, Nathan asked Harv and LG for everything they'd collected from the gamblers. After Harv put on his waist pack and got out, Nathan pulled away from the entrance and drove across the street. In the urgent-care lot, he recognized the same vehicle from the on-ramp and pointed it out to LG. Bag in hand, she slid out and approached the car. She touched its hood before looking into the rear window. *Smart thinking to check for engine heat first,* he thought.

She left the bag, grabbed the bundle of clothing, and hurried back to his Lincoln.

Delta had liberated light gray ski pants and coats, which would work well. Dawn was still a couple of hours away, but they'd be cutting it pretty close. Nathan would prefer to engage the twins before the sun came up.

Leaving the lot, he sensed LG's uneasiness. She was definitely pre-occupied. He couldn't blame her. Glen's murder still weighed heavily on her. All told, she'd done extremely well, and Harv's comment about feeling comfortable with her in combat was a strong confirmation. Harv wouldn't exaggerate, even for LG's benefit.

He figured she needed another task to stave off the depression that would set in during the quiet time. "While Harv gets our cab, take a look at ACH. It would be good to know what other highways or major roads connect to it."

"No problem."

His phone vibrated once with a text from Harv.

```
I asked the driver to sit tight for a minute.
Where are you?
```

Nathan told him to use the same street they came in on and look for his Lincoln just past a white, three-story building.

Nathan watched the cab approach in his rearview mirror. "I'll be right back," he said and got out.

CHAPTER 25

Linda turned to watch. She had to admit, McBride and Fontana made a formidable pair, but they seemed overly concerned about killing. When the situation called for it, you killed. Simple as that. She didn't have any regrets about the thugs at the dealership. She supposed Glen's murder had hardened her heart. More than that. It had cemented it.

McBride approached the passenger door of the cab and got into the front seat. Nothing happened for a good minute.

Then the driver's door opened and a small African American man got out. He slammed the door in anger and began walking back toward the hotel.

McBride also got out. The cabbie turned and said something, but McBride ignored him. After McBride slid into the driver's seat of the taxi, Fontana climbed out of the backseat and hustled over to the Lincoln.

"We're in business," he said, driving away from the curb. She glanced over her shoulder and saw McBride pull in behind.

"What'd you guys say to the cabbie?" she asked.

"We gave him two choices. We told him there was a national-security emergency and we were commandeering his cab and giving him a thousand bucks for his trouble, or we were taking his cab and *not* giving him a thousand bucks. He chose the former."

"You guys keep that much cash on hand?"

"Between the two of us."

"And if he calls the cops?"

"He won't."

"How can you be so certain?"

"Because I took his wallet and told him I'd overnight it back to him if he upheld his end of the bargain. I made it very clear if he didn't, we'd be paying him a visit later and explaining the error of his ways in the form of multiple broken bones and contusions."

I'm liking these guys more and more. "When you said you were getting a cab, I didn't think you were gonna jack one."

"We're improvisers."

"If you say so."

Fontana's phone rang. He put it on speaker.

"Pull over somewhere," said McBride.

"What's going on?"

"I need to yank the meter and leave it behind. It might be GPS enabled."

"You got it."

"Let's use our radios from here on."

She turned around and watched McBride tug and yank on the device mounted on the dashboard until it came free. A second later, the device flew out the passenger's window and clunked on the sidewalk along with its severed wiring.

"I'll bet he enjoyed doing that," she said.

"No doubt."

A minute later they were speeding east on I-10.

***

Nathan knew engaging the twins in the parking lot of the ski resort held all kinds of variables, none of which could be predicted, made worse by the absence of Delta Lead. As Cantrell pointed out, there was no guarantee both twins would be there unless they planned to leave immediately after picking up their brother, which was a strong possibility. Should the taxi be waiting in the lot? He believed the answer had to be yes. Why would Ashton stand around in the cold when he could stay in a warm cab and pay the driver to wait? He wouldn't.

Nathan was too big to play the role of the cabbie. Not one in a million taxi drivers were six foot five inches tall. Somewhere before arriving at the ski resort, they'd switch vehicles. Harv would drive the cab and LG would be in the back playing the role of Ashton. And that presented its own set of variables. The arriving vehicle would undoubtedly drive right up to the taxi. It wouldn't take long for Tomas or Ursula to realize LG wasn't Ashton, especially when she didn't immediately get out. Nathan figured he'd have less than five seconds to make his move or Harv and LG could find themselves in a meat grinder. He'd go over all the logistics again and get their input before they arrived at the ski resort. He didn't feel comfortable with Harv and LG being in the taxi, but if it looked empty when the twins arrived, it could spook them into bolting.

Tough call.

They had the advantage of darkness and were going to beat the sunrise by at least an hour. Still, the Bustamontes' headlights would light up the interior of the cab like a Broadway stage unless they drove in dark, which would be a strong possibility, especially if they didn't want to draw any attention to themselves.

So many ifs.

He doubted whether either of the twins would remember what he or Harv looked like. LG was a different story. She'd changed her appearance, but they'd still recognize her. If the arriving vehicle came in with its headlights on, Nathan had a backup plan. He'd take out the tires and try to shoot the windshield in a way that didn't risk hitting any occupants. *This op would be ten times easier if we didn't need them alive,* he thought. He supposed he would've taken the job anyway, even though they weren't contract killers anymore.

Half an hour into their drive, Cantrell called and said she still hadn't identified anything. The "cabin" clue hadn't helped. The term *wild goose chase* entered Nathan's thoughts, but they didn't have anything else going. Either they'd find the twins up there or they wouldn't; there was no sense worrying about it.

Harv agreed they should text Bustamonte well past the Cajon Junction. They needed to arrive at the parking lot first if they had any chance of pulling this off. If the twins had eyes on the highway, it could be a problem. They'd see a taxi drive past well before it was supposed to be there.

From what Harv told him, the ski resort was only about a ten- to fifteen-minute drive once they turned onto ACH from the 138. Harv thought he should send the text from Wrightwood, but that also held some risk. If the twins had the same idea of arriving first, they'd see the taxi sitting in the parking lot before it should be there.

They weighed the pros and cons and decided to chance it. It made more sense to send the twenty-minute ETA text from Wrightwood, which allowed them to arrive well ahead of the twins.

They stopped at the intersection of ACH and 138, changed into their 5.11 Tactical clothes, and then donned their ski outfits. Nathan's was a little snug, but manageable. They took a moment to view the ski resort on Google Earth. The resort was actually two separate ski areas along ACH. West Base and East Base. They were headed to the West Base's parking lot. The looping access road up to the parking lot, ski area, and lodge had the shape of an upside-down coffee cup, connecting to the highway in two places. For clarity, they named the two access roads. East loop and west loop. Approaching from Wrightwood, they'd use the east loop.

After switching vehicles, they resumed their drive.

As far as Nathan could see, the skies were clear. He rolled the window down a bit and freezing air rushed in. He welcomed its bite.

He couldn't pinpoint it, but something bothered him about Bustamonte's latest messages. He knew he shouldn't do it while driving, but he'd break his steadfast rule in this instance. He looked back at the recent texts, comparing them to the messages Tomas had sent before the car-dealership raid.

Tomas's tone was different, now: calmer, less harsh and vulgar.

He knew people released stress in different ways; maybe Tomas used foul language to alleviate his. The attacks against Cornejo's assets must've taken a toll on the man, especially given his brother had been at one of the locations. Now that Tomas believed Ashton was safe, he'd softened his tone.

Still, the texts almost seemed like they'd been sent by another person. He supposed Ursula could've sent them. But that didn't quite satisfy him either. Something didn't seem right . . . something he couldn't identify. It was like the feeling of being watched. And it wouldn't go away. He knew the only people watching him were Harv and LG, a quarter of a mile back. They'd decided to put some space between their vehicles, just in case.

He radioed Harv. "Pull over. We need to talk before we reach Wrightwood. I've got that nagging feeling."

CHAPTER 26

After situating the taxi in the middle of the ski resort western base's lot, Nathan parked the Lincoln in the southeastern corner, next to a couple of pickups. He'd checked their hoods and neither felt warm. Ultimately, Harv, LG, and he had decided that the taxi should be idling with its headlights on. Watching from the backseat, he wondered how long their wait would be. He'd sent the text to Tomas ten minutes ago and received a "be there shortly" reply. If Tomas had planned to arrive early, he ought to be here by now.

At least tire tracks weren't a major concern. The looping road leading in here and the flat area of the parking area had been plowed and it looked like a vehicle or two had already driven up. He saw the floodlights of several snow cats up on the slopes. The fresh tire tracks had likely been left by their operators.

At the fifteen-minute mark, Nathan began to feel some doubt. They'd timed the drive from Cajon Junction and it took just over twenty minutes. They'd exceeded the speed limit, but not by much. He considered his options and didn't have any. If the twins didn't show, they were out of business—barring a miracle from Cantrell's search—and the looming threat against LG, Harv, and him would continue.

On the eastern horizon, the faintest hint of dark blue had materialized. At least the lights of the parking lot remained dark. If Tomas arrived with his headlights off, he wouldn't be able to see the interior of the cab; its windows were totally black.

There hadn't been much conversation between the three of them. Everyone knew their roles. Now came the waiting game.

Nathan looked toward the highway with his night vision for the hundredth time; this time he caught a glimpse of headlight bleed in the treetops.

"We've got an approaching vehicle. Everybody stand by. It may not be our target, but be ready."

The highway couldn't be seen from the parking lot, but the ultra-sensitive device registered the headlight intrusion well before the naked eye could see it. Because the available light reflecting off the snowy ski slopes gave his night-vision scope more than enough light to see everything, Nathan had to remind himself that it was completely dark in this parking lot.

The right-hand windows of his sedan were down, but he couldn't yet hear the approaching vehicle.

Then something telling happened.

The headlight intrusion winked out.

Even if the car had turned off the highway, his NV would still see its illumination. Whoever approached had killed their headlights.

"I think we're on," he said. "The vehicle just went dark."

He heard it then, the soft crunch of tires on snow. The vehicle was definitely slowing.

He ducked low as it approached from the east loop leading up here.

A silver or tan SUV of some kind arrived. A big one.

Damn it. What if they noticed his open windows? He should've rolled them up.

The SUV eased past his position and he found himself holding his breath. He'd been on the wrong end of Kalashnikovs once this morning and wasn't looking forward to an encore performance.

Nathan squinted in concentration. He'd already lined up on the SUV with his .40 caliber Sig. Full-power ammo, this time. Nothing subsonic about it. If the driver turned on the headlights, he'd open fire.

The SUV slowed, then stopped about fifty feet short of the taxi.

Like a predator, it seemed to be stalking its prey.

Two armed men got out of the SUV.

Shit!

They leveled their AKs at the taxi and opened fire.

Stars of bright light erupted from their flash suppressors.

The roar crackled off the surrounding mountains.

"How did you know?" Harv asked.

"I can't explain it, I just did."

Harv and LG weren't in the taxi; they were sitting in front of him in his car.

As Nathan had predicted, the gunmen didn't bother to reload. They simply approached the shot-up vehicle, expecting to find shredded bodies inside.

"Now, Harv. Punch it."

Harv started the engine and raced straight toward the two gunmen.

Before Harv slid to a stop, Nathan was out the door.

"Hands in the air," he yelled.

The taller gunman didn't comply. He ejected the empty magazine and pulled another one from his coat pocket.

The other guy dropped his AK and ran for the trees.

Nathan heard three booms from his left as LG drilled the defiant gunman before he could insert the magazine.

"We need them alive!" Nathan had been half a second from shooting the man in the hip. "Harv, you're on the rabbit. LG, they might be wearing vests. Cover me."

Nathan sprinted to the downed man and rolled him over. A massive dark stain had already formed underneath his coat. No vest. This man was a goner. Fortunately, it wasn't Tomas.

Nathan heard Harv yell at the rabbit to stop at the same time a menacing sound made him cringe.

A sound he knew well.

The bullwhip crack of a supersonic bullet.

Twenty feet behind him, ice and snow exploded off the parking lot's surface.

"Sniper! Get cover behind the SUV!"

From the impact, he knew the shot must've originated from the ski area. He favored the quad chairlift as a location and popped three shots in that direction.

A second crack tore through the air. "LG!"

"I'm okay, but my underwear isn't!"

"I'm right behind you. Get behind that SUV."

The report of the rifle and crack of the passing bullet were nearly simultaneous, less than a half second. That meant the shooter was inside 250 yards.

The predawn twilight, coupled with his white clothing, were likely the only reasons he and LG remained alive.

The third shot hammered his ears and he could've sworn he felt the bullet's wake turbulence pass by his ear.

He huddled with her, his face inches from hers. "Stay down. I'm going to make an all-out sprint to get my rifle. I need you to look for the muzzle flash when he fires again."

"McBride . . ."

"Don't worry. I don't plan on getting shot. I'll need you to lay down suppression fire while I make the dash."

"We should go together. Fifty-fifty odds."

"I'm not in a gambling mood. Besides, I'm in command. Now stay here and watch for the flash. I think the shooter's somewhere near the quad chairlift."

Harv said, *"My rabbit's heading toward ACH. I'm on him."*

He estimated the distance to the chairlift to be around five hundred feet—plus or minus—not an easy shot for the sniper, given the low light conditions. Unless the shooter had a powered optical, it would be difficult to acquire targets in these conditions.

Nathan tried to recall the ballistic curve on an S&W .40 caliber. "Harv, what's the muzzle velocity of our .40s?"

"Around fifteen hundred feet per second, but it bleeds off quickly. They should go subsonic at around a hundred yards."

"I think we're about five hundred feet from the shooter. Half a second of flight time?"

"Yeah, about. Count on about four feet of bullet drop."

"LG, you're shooting uphill slightly, so add another foot. Hold five feet high and shoot at the base of the chairlift where the skiers load."

Harv cut into the conversation. *"Nate, I don't like this idea much."*

"I need my Remington to take that sniper out. We're both pinned and we're short on options."

Nathan didn't think Harv would say more about it, and he didn't.

"LG, maintain a constant rate of fire, shoot once every second or so. Drop back down if the sniper returns fire. The Sig's laser will work well with your NV. You should be able to see the beam in the atmosphere. Give it a try. Can you see its beam suspended in the air?"

"Yes."

This could be it, he thought, knowing some high-power rifle rounds cleaved through armored vests. Even if the bullet didn't have much energy left, it could still puncture his lung, perforate his stomach or intestines, or worse.

"Okay, do your best. Here goes . . . Now!"

Her Sig pounded the darkness. Again. And again.

On her third shot, he made his move, weaving back and forth as he ran to make himself a tougher target.

Twenty feet from his car, another supersonic crack hammered his ears.

He slid the last ten feet and positioned himself behind the right front tire.

The trunk of his car—where his Remington 700 lay—was exposed to the shooter. He couldn't access it without making himself a target again. He didn't beat himself up; a sniper could've been positioned anywhere and he couldn't have predicted there'd even be one.

Not all was lost. He'd seen the muzzle flash, but more importantly, he hadn't been shot.

But now he had to get his weapon. Even laser-sighted, his handgun was no match against a high-power rifle, and from the sound of the reports, a big one.

He should've kept it inside the car, rather than the trunk. He'd debated it and chosen the trunk in the event they encountered a cop. In hindsight, he regretted the decision and hoped it wouldn't prove too costly.

"Cease fire, LG. Conserve ammo."

The booming ended.

"Do you have the engine block between you and the shooter?"

"Yes."

"Watch your exposed feet. Use a front tire for cover."

"I'm already doing that."

"I'm going to need more cover fire to access the trunk. Keep down until just before you shoot. I saw the muzzle flash. The shooter's lying prone right where we talked about."

"I copy, but I can't see anyone."

"Don't worry about it. I just need you to be close, not exact. Your shots were landing a little short. Adjust your aim about a foot higher."

"Copy. I'm down to my last five rounds."

"Look for a landmark above and beyond your target. After you change magazines, wait for my signal and open fire on the same landmark, copy?"

"Copy. I'm reloaded and good to go."

"Stand by, LG. Now!"

When her handgun began booming again, he darted to the rear of his sedan, popped the trunk, and forced the lid open.

He grabbed the rifle case and maneuvered around to the front of the vehicle again.

A crack whipped by his position. The sniper's fifth attempt.

No doubt, the shooter had initially ducked for cover, then realized he had little chance of being hit.

Nathan flipped the latches, pulled the Remington from its foam slot, and powered on the scope. He set it for a combination of night vision and thermal imaging.

Since his optic was zeroed for three hundred yards, he'd hold low a few inches.

He cycled the bolt and came up. The long axis of his Lincoln was aligned about thirty degrees off the axis of the shooter's position. At least the open trunk didn't block his view.

"LG, hold your fire. I want our shooter to reappear."

She clicked her radio in response.

An eerie silence fell over the area and he thought he knew why. The box magazine capacity for most hunting rifles was five rounds. The shooter was likely reloading, one bullet at a time. Using a five-round stripper clip, an experienced marksman could get it done inside of three seconds, but he doubted this sniper was so equipped. If so, he should've taken more fire by now.

Calming his body and mind, he began taking a series of deep breaths. Being in a sniper's crosshairs had kicked his adrenal glands into high gear. He wasn't worried about a cold-barrel first shot. At this distance, it would be a negligible adjustment. Plus he kept his barrel clean and dry—no oil in the rifling.

He overruled the desire to rush things and settled into a comfortable shooting position.

Several handgun reports popped from the north.

Not wanting to distract Harv, he didn't ask about it. Besides, if Harv had taken a bullet, he'd say something.

As if on cue, Harv said, *"I'm okay. He just tried to use his cell phone. I convinced him otherwise."*

"Keep after him."

Nathan now had to wonder whether the shooter was relocating. *Patience,* he told himself. *Wait him out . . .*

Five seconds passed. Then ten.

Where are you?

He took his scope off the ski-lift mound and did a quick TI scan of the immediate area. No bright objects.

Twenty seconds, now. The shooter had to be relocating. It was also possible that LG had scored a hit, but he gave that low odds.

Time to be aggressive. He couldn't allow a sniper to remain on the loose.

"LG, I want you to support Harv. I'm on the sniper. If I have to kill him, Harv's rabbit will be the only live body we've got left to tell us where the twins are holed up."

"Remember, Nate," Harv said. *"I like my world with you in it."*

"I second that," LG added.

"I'll be fine. Get going. If Harv takes his man alive, we're going to need your skills if he doesn't cooperate. Do whatever it takes to find out where they came from."

"Count on it," she said.

Nathan slung his rifle across his shoulder, grabbed a handful of stripper clips, and stuffed them into his coat pockets. They were heavy, so he wasn't worried about them falling out. He ran through a quick mental checklist and made a beeline for the employee parking area. A huge medical cross was painted on a building to his left, probably the ski patrol's office. He'd head for that. From there, he should have a clear view of the quad chairlift and the surrounding area.

Handgun in hand, he changed his mind and diverted to a large covered sign displaying a detailed map of the resort and ski runs. Some kind of small building sat to the right of the map, probably a ticket office.

He ran straight toward the map kiosk, keeping it between himself and the last known location of the shooter.

The ski lodge showed no signs of activity at all. He began to believe the only employees on site were the two snow cat operators, and since they hadn't stopped, they couldn't have heard the gunfire down here. The building across the highway was a different matter.

Before moving out of the cover of the map kiosk, he used his thermal imager to scan the area again. No bright objects appeared, except for the snow cats. The TI easily picked up their engines' heat signatures.

Nathan had a native ability to memorize maps quickly. He didn't know how or why his brain worked that way, it just did. He burned the ski resort's layout into his mind, not bothering to learn all the names of the different ski runs, but making a mental note of their routes and the chairlifts supporting them.

He took a final look and saw a single bright signature appear from behind a tree to the left of the quad chairlift line. This was clearly the shooter; his rifle barrel glowed like a *Star Wars* lightsaber.

Nathan could've shouldered his weapon and dropped the man from here, but if Harv had to kill the rabbit, he'd need the sniper alive. His .308 delivered a lot of energy; even an extremity wound could cause a bleed-out. He'd seen it before. As long as he kept track of his prey, he had the option. Plus, he could keep Harv and LG from landing in the crosshairs.

"I've got eyes on the shooter," he said. "He's heading upslope."

Harv asked, *"LG, where are you?"*

"I'm just entering the trees north of the parking lot."

"Keep going north and cross ACH."

"I didn't have time to put my rifle case away," Nathan said. "It's sitting next to my car. When you collar the rabbit, make sure someone gets back there ASAP. Also pick up the dropped AK, don't leave it there. We're only a few miles from Wrightwood. If there's a sheriff's substation, response time could be fairly quick."

"I've got this guy," Harv said. *"He's not getting away. Let's send LG back for your car. She can meet me on ACH once I've collared him."*

"Sounds good," Nathan said. "LG, you copy that?"

"On my way back."

"My shooter's heading up the slope in a big hurry. Seems to know where he's going. Unless he tries to double back and line up on you guys, I'm going to keep following and try to intercept him."

"Do you want me to do anything with the dead guy next to the SUV?" LG asked.

Harv said, *"Leave him there."*

Nathan stayed in the trees to the left side of the chairlift. Every so often, the shooter stopped for a breather and looked downslope, but there was no way he'd see Nathan. Not without night vision or a TI.

Nathan was a ghost.

***

Harvey's runner seemed to be in pretty good shape. Fortunately, he was equally fit and had no trouble keeping up.

He wasn't overly worried about Nate. His friend had plenty of experience. Together, they'd chased adversaries through deserts, jungles, beaches, valleys, mountains, and cityscapes—with and without snow.

Harvey knew it was critical to not lose sight of his man for more than a few seconds at a time, but in this forest environment, it wouldn't be possible to keep his prey in continuous visual contact. The trees weren't terribly dense, but big enough to hide behind. In his favor, the twelve inches of fresh snow made trailing his mark easy.

He estimated the distance between them at 150 feet; an easy shot, but Harvey didn't want to shoot him if he didn't have to. The fact that the guy had dropped his weapon and fled meant he probably didn't have much stomach for fighting. But then again he'd been willing to gun down everyone in that taxi.

Harvey lost sight of his mark again and ducked behind a tree. If the guy had a handgun, he could find himself taking fire.

Putting himself into his prey's shoes, he knew the guy was running for his life with no wheels and no place to get shelter. He hadn't anticipated being chased on foot, so he was ill prepared for a prolonged exposure to the cold.

Harvey had given up issuing verbal commands to stop. The guy had ignored all of them. He hadn't seen the guy try to make another call, but he could be doing that right now. Harvey aimed at the man's last known location and popped off three rounds.

That did the trick. The guy came out from behind a tree and began running east, nothing in his hands. If he possessed a handgun, it ought to be visible.

Harvey changed direction, moving laterally toward the building on the north side of the highway. If his man intended to double back, Harvey planned to intercept him before he got there.

***

"Harv, my shooter just cut to the left. I think he's heading for the East Base of the ski resort. I'm closing on his position. Right now, he's no threat to you and LG. I'll make sure that doesn't change."

"My rabbit's also running east. Have you seen your man try to make a call?"

"Not yet. He seems more concerned about putting some distance between us. For now, he doesn't know he's being tailed but that will change soon enough if he tries to use his phone, if he hasn't already. LG, the keys should still be in the ignition."

"I've got your rifle case and the AK secured in the trunk and I'm about to pull out of the parking lot. Do you want me to stage somewhere? Sooner or later, employees are going to start showing up for work and there could be a deputy on the way."

LG had just voiced what he was thinking. The sooner LG got his vehicle out of there, the better. "Find a place to park on the west loop. Leave the headlights off when you drive out."

"Will do."

Nathan looked up the slope and marveled at the technology in his hand. The shooter looked like a yellowish ghost against a deep blue and purple background. Thermal devices don't register ambient light, only temperature variances. A thermal imager worked just as well in pitch blackness as it did in broad daylight.

"My runner's doubling back toward the building on the north side of ACH," Harv said. *"LG, stop about halfway to the highway. I want him to keep going in the same direction."*

"I'm the only car around. Nobody else is parked on the shoulder down here."

"If any deputies arrive from Wrightwood, they should turn into the east loop of the parking lot. Stay put for now and wait for Harv's signal to pick him up. I doubt they'll come in silent. We'll hear sirens."

"Copy. Standing by."

"Harv, if you have to shoot your man to keep him from making a phone call, do it. We need him alive, but don't risk your life over it. I'll do the same with my shooter."

"I've got an idea," LG said. *"The SUV might have an address on its registration. I think it's worth risking a look. I can be back at your sedan inside of a minute."*

"Harv?"

"The SUV could be registered anywhere or it might be a rental, but yeah, I think it's worth a look. LG, get the license plate as well. Cantrell can run it."

"Don't spend more than thirty seconds at the SUV."

"I won't."

"Harv, even if LG comes up with an address, we should still take our men alive if possible."

"Agreed. I don't think my runner has a weapon. He's been empty-handed since he bolted from the SUV."

"My man's still heading toward the East Base. It's possible they've got a second vehicle over there."

"If that's where you end up, we'll pick you up," Harv said.

Nathan clicked his radio. He half wished he could just shoot this guy and be done with it. An icy thought, he knew, but this clown had tried to snipe them and come within an eyelash of succeeding.

Acutely aware of time, Nathan knew they couldn't afford prolonged foot chases. If Bustamonte sent these guys to kill whoever showed up in the taxi, he'd be expecting a call or text soon. Nathan believed less than five minutes had passed since Bustamonte's men had shot up the taxi. Once they collared one of these guys, they'd force him to call Tomas with an update. Nathan would have the guy tell Bustamonte they'd been forced to chase one of the taxi's occupants into the trees, hence the delay.

He gradually closed the distance by angling up the slope to his left. Every time the guy looked back, Nathan froze and heard only the low rumble of the snow cats' diesel engines. So far, he didn't detect any sirens. If gunfire had been reported, any deputies stationed in Wrightwood should've been dispatched by now. The more likely possibility was that someone had heard the gunfire, reported it, but there weren't any deputies or CHP cruisers in the area. There was no way to know how much time they had unless he called Cantrell, and for the time being, he couldn't afford the distraction.

He looked upslope with the thermal and saw his man standing still. The guy appeared to be listening for sound.

Nathan pivoted his NV down.

And saw a bright glow illuminating the man's chest and face.

Shit!

Nathan brought his Sig up and activated its laser. A bright star of death blossomed on the man's chest.

The laser startled the guy and he dropped the phone. When he reached down to pick it up, Nathan fired.

CHAPTER 27

Nathan's bullet flew true and landed in the hole the cell phone had made. The snow erupted in the guy's face.

"Don't make me kill you!" he shouted. "All we want is information. Drop your rifle and put your hands on top of your head."

"*No hablo inglés!*"

"*No problema, hablo español.*" He repeated his previous command in Spanish as he moved upslope.

The man cursed in response.

Continuing in Spanish, he said, "I could've killed you. I've tracked you since you left the chairlift."

The man didn't move.

Nathan fired again. The bullet exploded the snow between the man's feet.

"This is your last chance. Is Bustamonte worth dying for?"

That seemed to get through. The man unslung his rifle, let it fall into the snow, and raised his hands. Nathan suddenly realized, this guy could *be* Bustamonte.

"Hands on top of your head."

The man complied.

"If you make any sudden moves, I'll drop you where you stand. Clear?"

"Yeah."

Keeping his laser painted on the guy, Nathan slowly worked his way farther up the slope and stopped twenty feet short. "Drop to your knees."

Nathan closed the distance and shoved the guy's face into the snow. He put a knee on the man's back, yanked one of his wrists behind his back, and held it there while he removed a pair of disposable cuffs from his waist pack. He used his penlight to look at the man's face. Definitely not Tomas. He searched the man's pockets and found a wallet, some keys, and a box of .30-06 ammo. Yep. It would've punched through his vest.

"Who are you?"

"I'm the guy asking the questions."

"Are you a cop?"

Nathan torqued the man's arms to the dislocation point and received a grunt of pain. He heard LG's radio traffic but didn't respond.

"What did I just say?"

"I heard you. You're the guy asking the questions."

"Where's Bustamonte?"

***

Harvey kept his runner in sight and kept closing the distance by cutting toward the building. His prey kept looking in the wrong direction. He was well out in front of the guy now. If the runner didn't change direction, he'd be able to tackle him in the next ten seconds.

That's it . . . keep coming.

The man continued to slog through the snow, looking over his shoulder.

Harv got behind a large tree and waited. Although he could see his own footprints, his prey couldn't. The near absence of light remained a huge advantage.

Timing his move perfectly, he swung his arm like a baseball bat and clotheslined the guy across the chest.

The man yelped in fear and landed flat on his ass.

Harvey pounced and clocked the man's jaw with an open hand. It wasn't hard enough to knock him out, but it stunned him. Before the guy could recover, Harvey had him rolled and pinned.

Two shots rang out from across the valley. He heard the pistol reports through his earpiece a full second before the actual sounds reached his position.

While Harvey handcuffed his man, he listened to Nate's exchange with the sniper.

Keeping his voice low, he asked his man if he spoke English.

The answer was no.

In Spanish, Harvey said he had no reason to kill the man as long as he cooperated.

"LG, I've got the rabbit in custody. Drive down to the entrance of the west loop. We'll be there shortly."

***

Nathan's sniper didn't have the physical address, but he knew where Bustamonte was. Yes, Ursula was there, along with a personal bodyguard.

He hauled the man upright and began marching him down the slope toward the highway. He'd heard Harv's exchange with the rabbit and formulated a plan. Right now, they needed to clear the immediate area and find a secluded spot along the highway.

They'd conduct quick field interrogations to be sure their stories matched.

Nathan thought about testing the man's assertion that he didn't speak English, but decided it wasn't necessary. He picked up the guy's rifle and slung it next to his.

"Harv, I'm giving you a line of sight to me. I'm about fifty yards west of the chairlift. Can you see my penlight?"

"Hang on, I'm relocating a bit . . . I've got you."

"I'm walking my man downslope toward the highway."

"The registration is a bust," LG said. *"Hertz rental. I took the contract. There's a garage door opener on the visor, though."*

"Good work," Nathan said. "Here's what I have in mind, but we need to work quickly."

***

Linda hadn't interrogated anyone in a long time, but Nathan admired how quickly she peeled their prisoners. She hadn't gotten overly rough, but the two men had discovered how sensitive some of their nerve clusters were. As it turned out, they had no stomach for pain. After verifying their stories matched, Nathan secured the bigger of the two prisoners to a pine tree using a pair of disposable cuffs. The man was far enough from the highway that no one would see him and the gag in his mouth would prevent him from calling out for help. Nathan had, however, allowed the man he'd tied to the tree to wear a winter coat—which they'd found in the SUV. The other prisoner would accompany them to the cabin in the SUV.

They assured the handcuffed man that as long as everything checked out, they'd come back for him. If he'd lied about the twins' whereabouts, they'd execute the man coming with them and the cuffed man's decomposed body would go undiscovered until summer. As it turned out, the two men were cousins so they had a strong motivation to tell the truth.

Perhaps it was Nathan's offhand comment about hungry bears wandering the woods that sealed the deal.

Nathan drove the SUV out to the highway while Harv followed them in his Lincoln. No cops yet, which was a blessing. They'd successfully forced their prisoner to call Bustamonte with an update. Bustamonte had sounded irritated at the foot chase, hence the delay, but pleased at the news that his men had killed everyone in the taxi.

Since they had no idea if Tomas could see the highway or surrounding roads from the cabin, they dropped Nathan's car off at a mom-and-pop gas station. Driving up to the cabin in two vehicles wasn't an option. The men they'd interrogated said they'd only brought the SUV. Before resuming their drive, all three of them quickly stripped off their ski clothing.

This was their first real chance to update Cantrell since the action at the ski resort, so Nathan asked Harv to do it. Nathan gathered from hearing Harv's end that Cantrell had changed her mind and decided to keep Delta active, in an emergency capacity only, but its ETA was twenty minutes at best. By his estimate, they were already a few minutes behind schedule. If they didn't arrive at the cabin within the next two or three minutes, Tomas would be gone, or waiting to ambush them.

He followed their prisoner's directions along a narrow street lined with pines and small, cabin-like homes with fenced yards. This tiny mountain community of Wrightwood looked like it could be anywhere in the country. The farther south they went, the more sparse the houses became.

The man told Nathan to turn left into the next driveway.

He noticed something right away: no tire tracks in the fresh snow.

It was obvious no vehicle had come out of here since the latest snowfall.

He hit the brakes and threw the SUV into park.

In English Nathan said, "Cut this idiot's balls off before we shoot him. They fed us a story; there're no tire tracks in the driveway."

"Wait!" the guy cried. "There's two driveways going up there. I took the shorter way down."

"I thought you didn't speak English."

The man pursed his lips.

"Why should we believe anything you've told us?"

"I was scared."

"Okay, I'll buy that. What else are you lying about?"

"Nothing, I swear."

Nathan was skeptical. "Where's the other driveway?"

"It's farther up the road, maybe two hundred meters."

He narrowed his eyes.

"It's the truth."

Nathan kept going, passing two driveways on the right that led to small cabins.

"How much farther?"

"It's the next one on the left."

"I really hope he's lying," LG said.

"I'm not lying!"

Nathan saw several tire tracks coming out of the driveway, but there was no sign of any cabin. The driveway sloped upward, but not too steeply. The SUV ought to make it without losing traction. To be certain this was the right place, he pulled to a stop and asked Harv to get out and check the SUV's treads against the tire tracks.

His friend issued a thumbs-up and got back in.

"See, I told you."

"Make the call," Nathan said.

Harv jammed his suppressed Sig under the man's chin. "This isn't our car. We don't care if your blood, brains, and skull fragments decorate it. Are you the person who normally talks to Tomas?"

"No, we all do."

"You sure you got your lines straight?"

"I know what to say," the man said.

Nathan turned in his seat. "If you go off script, it will be the last thing you ever do. Do you normally put it on speaker?"

"No, I mean, yes, when I'm driving. I didn't try to connect to the Bluetooth."

"Do you speak Spanish with Tomas?"

"Yes."

"Okay, make the call."

Nathan watched the man closely. Since he was nervous, he'd be acting a little different from normal, but Nathan could usually tell when someone was cooking up a story.

"I'm at the driveway."

"Ursy needs a haircut," Tomas said over the phone's speaker.

He mouthed two words to Harv: *code phrase.*

His friend jammed the silencer harder and squinted in pure malevolence.

The message got through.

The man said, "She looks fine to me."

There was a long pause, then Tomas said, "Get your asses up here. We're leaving before the cops put up roadblocks."

The call went dark.

Nathan nodded to Harv.

Without warning, Harv swung his pistol like a Frisbee and clocked the man in the forehead. The guy went limp.

"How do you know how hard to do that?" LG asked.

Harv shrugged. "Just a guess."

She smiled. "Let's get up there."

The driveway curved around to the left in a gentle slope but Nathan couldn't yet see the cabin. There were too many trees obstructing his line of sight.

"We'll pull up to the cabin like we belong there. I'll use the garage door opener on the visor and pull in. I'll enter the cabin while you two flank the exterior."

"My NV is picking up a substantial amount of glow up there," Harv said. "Probably exterior lights of some kind."

After twenty seconds or so, the trees thinned, and an open expanse of snow-covered driveway greeted them. Beyond it, a log cabin loomed in the twilight. Its orange exterior bulbs created a harsh contrast to the twilight background. No cars were present, but the tire tracks indicated the garage had recently been used.

The structure consisted of three levels, the entire lower level serving as a garage and basement. On both sides of the cabin, the ground sloped up to the ground-floor level. Above the basement, a huge window wall overlooked the canyon to the west. No one could get down from there without a ten-foot vertical drop to the driveway area. Despite the exterior lights, the cabin looked dimly lit inside.

"There's probably a rear door," Harv said. "I'll get back there and cover it."

"Everyone ready?"

"Let's do this," LG said.

Nathan pressed the garage door opener attached to the visor.

The middle of three roll-up doors began its journey.

Nathan stopped twenty feet short.

On the rear wall of the basement, Nathan saw an opening with stairs beyond.

Someone stood in the garage.

There was no way Nathan could avoid being seen. The security lights on the eaves of the roof blanched the entire driveway. He'd hoped no one would be waiting in the garage.

"Harv, LG, get your windows down, we've got company."

At the roll-up door's halfway mark, Nathan saw a nice pair of shoes, slacks, and a huge revolver.

When the door reached head height, he recognized the man they wanted.

Tomas Bustamonte.

Hoping to buy an extra second of time, Nathan flashed the headlights in a friendly way. It didn't work. Bustamonte frowned and raised his weapon.

"Get down!" Nathan yelled.

He stomped the accelerator and the SUV answered the call.

Tomas fired as they crossed the garage's threshold.

Nathan closed his eyes and jerked his head down to the right as the windshield exploded.

He kept his foot on the gas, hoping to plow Bustamonte before he retreated into the stairwell.

Remembering the air bags, he slammed the brakes before the SUV smashed into the wall.

Harv and LG fired from their open windows, but their shots missed low when the car jerked to a stop.

Nathan clenched his teeth as Bustamonte bounded up the stairs.

LG yelled, "Shit!"

He kept his voice calm. "We stick to the plan. Get your bearings. This garage faces west."

"Nate, we—"

"We can't let them escape. We end this here and now. LG, take the south side, Harv, you're on the north. Circle around and get to a position where you can cover the corners. We'll call the three levels basement, ground, and second. Get going!"

Nathan hustled over to the door leading to the interior of the house and flattened himself against the wall. No noise came from inside.

He looked around and found what he needed near the washing machine. He grabbed the winter parka hanging from a coat hook.

He ran toward the door, purposely making loud footfalls. He stopped short, tossed the parka across the opening, and was rewarded with a booming report. The weapon sounded like a small cannon, probably a magnum. The coat jumped as the bullet perforated its form and skipped off the concrete.

"Nathan!"

"I'm okay, Harv. He's still in the stairwell." In Spanish, Nathan yelled, "Give it up, Bustamonte. You and Ursula can walk out, or be carried out, we don't care which."

His answer came in a string of vulgarities that would have impressed the most seasoned of Marines.

Nathan switched his Sig to his left hand, figured out the right angle to shoot, extended his arm through the opening and fired.

Figuring his shots had forced Bustamonte to duck for cover or retreat, he pivoted into the stairwell. Halfway up, the stairs changed direction to the left. Seeing a concrete block wall, he fired twice more at a safe angle, hoping to score a shrapnel hit. If nothing else, it kept Tomas from reappearing.

He heard a handgun boom from the east side of the cabin.

"Harv?"

"Someone just tried to leave through a rear door back here. I convinced him otherwise. I'm working my way toward the northeast corner. I had to duck under a kitchen window next to the door. There's not much of a backyard out here, just a retaining wall about ten feet from the cabin. The mountain slopes up from it. There're stairs coming down from the second-floor deck. From the layout of the windows further along the ground-floor wall, I'd say I'm looking at a large bedroom, not multiple rooms."

"LG, do you see any doors?"

"No, just windows. I'm at the southeast corner. The retaining wall extends over to my side. I had to duck under some windows too. I don't have eyes on Fontana."

"I'm not seeing any footprints," Harv said. *"No one's been out here."*

"I concur," LG said.

"I want both of you to break windows on my command," Nathan whispered. "Shoot at an upward angle toward the ceiling to avoid cross-fire. I'm hoping to flush the twins toward me."

His radio clicked twice.

Nathan steeled himself. If he was going to take a bullet within the next few minutes, now could be the time. He'd come close at the Expo line, but this was different. Every room inside this cabin was unknown and every corner blind.

Moving silently, he ascended to the landing and took a quick glance around the corner.

No one there.

He could see the ceiling beyond, but little more. Keeping his gun aimed at the top of the stairs, he ascended slowly, ducking lower as he gained elevation.

His cone of vision widened. Directly ahead, he saw a dining room table and a kitchen beyond. It looked like the living room lay to his right.

He had an idea, something Delta had suggested at the dealership.

"Stand by, I'm going to kill the power."

"A loss in power might trigger the alarm system," Harvey said.

"It's a risk we're going to take. If the twins don't have night vision, it will give us a huge advantage."

He hurried back down the stairs to the garage and hustled over to the circuit-breaker box. "Deploy NV."

Nathan opened the panel and located the master breaker at the top. "Now!" Nathan whispered. "Bust as many windows as you can."

The breaker made a clunk sound and the garage went black.

He hurried back to the midpoint landing of the stairs. Using the same technique, he reached around the corner and fired three shots toward the kitchen area.

The sound of shattering glass filled the cabin. *Tonight hasn't been a good night for windows,* he thought.

He risked a quick glance over the top step.

No one in sight.

Something thumped across the floor.

He saw the object in his NV, its menacing shape unmistakable.

An M84 stun grenade.

Headed straight toward him.

"Banger!" he yelled.

CHAPTER 28

This was going to be bad.

Nathan flattened himself on the stairs and lowered his head onto a step.

The cylindrical object brushed his head, glanced off his back, and—

Detonated.

The deafening blast compressed his eardrums to the bursting point. It felt like he'd taken a sledgehammer blow to the back of his head.

His left calf ignited with the collective sting of a thousand hornets.

He pushed himself down a few steps just as a handgun boomed.

Behind him, the block wall exploded.

The stinging on his calf grew worse.

Shit, his pant leg was on fire!

He reached down and swatted out the flame with his free hand.

Not all was lost. Only one of his ears took the full brunt. The ear with the speaker had been somewhat spared. The choking effect of burned powder, clothing, *and flesh* assaulted his lungs. He should've anticipated this. Good thing nobody was counting his mistakes because he'd made a slew of them.

Even through the disorientation and shock, Nathan's mind kicked into high gear. He aimed his Sig toward the kitchen, put desperation in his voice, and yelled, "I'm hit! I'm hit!"

No one appeared.

Harv said something, but he had no idea what.

He couldn't hear himself, but whispered, "I'm okay. One of them's in the kitchen. I was trying to draw him out."

He needed more time to recover. That damned grenade had thrown off his equilibrium. He'd managed to close his eyes in time, but the million-candlepower flash had penetrated his free eyelid and probably damaged his NV scope as well.

Like something out of a recurring nightmare, he heard the same thumping sound again.

You're kidding me!

A second grenade skipped over his head.

Fortunately, this one was moving faster. It smacked the wall behind him and dropped onto the midpoint landing.

Here we go again!

He buried his head into his forearm as the second device detonated.

His unprotected ear took another pounding and he wondered if he'd suffer permanent hearing loss.

Rage overpowered the fresh agony in his head.

Screw this.

He came up from his crouch and charged up the basement stairs, firing as he ran. His calf felt like charred skin was peeling off, and probably was.

His mind registered movement to his right beyond the kitchen, from an opening to a hall or other room.

A big man had pulled the pin on a third grenade! It couldn't be Bustamonte—this guy was Harv's size and wearing different clothes. The twins' personal bodyguard? Fair game then.

Nathan activated his laser and painted the man's chest.

The guy saw the bright dot, dropped the grenade, and pivoted out of sight just as Nathan fired.

He averted his eyes as a third explosion rocked the cabin.

Had he nailed the guy? He didn't know.

The place fell into eerie silence, intensifying the ringing in Nathan's head. He wondered if blood was dripping from his injured ear. Not wanting to stay exposed, he backed into the stairwell and crouched. Now that the threat from more stun grenades had been eliminated, this became a defensible position. Despite the disorientation, he directed his aim at the spot where the bodyguard had disappeared and fired two shots.

"Nate? Check in. Can you hear me?"

That sounded like Harv. He cranked the radio's volume to maximum.

"Nate, you okay?"

"Just smarting. The first grenade burned my calf. It was their bodyguard; he just ducked into a hall or room off the kitchen on your side."

"Where are you?"

"In the basement's stairwell. My head's reeling."

"LG," Harv said, *"can you work your way into the house and support Nathan's position?"*

"Yes, I'm looking at a large living room. I can get in through a window."

"I'll give you cover fire when you come in," Nathan said. "Harv, are you in crossfire danger?"

"No. The walls are super thick. They could escape out this side of the house if I don't keep eyes out here."

"Do you see any other doors on the ground level?"

"Not yet. I haven't looked around the southeast corner yet."

"LG?"

"All I'm seeing are windows along the south side of the cabin. No doors."

"Harv, maintain position. LG, advance into the living room when you hear me open fire. Verbal copies from here on out, my ears are toast."

"Copy, standing by."

Nathan began shooting the corner where the bodyguard disappeared. Dust and chunks of gypsum blasted away from the wall.

"I'm inside," LG said. *"I saw your muzzle flashes. I'm directly to your right on the other side of the wall. I can see the kitchen and dining room. There's a loft directly above me with a solid half-wall. I can't see if anyone's hiding up there."*

"You need to clear it. I'll maintain position until you've done that."

"Copy, the stairwell to the loft's on my left. Can you cover the stairs coming down from the second floor on the other side of the living room?"

"Yeah, I can see the landing from my position."

"Copy, on the move."

Nathan didn't like being stationary, but his senses were still out of whack.

It happened so quickly, he couldn't line up on the threat in time.

A hand holding a Mac-10 reached around the corner where the bodyguard had disappeared.

"LG! Get down!"

The weapon discharged in a booming roar of twenty rounds per second.

Nathan ducked as dozens of bullets sprayed his position and the living room. Some of them found the concrete block wall behind him. Something stung the back of his neck, but he ignored it.

LG cried out. And it didn't sound good.

The barrage ended.

Throwing caution and pain aside, Nathan charged the kitchen, firing at the corner as he ran. He intended to kill the shooter before the guy could reload and send another salvo.

"Shit! SHIT!" LG yelled. "I'm hit."

"Stay there. I've got this." He had five rounds left and he intended to puncture flesh with every one of them.

He entered the kitchen and pivoted into the opening of the hallway.

In the process of reloading his machine pistol, the man snarled with fury at the bright dot on his torso.

Nathan calmly said, "Lights out, dirtbag."

As fast as he could accurately pull the trigger, he fired all five rounds into the man's chest.

The man stiffened as if being electrocuted, then slumped to the floor. The Mac-10 spilled out of his hands.

Now wasn't the time to admire his marksmanship. His weapon needed ammo.

He dropped the mag, jammed a full one home, and thumbed the slide.

"Harv, the bodyguard's down," he whispered. "I need to clear the rest of the ground floor before helping LG."

"Copy."

"LG, where are you hit?"

"Right hip," she groaned. *"I haven't cleared the loft, but if anyone's up there, I'd probably be dead."*

"Can you cover the stairs coming down from the second level?"

"Yeah, but don't ask me to tackle anyone."

Nathan looked around. *Jackpot,* he thought. Sitting on the kitchen counter were three more bangers. He stuffed them into his waist pack.

Staying on the offensive, he rushed down the hall, dropped to his back, and kicked the first door with both feet. His calf screamed in pain as the door flew open and banged the wall. An empty bathroom greeted him. He eased down the hall to the second door. Using the same technique, he breached it.

No one shot at him, but cold air gushed out of a large bedroom.

"I've got eyes on you and this side of the bed," Harv said. *"It's clear."*

Nathan pointed to his own eyes, then pointed to the closet. Staying low, he moved deeper in the blackness and checked an open closet door. Nothing. Not even clothes. Only one door left—likely a bathroom.

He eased along the wall and peered in at waist level. An open shower curtain revealed an empty tub. Next to the toilet, a small cabinet—too small for an adult to hide in—supported a sink.

"Unless someone's hiding in a kitchen cabinet, there's no one on the ground floor. The twins must've retreated upstairs hoping to escape out the exterior deck above you."

"Any sign of Ursula? Clothes, anything like that?"

"Nothing. LG, I'm coming to you. Harv, stay there and keep eyes on the stairs and second-floor deck."

"Copy."

He found LG clutching a bloody mess, put a finger to his lips, and hustled up the loft's stairs to be absolutely certain no one hid up there. No one did. He returned to LG and used his Predator knife to cut away her pants. Two of the Mac-10's bullets had cleaved into her right hip. It didn't look as though any major arteries or veins had been severed, but her pants were soaked.

"Keep pressure on it."

"Ya think?" she gasped.

"I'll be right back. Cover me."

He patted her shoulder and ran for the couch, the burned flesh of his leg stinging worse than before. The opening of the stairwell leading up to the second level loomed large. Ursula or Tomas could appear at any moment. So far, they hadn't.

He grabbed a sofa cushion and limped back to her position. "Unzip it while I cover us."

She wasted no time removing the foam. Her bloody handprints created a stark contrast to the light-colored leather. He adjusted the focus on his NV and went to work.

Using his Predator knife, he sliced the seams of the cushion's cover. It was now long enough, but its shape was wrong. He cut pieces out, creating a reverse hourglass shape. Working quickly, he placed the wide portion of the leather over the wound's puncture and tied the narrow strips on the opposite side of her hip. "Be right back."

He made a trip over to the fireplace and back. After forcing the iron poker under the knot, he gave it a 360-degree turn, tightening the tourniquet like an oversized garrote. LG moaned, clenching her teeth.

"I'm going around one more time."

He manhandled the poker through one more turn.

"Shit, McBride, you're killing me."

"All done. Keep it from unwinding."

"Where'd you learn this?"

"The Marines, of course."

"Well, Semper fucking fi."

"Harv, you copy all of this?"

"Affirm. Sounds like LG's okay."

"I've got her bleeding under control. She took two to the hip." He grasped her shoulder. "You're out of the fight. Stay here, that's an order." He showed her one of the grenades and smiled. "I've got two more of these. Harv and I are gonna take out the trash."

She grimaced in pain. "May I quote Fontana?"

"Of course."

"I like my world with you in it."

"Me too."

"Why haven't they attacked?"

"They're on the second floor and want us to go up there, which puts us at a big disadvantage. Hang tough, LG. I need to send a text to Cantrell. Can you cover us for a sec?"

"Yeah." LG pivoted to her good side and pulled herself up so she could see over the sloped half-wall that also served as the stair rail.

He had a good cell signal and sent:

```
Engaging the twins. LG seriously wounded
```

"There's no activity out here," Harv said, *"but a few lights have come on in the cabin to the north. It's a good bet deputies are on the way."*

Ignoring the hideous sensation on his leg, he limped over to the sofa and crouched.

Keeping his voice low, he said, "I'm in the living room and I've got eyes on the stairs down to the garage. They can't escape in this direction. LG's got my back. I'm going to clear a door near the stairs. I think it's a coat closet. The door you're guarding leads into the kitchen. Stand by: I'm going to test my theory."

"Copy."

Nathan grabbed a coaster from the sofa table and hurled it across the room. It bounced off the floor and smacked the door.

"Did you do that?"

"Yes. LG, you've got living room, dining room, and kitchen." He hurried over to the suspect door near the basement stairs, stood to the side, and ripped it open. Several coats and umbrellas greeted him. He looked across the living room to the stairs leading up to the second floor and knew he'd have to go up them. No time like the present. He was about to make his move when his phone vibrated.

"LG, you still good?"

"Yes."

He ducked into the pitch-black stairwell leading to the garage, pulled his cell, and looked at the text from Cantrell.

Ambulance, Delta, and FBI SAs on the way.
Local law enforcement will stage at street
until Delta and feds arrive. ETA 15 minutes.
I need the twins alive.

No shit, Sherlock. He instantly regretted the crass thought. His damned leg felt like a blowtorch was at work. Surprised Cantrell had brought in the FBI, he relayed the info to Harv and LG. Thinking about it more, it made sense at this point. Delta had no law-enforcement powers.

"Nate, you shouldn't clear the second floor by yourself. If LG's got this door, let me help you. We can leapfrog it."

"I need you out there. I'll be okay. I have a few surprises in store and it's super dark in here."

Nathan started toward the second-floor stairs, then stopped.

Why not give the twins a taste of their own medicine?

"Harv, I'll meet you at the door leading out of the kitchen. Are you at any risk of being fired upon from any of the windows upstairs?"

"No. If they open or break one, I'll hear it."

"I'll be at the kitchen door in the next few seconds."

"Copy. Standing by."

"LG, you're still on the stairs to the second level."

"I've got them."

Nathan hurried over to the door next to the refrigerator and cracked it a few inches. "Take these," he whispered, handing Harv two of the bangers. "Head halfway up the stairs out there and stand by. We're going to flush them into the living room."

"Too bad we don't have any tear gas."

"Maybe we do. I'll be right back." He used his penlight to search the cabinet under the sink and hit pay dirt. He grabbed a can of oven cleaner and a plastic bottle of ammonia.

He rejoined Harv at the door. "I'm going to secure this can to a banger with duct tape. Hold it in place for me."

Working quickly, he bent the safety handle a little outward, removed the tape from his waist pack, and wrapped several layers of tape around the can and the grenade. He made sure to keep the tape under the safety handle so it could fly free when deployed. He repeated the process with the bottle of ammonia.

"Shit," said Harv. "This might work."

"We're going to find out."

"If it starts a fire?"

"Then our beloved twins will be forced to come down. Up you go. Shoot out the window first. Send the other banger through a different window." He looked toward the stairs leading up to the loft and saw LG peering over the half-wall.

"Need I remind you guys I'm not in any condition to run wind sprints?"

"Don't worry, LG. I'll carry you."

"At least I'm properly dressed this time."

"Stand by," he told her. "We're about to heat things up."

Nathan positioned himself at the corner of the kitchen where he had a clear view of the second-floor stairs.

"I'm ready," Harv said.

"Do it!"

CHAPTER 29

Nathan heard Harv's handgun boom. A few seconds later, a loud bang rocked the second floor, followed by a shrieking whistle.

The can of oven cleaner. Glorious!

It probably seemed like a demon was loose up there.

Harv's pistol sounded again, followed by a second explosion, not as loud. The ammonia grenade.

A female scream rang out.

Nathan yelled, "Hey, Ursy? How do you like us now?"

He heard stomping above his head, from more than one person, then violent coughing.

Even if the oven-cleaner grenade didn't start a fire, the fumes had to be overpowering. The ammonia made it even worse.

Automatic gunfire erupted followed by a thump of some kind.

Harv's handgun boomed again.

Nathan was tempted to rush up the stairs, but he didn't want to breathe any of the toxic gas. The glow from the stairwell ended, meaning the place probably hadn't caught fire. Either that, or it hadn't spread yet.

"One of them just tried escaping out to the deck. I forced them back inside."

"Good work, Harv. Stay there for now."

He heard more coughing and choking, louder this time.

Something thumped down the stairs. His NV registered the bouncing light source as a flashlight, not another banger.

Automatic gunfire followed.

"LG, get down!"

The wood floor of the living room splintered as dozens of slugs destroyed its surface. All the bullets missed LG's position, but that would change as the shooter reached the ground floor.

In the eerie light from the flashlight, Nathan lined up on the stairs' landing.

What happened next took him utterly by surprise.

The ceiling exploded in an oval shape of dust and debris.

One of the twins was firing blindly through the floor. Nathan dived to his left and ended up against the kitchen's island.

Looking like a war refugee, Tomas bounded down the stairs and entered the living room with a look of pure hatred and rage. The oven-cleaner grenade must've detonated right next to him; his burned pants still smoldered and his shirt was charred.

His right hand held a huge revolver, his left a Mac-10.

Nathan saw LG pull herself upright from her cover and aim at Tomas.

Her bloody hand slipped off the rail and she fell out of sight.

Tomas tossed the empty Mac-10 aside and pointed the revolver at her.

Knowing the magnum's bullets would easily penetrate the half-wall, Nathan yelled, "Tomas! Over here!"

Before he could fire a wounding shot, the ceiling erupted again, and again. Nathan found himself in a maelstrom of wood splinters, chunks of drywall, and dust.

Something hit his cheek, causing him to flinch and lose his aim just as he fired.

Tomas turned to him, madness lighting his eyes.

Nathan watched in horror as the muzzle of Tomas's revolver ignited with a thunderous roar.

He heard LG scream his name.

The impact hammered him so violently, he thought he'd pass out. He staggered back, lost his balance, and felt the back of his head smack the granite countertop. His vision grayed, then went dark. His final thought before losing consciousness was a desperate prayer that Linda wouldn't kill Tomas . . . that he wouldn't die in vain.

***

Harvey heard multiple bursts of automatic gunfire roar from the interior of the cabin, followed by a single thunderous report.

From the frantic tone of LG's scream, he knew Nate was down. He felt it as surely as the sun would rise.

Throwing caution aside, he bounded up the stairs to the deck and kicked the door.

An empty bedroom greeted him, along with a noxious smell.

He heard the sound just in time, a cycling bolt.

He dived to the floor as the wall to his left exploded in a linear string of eruptions.

A scream of animal-like fury overpowered the roar of the machine pistol on the opposite side of the wall.

Harv shimmied on his stomach into the hall. Without hesitating, he ran to the next door and rushed into the adjacent bedroom where he'd thrown the second grenade.

Ursula.

Her face wet with ammonia, she wiped her eyes and cursed. When she attempted to reload the Mac-10, Harvey struck her jaw with the butt of his Sig.

He kicked Ursula's weapon aside, grabbed her by the hair, and dragged her out of the bedroom and down the hall. Flailing and screaming, she tried to bite his arm. He flung her against the wall and belted her in the face again. Her eyes rolled and she went limp. Had they not needed this woman alive, he would've slit her throat.

He stopped at the top of the stairs to the living room. "LG!" he yelled.

"I'm okay."

"Where's Tomas?"

"Dead."

Shit.

Not caring about Ursula's head, he switched his grip to her ankle and hauled her down the stairs.

Tomas lay on the floor, a puddle of blood growing next to his chest.

Bloody handprints smeared the half-wall of the stairs where Linda stood. She took a step into the living room, and nearly fell.

Harv left Ursula next to her brother and rushed to Nathan's side.

He reached down and felt for a pulse.

Behind him, Ursula screamed.

***

Hatred boiled in Linda's soul, strong and deep. She'd wanted this opportunity for years and here it was. One down, one to go. She hobbled over to Ursula and winced at the overpowering smell of ammonia. The woman had seemed unconscious, but now she stirred. Writhed, really, no doubt from the chemical cocktail burning her face and eyes. *You poor thing,* she mused. *I'm happy to end your suffering.* Ignoring the hideous sensation in her right hip, she pressed her Sig against the woman's temple.

"Time to die, Ursy."

Squinting in agony, Ursula looked up. "You!"

"Stop," Fontana yelled. "Damn it, LG, don't do it. You know we need her alive."

"She just killed McBride!"

"He's not dead. Just unconscious."

"You're just saying that so I won't kill her."

"It's the truth. Lower the gun."

She shook her head. "She deserves to die."

"So this was your plan all along? You used us?"

Linda didn't trust herself to answer that.

In the eerie light coming from the fallen flashlight, Fontana took a step forward.

She pressed her pistol tighter against Ursula's head.

Fontana holstered his pistol and held his hands out. "One minute, that's all I ask."

She felt herself breathing hard. "What difference will a minute make?"

"Lower the gun, okay? She's not going anywhere."

She didn't move.

"Killing her will leave a wound that won't heal."

"This bitch is pure evil. She tortured Glen and tried to kill McBride in Caracas. She sold children into sexual slavery. She's pure evil!"

"I was trying to kill *you,* not that big dumbshit!"

"Don't listen to her," Fontana said. "Focus on me."

"You're a whore! You spread your legs for my brother."

Her finger tightened on the trigger.

"Don't do it, it's what she wants."

Ursula issued more insults and foul language, first in English, then in Spanish.

"Eyes on me, Linda. Tune her out."

"She has to die."

"The price is too high."

"Too high?"

"To yourself, to Nathan."

"I'll gladly pay it."

"You can't."

"She's lying about Glen's rescue."

"Think about it, Linda. In Caracas, Ursula could've shot any of us in that house. We were in the kitchen. I was on your left. Nathan was in the living room, near the television. Ursula lined up on you from the hall right after you shot the old man on the couch."

Ursula twisted on the floor, trying to stare Linda in the eye. "Old man? He was my father!"

Fontana narrowed his eyes.

"You didn't have to kill him. He trusted you, let you into our family."

Linda pistol-whipped the side of Ursula's head.

"The old man on the couch was their father?"

"Why does that matter?"

"But you knew?"

"He was reaching for a gun! What would you've done?"

"The same thing, but I didn't have to make that decision. You did. This is different. You don't have to kill Ursula. You gave us your word. No summary executions."

"Don't you want her dead?"

"Cantrell needs what's in her head. Look, no one will ever know. If you kill her, I won't say anything, but there's one condition."

"What condition? What are you talking about?" She didn't want to hear any of Fontana's bullshit. Ursula had to die. Simple as that.

"You have to use your knife."

"My knife?"

"I'm going to repeat what Holly once told Nathan when he faced the same thing. I wasn't there, but he told me about it."

"I'm in no mood for a lecture, Fontana. Say what you have to say and be done with it."

"I want to see you kill her with your knife. Up close and personal."

"What the hell are you talking about?"

"You heard me. I want to see you slice her throat from ear to ear. I want to hear the gurgling of her lungs. I want to see her blood spurt onto the walls. Go ahead, show me how tough you are. I want to witness the real Linda Genneken at work. Apparently the woman I thought I knew doesn't exist."

"Spare me the drama, Fontana. I'm in no mood."

"Having the power of life and death in your hands is like heroin to an addict, but there's no twelve-step treatment plan. Once you kill, you can't get that life back. Nate and I fight it every day of our lives. Don't give in to it. You're in a lot of pain and you're losing blood." He nodded to her foot. "Your boot's overflowing. Close your eyes, LG, and focus on my voice. Shut everything else out."

"We don't have time for this." She shuffled back a step and painted the bitch's face with her laser.

"Close your eyes and focus on my voice."

She shook her head. "I can't."

"Life is about choices, Linda. Every day." Fontana took a few strides forward.

"She had Glen murdered!"

"Killing her won't bring him back."

Linda couldn't listen to this. Ursula had to die.

"You need to trust me, like you've never trusted me before. You and I? We've been through life and death together. I'd never lie to you, or try to deceive you. Ursula's not going anywhere."

She could feel her rage radiating like white-hot iron. Killing this bitch was the only way to purge it. Nothing less would work.

"Focus on my voice. Lock everything else out."

She squinted.

"Eyes on me, right here." He pointed to his face. "I know what you're feeling. The anger and rage. It makes you want to scream until your throat bleeds. Killing Ursula won't release it; it only makes it worse. You'll hurt yourself. Hurt your country. Doubt and regret will haunt you for the rest of your life because you did something that can't be undone. The feeling festers and gets worse with time. It'll consume you like cancer."

"I have to kill her. I have to!"

"Is that what Glen would want?"

She didn't answer.

Harvey stepped forward and put a boot on Ursula's neck. She groaned in protest, but he didn't ease off.

"Close your eyes and focus on my voice." He reached out and put a hand on her shoulder. "This is it, Linda. Your soul's at stake. Everything in your life hinges from this moment forward."

She shrunk away from his touch, then cried out at the pain in her hip. "It's just you and me," she breathed. "No one has to know."

"The price is too high."

"But no one will know!"

"You'll know."

"I can't . . ."

Ursula started another tirade, but Fontana stepped heavily on her throat until she went slack.

"Stay with me, Linda. Close your eyes and listen to my words . . . that's all I'm asking you to do. If you still want to kill her afterward, I won't stop you."

Trying to do what he asked, she forced her eyes shut.

Fontana spoke slowly. "Take a deep breath and set the pain aside. I know it hurts, but focus only on my voice, lock everything else out. Picture yourself in a forest of fall-colored trees."

She shook her head. *"I can't do this—"*

"Keep your eyes closed and stay with me."

"Please—"

"You're still under the trees. There's a slight wind blowing. A gust frees some of the leaves and they begin to flutter down to the ground. See them as they tumble through the air. Rays of sunlight brighten their colors. Feel the sensation as they brush past your skin and gather at your feet. Each one drains a tiny piece of anger and carries it away."

Fontana's voice held a calming, almost hypnotic tone. She frowned, but kept her eyes closed.

"Hundreds are falling. Then thousands. Hear the sound they make, see their swirling patterns on the ground. Anger doesn't control you; you control it. There're a million reasons to kill her, but only one reason not to."

She relived the fight earlier that evening, the mercenary's bullets piercing Glen's chest. His concern for their dogs. His unconditional love of her. She'd said some horrible things to him over the years when she'd been angry, and he'd always forgiven her. Fontana was right: pulling the trigger would haunt her for the rest of her life. Glen wouldn't want that. His memory would be tainted. She might even blame him for what she'd become.

She felt the tightness in her face ease.

Her free hand unclenched.

And she lowered the pistol.

"Welcome back, Linda."

"Accountability," she whispered and opened her eyes. "That's a damned good trick, Harvey."

"What happened to calling me Fontana?"

"It's been suspended until further notice."

"I can live with that."

"I was going to do it, but I'm glad I didn't. So where did that falling-leaves business come from. You just make it up?"

"Nathan's used it for years. He calls it his safety catch. A company shrink gets the credit."

She sat heavily on the couch, wincing at the lancing pain. "You guys continue to amaze me. Just when I think I've seen it all, you come up with a bunch of leaves. Killing Ursula wasn't going to make me feel better, I know that now. Thanks for talking me down."

"Don't shortchange yourself. The decision was yours alone."

She looked at McBride.

And in that moment, they communicated without words.

Each knew what the other thought and felt.

It was one of those mysterious human experiences that defied understanding.

"Am I that transparent?" she asked softly.

"Actually, LG, you're pretty guarded."

"When I was drugged, did I, you know . . . say anything I shouldn't have?"

"Nathan said you told him you loved Glen."

She closed her eyes against the pain. "I did love him. He was a good man."

"You two had a great life together. You'll always remember the best times. Come on, let's apply Nate's tourniquet again before you bleed to death."

"He's really alive? You weren't just saying it?"

Harvey looked up while he secured Ursula on the floor with plasticuffs. "To quote a line from a movie, Marines are not allowed to die without permission."

They both heard it, an approaching siren. Probably a fire engine.

"We're going to have company soon." He stood and looked at Tomas.

"I didn't have a choice. He was about to shoot Nathan again."

"Don't second-guess yourself. You did the right thing." He came to her side and got the makeshift tourniquet back in place.

"Ouch. I've never been shot before. This really sucks."

"Welcome to the club."

"This is one membership I could live without. We did well, didn't we?"

"Yeah, LG, we did well."

"I miss it. Being in the CIA."

Harvey nodded. She knew he missed it too.

"How's Nathan?"

"Out cold. He's been concussed many times so he's more suscep-tible to brain trauma. He may have some fractured ribs, but the vest saved his life. He'll be okay."

"I'm glad to hear that. I mean . . . about him being okay."

Harvey smiled.

"He took a bullet for me again," she said. "I guess I've always known what happened in Caracas, I just didn't want to accept it. Nathan forced Ursula to shoot him, not me or you."

"Our definition of friendship is the willingness to die for each other."

"I guess I'm Nathan's friend."

"You most certainly are. You good for a sec? I need to contact Cantrell."

"This burns like all hell, but I'm good." She tried to smile but knew it looked like a grimace. "Thanks for saving me from myself, Harvey."

He gave her arm a squeeze. "I'm gonna turn on the power, check on Nathan, and grab his phone."

She looked at Ursula's prone form. *I'm not like you.* The last six hours replayed in her head again—from waking up at midnight to here and now. It seemed surreal. Many people had died getting to this point; she hoped it had been worth it. Everything Harvey said was true. For the first time in her life, she understood the true nature of death. Underneath the pain, a sadness washed through her and she wiped tears. She'd honored Glen's memory, but he remained gone. When the lights came on, the full scene snapped to life. Blood and destruction everywhere.

Harv returned to the couch and handed her the phone. He mouthed, *Cantrell.*

"I'm here, Director."

"Thank you, Linda." The phone was on speaker.

"You're welcome."

"I'm very sorry about Glen."

She looked at Harv, uncertain what to say.

"There's no way to express in words how important the situation is, so I won't try. You three have done outstanding work, and I won't forget it. Follow Harvey's lead. I've instructed him to stay with you during the ambulance ride and in the hospital. When you wake up from surgery, he'll be there as well."

"Surgery . . ."

"Hopefully, your hip isn't shattered. We'll take care of everything."

"Thanks."

The call ended and she stared at the phone. "She doesn't say goodbye."

"No, she doesn't."

CHAPTER 30

FOUR DAYS LATER

Cantrell placed the phone in its cradle and sighed. Her interrogation team hadn't made any tangible progress with Ursula. They'd tried everything legally allowed and Ursula still hadn't broken. The woman was driven by pure, malevolent hatred. Human life meant nothing to her, not even her own. Not breaking had become her sole reason for living. Cantrell had seen this level of resolve before. It was fairly common to radical jihadists. On the other end of the spectrum, the would-be abductor they'd captured at Genneken's house hadn't been driven by fanatical ideology or hatred, so breaking him had been easy.

Before calling DNI Benson to give him the bad news, she figured she'd update McBride first—not a pleasurable call to make, but he deserved the truth. He'd risked his life delivering a live prisoner; they all had.

Not all was lost. Cantrell hadn't given up hope, though, because Ursula had initially warmed at being offered a new identity and relocation, but she wasn't naïve. Ursula made it clear she knew how the game worked. Once the CIA had what it wanted, her usefulness terminated and the CIA would have no reason to fulfill its end of the bargain. She'd also expressed fear of being tortured to death by Cornejo if he ever found her.

Unless Ursula could definitively finger Cornejo for the kinds of crimes that would put him behind bars, he'd sail into the presidency and become the leader of thirty million people. The nuclear threat would remain and Iran would have an open path to a bomb. Not a pleasant thought. Dethroning Cornejo after the election would be much more difficult—if not impossible—because he'd be in control of the judiciary. Evidence and witnesses would disappear and judges would receive grocery bags full of cash. The time to stop him was now, before he took the presidential oath.

I wish we could just kill the SOB, she thought.

Frustrated didn't begin to describe how she felt. It sickened her that Cornejo remained untouchable. Thinking about the suffering of children sold into sexual slavery made her skin crawl.

She squinted in thought. Why not? She had nothing to lose at this point. The decision made, she picked up the phone.

***

Nathan shook his head after ending the call. Ursula hadn't broken and there was no indication anything would change before the election took place in less than a week. Cantrell had asked if he and Harv would talk with LG once more about anything she might have on Cornejo.

Desperate times . . . desperate measures.

Although reluctant, LG had agreed to stay in Nathan's La Jolla home during the first week of her recovery. She needed help with every-day activities and Angelica was more than happy to assist her. He'd come by every day to check on LG, but he spent the nights in his smaller Clairemont house, a way of granting his houseguest a measure of privacy. Having been through an ordeal few ever faced, LG needed time to decompress. He had, however, gotten to know her a whole lot better over the last few days.

When he'd arrived this morning, Linda looked positively radiant, and judging by their behavior, her two German shepherds had become quite chummy with Grant and Sherman.

Nathan invited Harv to join them for breakfast, and here they were, all sitting at the kitchen's island with two giant schnauzers at their feet. Linda's dogs preferred to spend their time exploring his property in search of an elusive jackrabbit that Grant and Sherman had long ago given up trying to catch.

Linda knew what was coming; he'd told her about his call with Cantrell.

He'd also talked to Harv and they'd both agreed to keep the conversation as amiable as possible. Based on the direction they needed to go, a tenuous task at best.

Harv looked at LG. "I hope you haven't been spoiling Nathan's mutts."

"Well, maybe a little."

"How's your omelet?" Nathan asked.

"It's really good," she said. "I like the chili; it gives it a nice kick. I can safely say this's the best omelet I've ever had."

"Glad you like it. Angelica told me how to make it. It's my first attempt."

"Well, you looked like a pro cooking it. I'm impressed."

"Thank you."

"How's your noggin? You nailed that countertop pretty hard. It sounded like a dropped melon."

"It's a good thing I hit my head—I could've been seriously hurt. Truth be told, my calf is bothering me more. I lost more skin," he pointed at his face, "and I don't have all that much to spare."

LG smiled and he liked the way it looked. Despite being on crutches, she somehow seemed more at peace.

No one said anything as they ate, but LG eventually broke the silence.

"I guess I'm not surprised Ursula won't talk," she said. "Probably figures she's got nothing to lose. She and Tomas were pretty close."

"I know we've asked you a bunch of times, but let's talk through it again."

"I'm as baffled as ever. Coming after me like Cornejo did makes no sense unless he did it for purely personal reasons."

"Which is a distinct possibility," Harv added. "You're familiar with Occam's razor?"

"Yeah, all things being equal, the simplest answer tends to be the correct one. If all he wanted was to shut me up, he could've killed me with a ton less fuss, don't you think?"

Nathan nodded. "I know you're burned out on it, and it's a difficult thing to relive, but let's give it another try."

She shifted in her seat, trying to get comfortable, and gave Nathan a curt nod.

"The security alarm woke you and you spotted the intruders in your yard. They used bangers to stun you, then attacked."

"I told Glen to get in the closet and I fought off the gunmen until I got tased."

"Once they had you, they handcuffed you and injected the Ketamine. You told us you remembered the guy called you Little Peach."

She closed her eyes for a few seconds—obviously a bad memory. "That's useless now. We know it was Tomas and Ursula."

"Why Little Peach?"

"I had a dog named Peach at the time, a toy poodle. I called her Little Peach. She was apricot color, but I didn't think Apricot was a good name."

"So you told Tomas about your dog?"

"Yes. He thought it was a good nickname for me. I didn't like it, but I needed to stay in his good graces. I don't see where this is going."

"I'm not sure either, but let's stay in Caracas. After we rescued Glen, did he ever tell you why the twins beat on him?" Nathan needed to steer the conversation gently.

"No. I didn't see him at all after he got back."

"And you never knew him prior to the mission?"

"No."

"How did you two get together after that? It's not like he could look you up in the phone book."

She looked hesitant, as if she didn't want to answer. "I asked Cantrell for his contact info."

"Because you were interested in him?"

She sighed. "Yes. Where's this going?" Her tone held some edge.

Nathan looked at Harv. "We've been operating on an assumption that Cornejo was after you. What if you weren't his endgame?"

"Then who? You guys?"

"Glen."

"That's crazy. He didn't know anything about Cornejo."

"Cantrell told us there have been a bunch of other murders *and* kidnappings related to Cornejo's bid for the presidency."

"I still can't believe he'd be after Glen."

"Did Glen ever tell you why he was in Caracas in the first place?"

"He went there for vacations. He liked it there a lot."

"It's a beautiful city," said Harv.

Good job, Harv, he thought. It was the perfect comment for the moment. It removed some of the tension.

"How many times did he take vacations down there before we rescued him?"

"A bunch. I don't know the exact number, he never told me." She sounded a little resentful.

Nathan held up a hand. "And he spoke Spanish?"

"Yes."

"Was there ever a ransom request from the twins?"

She shook her head.

"Doesn't that strike you as odd?"

"Not really, Cornejo had all the money he needed."

"Right, so why kidnap Glen?"

Linda didn't say anything, her mind clearly working.

"Did you guys ever talk about it?"

"I tried a few times, but he wanted to put it behind him and move on. I didn't push."

"For the moment, let's assume Glen was the target, not you. Would you agree if they wanted him dead, they could've easily done it?"

"They *did* kill him."

"But you said he attacked the gunman who'd captured you. Maybe killing him wasn't their plan."

She just stared.

"What if they wanted to render Glen, not you? Getting their hands on you was just gravy, so to speak."

"No, that can't be right. He didn't know anything."

"I know this is painful, LG, I'm sorry."

She put her fork down with some force. "You're the ones who brought up Occam's razor. Aren't we getting a little presumptuous here?"

He needed to slow things down. "Let's go back to the chain of events. You were both in your bedroom when the alarm went off. What did Glen say?"

"What did he say? I don't know. He asked who I was texting."

"What else?"

"He mentioned our dogs . . ."

"What about them?" He remembered the dogs being one of the first things Linda mentioned when he found her in the kitchen.

"He didn't like leaving them in the bedroom, but I didn't want them following us, so I locked them in the closet."

"Did he say anything else?"

"No, I told him to be quiet. When the bangers went off, I told him to hide in the linen closet because I didn't want him slowing me down."

"After the fight in the kitchen, did he say anything more?"

"Why are you guys making me relive this? He's dead!"

Harv stepped in. "Easy, LG. We're not ganging up on you."

"I just hate thinking about it."

Neither of them said anything, giving her some time.

"He told me he was sorry."

"Sorry? You mean about the attack?" asked Nathan.

She closed her eyes.

"I'm sure he didn't blame you for it."

Across the table, his friend held up a hand. He nodded and didn't say anything. He knew Harv wanted LG to work through the events without any coaching. Anything else might taint her recollection.

She pressed her eyes tighter. "He was worried about our dogs again. He told me to get them out. Then he said he loved me. I told him not to talk and that I'd call an ambulance . . . I hated lying to him. I felt so helpless. The Ketamine had begun to work on me. If he said anything more after that, I can't remember it. I don't even remember anything I said with you."

"You asked if your dogs were okay. I heard them barking and you told me they were in your bedroom closet."

"I can't remember any of that. It's like it never happened."

"You told me their collars were in a kitchen drawer, their leashes too. I passed that on to Cantrell. It's how her team handed the dogs off to Harv before you woke up."

"It's scary not remembering stuff like that."

"To take your dogs out, you have to put their collars on, right?"

She nodded. "Collars and leashes. We always did, even on short trips."

"I do too," Nathan said. "No matter how well-trained your dogs are, you want their collars on for ID purposes. They could—"

LG's face changed. "Oh, dear Lord."

"What? What's wrong?"

She got up from the table. "Their collars! The crosses!"

"What about them?" Harv asked, also getting up.

"Glen said it a bunch of times: 'Never thumb your nose at them, they might save your life someday.' What if he didn't mean that figuratively as a Christian, what if he meant it *literally*?"

Nathan frowned.

"Their crosses!" She almost fell, trying to get up on her crutches so quickly.

He and Harv followed her toward the front door. "Slow down, LG. You're going to fall."

"Elsa! Morgen!" She left the door open and hobbled out to the driveway. Grant and Sherman bounded out behind her.

"What's going on?" Nathan asked.

"I saw an email on Glen's computer a long time ago. It was from a company that made custom thumb drives. Elsa! Morgen!"

Her shepherds came trotting around the corner from Nathan's garage, their white crosses dangling from their collars.

"When I asked him about it, he said he'd decided not to order them, but the email was a receipt. I never made the connection because there wasn't a drawing of the crosses. He gave them to our dogs as Christmas presents. Don't you see? What if you're right? What if Glen was the target, not me?"

"Then he had something Cornejo wants," Harv said.

She unhooked one of the dogs' crosses and examined it. "There's a tiny seam in the middle." She tried pulling at it, but it wouldn't budge.

"Harv, give it a try," Nathan said.

Harv pulled at it with some force and it wouldn't come apart. He produced a small pocketknife, forced its blade into the seam, and twisted.

When it separated, the three of them stared at the USB connection in stunned silence.

Nothing needed to be said.

They hurried into the house and went upstairs to Nathan's small office. He felt his stomach tighten with that tingling again as he plugged it into his Mac.

He clicked on the drive and received a password screen.

"Crap," he said. "Linda?"

"I don't know."

"Is there something you both use? A gate code, anything like that?" Harv asked.

"We don't have a gate at our driveway. The only thing I can think of would be our security-alarm code." She gave it to them.

Nathan tensed as he entered the numbers. "It worked."

A list of files appeared, most of them Excel and Word. The first one was a video, dated five years ago.

He double-clicked it.

CHAPTER 31

Glen's face filled the screen. LG put a hand over her mouth and leaned into Harv.

"Linda, if you're viewing this video, I'm probably dead or missing and Daniel Cornejo is likely behind it. Please know how much I've always loved you. When I first saw you in Caracas, you took my breath away. You weren't only my rescuer, you were the most amazing woman I'd ever met. We would've had beautiful children had we been able to. I loved you with all my heart, mind, and soul."

Nathan paused the video, looked at Linda, and knew at a glance she'd never had a clue. Her expression couldn't be faked.

She looked from him to Harv and didn't say anything. She didn't have to.

"Everything makes perfect sense now," Nathan said. "If you don't want to watch this—"

"No, I need to."

He resumed the video.

"Nathan McBride and Harvey Fontana came out of retirement to help rescue me. If you two are seeing this, please accept my deepest thanks. Please look after Linda."

Glen tried to smile, but it looked forced.

"We fought a lot because we're so opposite, you and me. You were always hotheaded, passionate. I was calm and collected. Some would've said 'cold.' They say opposites attract, it's hard to argue with the truth. And you deserve the truth.

"I first met Daniel Cornejo at a Caracas resort. We got to talking and he said he needed a good investment consultant. Please believe me, I didn't know what he was. By the time I did, it was too late. I was already in over my head. I won't make any excuses, but I was seduced by the prospect of having such a large client. My business was floundering and Cornejo was like a dream come true.

"Contained on this flash drive are the personal financial records I stole from Cornejo's computer."

Glen averted his eyes from the camera and shook his head slowly. Then he faced the camera once more.

"When I first saw these files, I couldn't believe the numbers. As you'll see, his cocaine-smuggling income was over a million dollars a day, and he used his oil-drilling business to launder much of the drug money worldwide. He bought gold bullion, original art, expensive antiques and coins . . . you name it. He must have five or ten tons of gold in his wine cellar. He took me down there once. It's like a labyrinth. As Venezuela's attorney general back then, he was untouchable. His enemies had a habit of disappearing, like I almost did."

Glen paused and his face reflected pain. It looked like he was about to melt down.

"I hated what his wealth represented, but that's no excuse. Stealing is wrong, even when it's from a man like Cornejo. Over a period of three years, I siphoned over forty million dollars from his accounts. I'm not proud

of what I did, but please believe what I'm about to say: I didn't keep any of it. I gave all of it to charities. Every last penny. I thought if I could put some of his money to good use, it might make up for some of the horrible suffering he'd caused.

"It was my own fault, being kidnapped. Cornejo invited me down to discuss some new investments he wanted to make. When I arrived at the mansion, Tomas and Ursula Bustamonte were waiting because Cornejo had discovered the missing money. Ursula beat me for days but I knew as soon as I caved, I'd be killed. I'm not sure I could've held out much longer. I'd befriended many of his staff and one of his young female servants got word to the FBI that I was being held. She knew I was an American. Had she not done that, no one would've ever known my fate. When he found out someone betrayed him, he went crazy. He tortured his staff until he found out who did it. The poor woman died horribly and her death will always weigh heavily on my conscience.

"After we started dating several months later, you told me Cornejo put a bounty on your head. When you said he offered to double it if you were delivered alive, I knew I had to act. I sent him copies of the files I'd stolen and told him he was safe as long as he left you alone. I should've turned everything over years ago and faced whatever consequences I deserved. Instead, I turned the files into our insurance policy. If he left us alone, I'd leave him alone. These flash drives aren't the only copies. Others have them too. Sleeper measures to insure that, if anything ever happened to me, Cornejo would be exposed. You have to understand I did it to protect you. I'm sorry I never told you.

"The Word file called NOMBRES contains a list of people who Cornejo might consider threats. I wasn't his only consultant; there were at least half a dozen others all over the world. You'll be shocked to see how much money the man laundered. The numbers are hard to wrap your head around.

"The file called NINOS contains hundreds of portrait-type photos taken with an early digital camera. None of them are pornographic but

the numbers under the pictures with lots of zeroes must be prices. Once I saw them, I knew I had to get out, and did. I have no idea why Cornejo kept them, maybe he planned to blackmail the buyers someday. There are other files as well. Cleverly hidden records of extortions, ransoms, and what I believe are contracts for murder.

"There's more you need to know, but I don't know if it will be useful. Tomas and Ursula Bustamonte are his illegitimate children. The man you killed on the couch was their adoptive father. The twins were Cornejo's flesh and blood, but he never told them because he didn't want to share his wealth."

He paused for a few seconds.

"Nothing I can say will justify what I did and I won't make any excuses. All the charitable donations in the world aren't enough to undo what I did, but I'd hoped it would at least purge some of the guilt I felt. It never did.

"I've asked God for forgiveness. I hope you can forgive me as well. I love you, Linda. I always have. I hope you'll find it in your heart to forgive me and remember the best times we had together."

The video ended. No one said anything for a few seconds.

"He wasn't a bad man," she whispered.

"Harv and I know that, but we need to call Cantrell right away and send these files to her. Maybe she can save some of the people on the list."

Linda stared at the list of files. "After he'd been given his new identity, he bought the house in La Jolla. We had our first date in it. He made me dinner. He was always secretive about money. I never asked him about it. Maybe if I had—"

"None of this is your fault," Harv interrupted. "Don't start second-guessing yourself. It's going to take you a long time to process what we've just seen."

She turned to face them. "I don't know if I can be alone right now."

Harv put an arm around her. "We'll always be here for you."

CHAPTER 32

46 HOURS BEFORE THE ELECTION

Nathan answered his phone. Cantrell.

"Turn on CNN."

Nathan hurried into his living room, pressed the remote, and found the right channel. The tail end of the aerial clip zoomed, showed a man being taken in handcuffs from a huge mansion. Nathan recognized it—Cornejo's palatial house in Caracas. The camera angle wasn't great, but Cornejo's face couldn't be mistaken. He turned the volume down and read the news ticker along the bottom of the screen.

VENEZUELAN PRESIDENTIAL FRONT-RUN-NER DANIEL CORNEJO ARRESTED IN CA-RACAS MANSION. CHARGED WITH RACKE-TEERING, EXTORTION, CHILD TRAFFICKING AND MURDER.

The news ticker started again.

"You got him," Nathan said.

"No, *we* got him. It's the lead story around the world. I wish you could see things around here. This is huge."

"I'm glad it was worth it."

"You have no idea. Ursula got on board when we told her that Cornejo was her biological father. We got tons of testimony and leads on more caches of information that she and her brother had stashed away. That, plus the thumb-drive documents, will mean Cornejo's going to prison for the rest of his life. Venezuelan authorities are going to do their best to locate as many of the children as possible."

"What about Ursula?"

"She got spared a needle. Part of our deal. Don't worry, she'll never see daylight again."

"I'm assuming they raided his basement?"

"Yes. They found over one hundred million dollars of gold bullion in his cellar and another three hundred million in other stuff. Seems he was quite the pack rat."

Nathan shook his head. So much wealth, so little compassion. "So where does this leave Venezuela?"

"Acting president Cadenas is on a solid path to victory now. You didn't hear this from me, but ever since Garmendia's incapacitation, the state department's been conducting secret negotiations with him. He's anxious to normalize relations."

"For a price, of course."

"It's how the world works, but in this case the price won't be high. Venezuela's economy's on the brink of collapse, after all."

"And the nuclear issue you mentioned?"

"Nipped in the bud. Let's just say it's not a banner day in Tehran. DNI Benson's briefing with the president went well and your names were mentioned. Needless to say, our commander in chief remembered you guys and wanted me to personally offer his thanks. Now it's my turn. Thank you again, Nathan. Please extend my gratitude to Harvey and Linda."

"I will. She doesn't want to stay in La Jolla. She needs a fresh start somewhere." He hoped his message was heard.

"We can always use another good analyst."

He ran his hand along Sherman's back. "I think she's game. Harv and I are coming out there next week. Harv wants to see your algorithm at work."

"I'll make it happen. What about you?"

"I'm heading over to the Hoover Building. Holly's arranged a personal tour. I've never been in it."

"Don't even think about buying your airfare or hotel stay. It's on us."

"I'll accept it, with no strings."

"None offered."

"I need a small favor."

"Name it."

"I need a name and address." He told her why.

"Be careful, Nathan. That may not go so well."

"I trust my instincts."

"I'll send you a text in a few minutes. Good luck with it. I've got to run. I'll say it this time. Goodbye, Nathan."

***

Nathan arrived in the Santa Monica area a few hours later. He didn't know what to expect from the meeting, but it was something he needed to do. After parking a few blocks away, Nathan walked along the sidewalk. The Wounded Warriors ball cap he wore helped mitigate the grooves on his face. He didn't think of himself as a wounded warrior per se, but he believed in its trademarked statement: *The greatest casualty is being forgotten.* Not in this Marine's world. Nathan thanked vets wherever he ran into them. If uniformed service members dined in a restaurant with him, even at a different table, he picked up their tab. And it didn't matter how many there were. Four or forty, he paid the bill. There were few absolutes in his world, that being one of them.

The stop he'd made before this one went surprisingly well. Again, he hadn't known what to expect, but it was also a visit he'd needed to make.

The day was bright, with no signs of the previous storm that had carpeted Southern California. Staying on Pico, he crossed 26th and saw his destination ahead: Santa Monica Car Wash. Buried in their electronic worlds, not one of the cell-phone addicts sitting in the waiting area looked up as he strode past. Fine with him.

He spotted his mark drying off an expensive sedan. Without hesitating, he approached the kid.

"Remember me?"

Oliver Kline looked up with a confused, almost frightened expression. Then recognition hit. The kid didn't say anything and kept wiping the sedan's door panels.

"You don't have to talk to me. I'm just here to give you this." He extended his hand. "It's a new Samsung Galaxy S7. All yours. All you have to do is activate it with Verizon."

When the kid didn't take it, Nathan set it on the trunk of the car. Oliver eyed it while wiping the bumper.

"I took your phone, so I'm replacing it. Simple as that."

Oliver looked him in the eyes and he saw the same intelligence he'd seen in the alley. Nathan turned to go.

"Is this your Lexus?"

It isn't much, he thought, *but it's a start.* "I'm parked down the street."

The kid moved around to the far side of the sedan. "How'd you find me?"

"Your mom."

"My mom? How'd you— My cell phone."

Nathan smiled and nodded.

Oliver didn't say anything for a few seconds. "I told her what happened. She was really pissed. I got grounded for a month."

"You'll live. When I told her I was the man from the alley, she wrapped me up in a bear hug that would make my girlfriend jealous."

"Yeah, she's pretty strong."

"We had a long talk. She worries about you. A lot, actually. She says you don't listen."

He looked down.

"Look, if you keep out of trouble and stay on the straight and narrow, you've got a job waiting for you in my company."

"What kind of job?"

"Let's just say you'd be helping people stay safe. It's a good job. I think you'd like it. I get hundreds of applications for a single slot."

"Where did you learn to fight like that? I couldn't believe how fast you were."

"The United States Marine Corps."

"For real?"

"For real."

Oliver looked around and lowered his voice. "I was really scared. I thought you were going to kill us."

"How're your friends doing?"

"Uh . . . they're not really my friends."

"You told them you were going back to school, didn't you . . ."

"They called me names."

"Names won't hurt you, bullets will. Look, I'm not here to give you any fatherly advice. You already know what to do. The job offer is real, Oliver. No BS."

"Did you tell my mom?"

"Yes."

"What did she say?"

"I got another bear hug, *and* a kiss. I had to reward her for it: anyone who gives that good of a hug deserves a payback. I gave her the money for your driver's-ed classes."

Now he looked genuinely confused. "Why'd you do that?"

"She said she couldn't afford it. Let's just say I consider it an investment."

They fell into silence again.

"I was a lot like you at your age. Defiant and stubborn. Nobody could tell me anything. I started fights, got into trouble, and ditched school. I was also horny as all hell."

Oliver smiled.

"I see you know what I mean. You're at a tough age. There's good news and bad news. The good news? You'll outgrow it. The bad news? Life doesn't get any easier."

"What happened to not giving me fatherly advice?"

"Okay, you caught me. It's one of my many character flaws."

Oliver grabbed the phone and pocketed it. "It was gonna take me forever to save enough money. Thanks, man."

"You're welcome. I want you to promise me something."

"What?"

"I want you to do a Google search with the words 'poverty in the Congo' then click on the images. Poverty in the Congo. Got it?"

"Why do you want me to do that?"

"You'll know why when you see the pictures. Promise?"

"Yeah, I promise."

"America's an amazing country."

Clearly, the young man didn't know what to say.

"You making minimum wage?"

"Yeah, it sucks." He looked around. "I don't speak Spanish."

"Don't worry, the language of work is universal. I had the same job at your age."

Oliver finished drying the sedan.

"Think I'll ever be able to buy a car like this?"

"I don't doubt it for a second." Nathan offered his hand and Oliver shook it.

With that, he walked away and didn't look back.

Oliver's world was small, but Nathan had a feeling it was about to get a whole lot bigger.

AUTHOR'S NOTE

Writing a thriller series is challenging on a number of levels. Over the years, I've received quite a few emails and letters from folks who think I don't need to describe Nathan's unique features—namely his 6'5" size, deep blue eyes, and scars marring his face and torso—in every book. One very kind lady said I didn't need to keep reminding readers about the horrible ordeal he endured. This is where the challenge of being a series author comes into play.

Each Nathan McBride novel needs to be a freestanding story. For many readers, *Right to Kill* is their introduction to Nathan's world and its supporting characters. By necessity, new readers need to "see" Nathan and Harvey, both physically and emotionally. I can only ask the series veterans to be patient when reading material they already know.

Nathan's world is big. He knows all too well that evil exists and he steps up to confront it with no expectation of receiving anything in return. Some might say that's a definition of a hero.

In my humble opinion, thriller heroes need to be larger than life, yet flawed and vulnerable. Nathan McBride makes mistakes, simple as that. Some of them put him in mortal danger. Nathan isn't a "win at all costs" man. His sense of right and wrong often conflicts with a deep, ethical question: When is it okay to kill?

My personal heroes are not athletes, musicians, or actors. My heroes are our military service members, law enforcement officers, and federal special agents who put their lives on the line to keep America safe from its enemies.

I sleep well because they often don't.

My freedom isn't free; it comes at an extremely high price.

I'm a firm believer in the Wounded Warriors Project trademarked statement: "The greatest casualty is being forgotten."

The dedication at the beginning of this novel is from the heart. It's my desire to honor one of our nation's most cherished fallen heroes. Rest in peace, Special Warfare Operator 1st Class Charles Keating IV, you've earned it.

ACKNOWLEDGMENTS

My wife, Carla, is kind, patient, and industrious. I spend countless hours in my studio writing these novels and she's working behind the scenes to keep our household running. I couldn't do my job without her. Carla gets as much credit as I do, and it's well deserved. I have a lapel pin that says: "I'd be lost without my wife!"

Ed Stackler has been my freelance editor from the beginning. He's worked on every Nathan McBride novel and these stories wouldn't be the same without him. Simply put, Ed is the best at what he does, and I'm fortunate to have him in my camp.

Dick Hill is the voice of Nathan McBride in the audiobooks. He's not only a trusted friend, he's the guidepost for my writing. I have Dick's narration in mind when I compose a manuscript. If I don't think it will sound right with Dick reading it, I edit the manuscript until it does.

Thanks is owed to Tom Davin, CEO of 5.11 Tactical, for allowing me to plug his products in Nathan's adventures. He's not only a terrific businessman and friend, he's a Marine! Tom served with the 1/1 (First of the First).

Dr. Douglas Reavie, M.D., F.A.C.S., and his wife, Janice Reavie, CRNA, MSN, are real people and they graciously allow me to put them in my books. Thank you for helping me with the opening home-invasion scene.

Linda Genneken is physically based on a real person. Linda won an auction to be a character in *Right to Kill* and the money was donated to the German Shepherd Rescue of Orange County. Over the years, she and her husband have helped countless dogs find loving and permanent homes. Thank you, Linda, for all you do to make the world a better place.

The Thomas & Mercer team does an amazing job. Amazon Publishing, Inc., isn't some giant nebulous thing, it's made up of people—good people—and I want to acknowledge and thank them:

My editor, Gracie Doyle, Editorial Director of Thomas & Mercer

Sarah Shaw, Author Relations Manager

Jacque Ben-Zekry, former Marketing Manager, now Editor

Marlene Kelly, Lauren Edwards, and Laura Costantino, Marketing

Timoney Korbar, Producer of Kindle Most Wanted

Dennelle Catlett, PR

Jeff Belle, Vice President of Amazon Publishing

A warm thank-you is also owed to my readers; you folks aren't taken for granted. My goal is to deliver the best product I possibly can. Unfortunately, speed isn't my forte. I can't crank out a novel every few months. I admire authors who can. I'm just not one of them. Thank you for hanging in there with me.

If you're looking for other authors who'll grab your attention and keep it, I'm happy to recommend the following:

Blake Crouch's Wayward Pines Series

Robert Dugoni's Tracy Crosswhite Series

Kendra Elliot's Bone Secrets Series

Marcus Sakey's Brilliance Trilogy

T.R. Ragan's Lizzy Gardner Series

Barry Eisler's John Rain Series

Sean Chercover's The Game Trilogy

Alan Russell's Gideon and Sirius Series

And newly discovered Matthew FitzSimmons—I gave Matt a well-deserved blurb.

I know all of these authors and they're fantastic storytellers—I wouldn't recommend them otherwise!

A final note. Yes, there will be more Nathan McBride novels. I'm hard at work on book seven.

ABOUT THE AUTHOR

USO Tour Operation Thriller II, Bagram Airfield, Afghanistan

Andrew Peterson is the #1 Amazon international bestselling author of the Nathan McBride series. An avid marksman who has won numerous high-powered rifle competitions, he enjoys flying helicopters, camping, hiking, scuba diving, and playing a questionable round of golf. Peterson has donated more than three thousand books to troops serving overseas and to veterans recovering in military hospitals. A native of San Diego, he lives in California's Monterey County with his wife, Carla, and their giant schnauzers, Elsa and Lilli.

For more info about Andrew Peterson, please visit his website: www.andrewpeterson.com

Facebook: @andrew.peterson.author

Twitter: @apetersonnovels

Goodreads: www.goodreads.com/Andrew_Peterson_Author